# CHAINED

*The Realm of Wind*

*—book 1—*

Trigger warnings: bullying, verbal abuse, torture, physical pain, unwilling confinement, claustrophobia, overeating, hunger, gore, terror attacks (mention), imprisonment, gun violence, hostage situation

This is a work of fiction. References to real people, locations, events, organizations or establishments are intended for the sole purpose to provide authenticity and are used fictitiously.

# Chained

**The Realm of Wind Book 1**

Discover the Tales of Earth and Leaves series

*Tales of Earth and Leaves*

*Tales of Fire and Embers*

*Tales of Forever and Now*

*Tales of Wind and Storm*

*Tales of Water and Blood*

Discover *Love, Will, an LGBT historical fiction*

## Day 0

They gave me a fucking faerie. This cannot be happening. Not to me. Not now.

I worked my ass off day in and day out. I excelled at everything because they gave me no other choice. There was no other choice for someone like me.

An outsider to my own race. A stranger in the Human Realm. An immigrant.

But to do this to me? Now? When I was on the cusp of reaping the rewards for eighteen years of hard work. It's got to be a joke.

I knocked on the general's office door again, even though I knew what I was putting myself through. How he never wanted to be disturbed during his meditation hours. Though we all knew by now that the old man was probably snoring in front of the TV after inhaling junk food. Ever since his wife decided he needed to get on a healthier lifestyle after that heart attack, General Milosh implemented these 'meditation hours' as he liked to call them and none of us had the right to disturb him.

He even gave specific instructions, we could only do it in case of fire, death, or war.

None of these were happening to me. Yet.

But I knocked again, and again and again, determined to wait until he finished his snoring session, or he got so sick of me that he moved his fat ass and opened the fucking door.

Luckily, it was the latter.

"Who died?" General Milosh scanned me through those bushy eyebrows that mixed with his lashes. Their thickness, along with the darkness of his eyes made him look invincible. Unstoppable. Even for his old age. Everything that I wasn't. That I wouldn't be for a long time.

"Sir," I jumped into action, knowing I had about five seconds before he lost his patience. And he was known for the aftermath of that action.

"Harrow," he furrowed those brows deeper at me. "Who died?"

"Sir, I need to talk to you. There has to be a mistake, I can't possibly—"

The smack against my cheek came with unexpected force, instantly silencing me. I hadn't received a strike like that in years. My jaw forgot how to properly lock and distribute the pressure, making my lips get the better part of the hit.

I sucked at my bottom lip, the tang of blood all too familiar. Reminding me where I was. Whom I was speaking to. Who I had the nerve to disturb. Still, I did not back down. I did not shy away from the pain. I had gotten to live with it most of my life and it slowly, forcefully, became a friend rather than a thing of nightmares. If there was pain, it meant that I was still alive. If I was still alive, I could fight. Escape. Win.

"Sir," I insisted with newfound commitment.

"For fuck's sake, Harrow," Milosh sighed, probably guessing that he would sooner or later have to deal with me.

Stepping back, the tall mountain of a man allowed enough room for me to squeeze past him and enter his den. The general's office we all dreamt of owning one day. The invincibility such a position offered in the Realm, for generations to come. One I needed to earn for myself. For my family.

Not wasting a second, I started speaking, sharing the facts and carefully avoiding my feelings. He already knew the humiliation, there was no point in wasting breath to tell him facts he already guessed.

"Sir, there must be someone else. Something else. Anything else, but not a faerie. I can wait another season, I can help support the unit, I can..."

I stopped. He had already lost interest.

"Harrow," he sighed. That sigh I knew all too well. That sigh that brought a rain of insults whenever he spoke to me like that.

"Sir," I heard myself saying again, not knowing why.

"How long have you been a Captain for?" he asked to my surprise. He was the one who ranked me, after all.

"Three years, sir."

"How many years have your colleagues been captains?" Again, a question he already knew the answer to. I was the youngest captain to complete the training and gain merit to a major appointment trial. I knew this and he knew it too, so what was the point in asking? Still, I had no choice but to answer a direct question from my superior.

"Longer than me, sir."

"Did Wood, Pecknam or Castro get their appointment trials during these minutes you have wasted and I'm somehow not aware of it?"

"No, sir." The way he looked at me, the evident disgust in his eyes, his body language, even the tilt of his lip, made me want to throw up. I should have been used to it by now. After all, I had been treated like this all my life. But somehow, my brain picked this exact moment to think about watering my eyes. Just because I needed even more embarrassment. Knowing what was coming, I braced myself for the blow. Pressing my lips together, I squeezed my tongue to the roof of my mouth and waited for the insults that would be coming. For the hate I had to swallow every day. Every time I walked the corridors.

"Do you think I want to have a Windling cunt in my unit, Harrow? Do you honestly think, if the choice were up to me, that I would put you in front of one of my boys? Young men I trained from childhood, deserving to be here?"

OK, it wasn't that bad. *Windling cunt* was a walk in the park. Nothing compared to being denied food for days, having to work three or four hours extra every shift or return to my bunk at three in the morning to find my pillow filled with faeces.

"No, sir," I replied, somehow content with this new information. I didn't get a faerie because Milosh wanted to humiliate me. The disgust on his features told me he would happily trade my place with one of his boys, as he so clearly put it.

"Get the fuck out and go do your job."

By the time I nodded in greeting and turned around, the general had time to reconsider my humiliation and send a mouthful of phlegm down my neck. Great, now I had to shower again.

But that part of me, the one that kept pushing, the one that loved to embrace the pain and humiliation, turned to the general.

"Thank you for your time, sir. I look forward to your hands touching me again. Next time to hang the major epaulettes on my shoulder," I threw him a dashing smile.

"Get the fuck out, Harrow."

"With pleasure, sir."

I stepped out and shut the door, feeling a little bit more excited about the person I was going to spend the next month with.

I walked the hallways back to my assigned room, chasing away memories that always found their way back in the most unfortunate moments.

When I first arrived here, frozen and full of mud and terror. When I was first assigned as a guard and forced to standpost by the frozen lake all winter long. How my jacket and boots turned up either ripped to pieces or filled with rat intestines or half-chewed leftovers to attract the wild animals during the night.

Wolves did not scare me anymore, that was for sure. They were no match for twelve-year-old boys and the cruelty they inherited through the human blood they cherished beyond anything else. Not that my blood was not the same as theirs, but it was seen as polluted because I was born in a different place. In a faerie place.

I made a right turn and walked past the garden entrance and towards the bridge that leads to the new cabins, meant for the comfort of new recruits of distinguished families, commanders and higher ranks. I looked at number 17, the small cabin I had my eyes on ever since Commander Vancozia lived there. The first and only woman to do so.

Her cabin always smelled nice, she always had a fire burning and the stove running and whenever she did not have to fight the monster that haunted us, she spent her time working in her small garden or planting flowers in front of her cabin.

Everyone hated them but no one dared touch them. No one but me. I lived for their colours, for their beauty and snuck out every chance I got to spy on the woman. The cabin emptied after her passing, and no one wanted number 17. It looked in dire need of repairs, but that's why I'd been working my ass off for so many years.

Everything I did not send to my family, every uniform allowance or bravery bonus went on a secret card, opened in a regular bank, so the military could not find it using my name. I was one month away from earning the right to request the keys to this cabin, to claim number 17 as my own. To be mine until my passing. If I were to judge by the dozens of attempts on my life these fuckers made, I was one lucky cookie and hoped to have that cabin for a long, long time.

"Hey E, I heard about your appointment trial," Veronica came bursting in, forcing the door off its hinges because why wouldn't she? After all, this was not her room, she did not care one bit about the damage she could cause around her.

She called me E, because Ellyana was somehow too much for her to say. Too much for everyone to pronounce. I knew they hated the origin of my name, I myself had despised it since it brought me so much sorrow. Everyone who spoke to me without shouting an order or needing to address me for an official matter had reduced me to an initial.

"Hey, Veronica," I half-turned and replied, my hands still working to wrap all the T-shirts I had piled on my bed. Enough to last me a month.

"A faerie, huh?" she placed her ass on the mattress, uninvited as usual, and blinked at me with curious eyes, probably wondering why I was so calm and not bawling my eyes out crying with the news.

Because it didn't come from fucking Milosh, that's why. Someone above, someone with power in our realm thought of me instead of not one, but three of their own. Because I was finally on the right track, finally doing something right.

"Yeah, but at least I can get a cabin and better wages, so…" I shrugged, ignoring her, and placing my full attention back to my clothes. Were five pairs of jeans enough?

"I know but, a faerie?" she kept insisting, her curls dropping ostentatiously down her shoulder while her big eyes blinked at me with lazy curiosity.

I knew what she was trying to do, what she was trying to raise in me. But that monster was too well trained to come out with such an amateur calling.

Veronica and mine's relationship was complicated. She was the only other woman in our unit, so we were left with no other choice but to train together and bond over period cramps, but where I was skinny, formless and despised, she was a dashing apparition that caused everyone to mellow. She never had to finish her chores or conduct all her exercises because one clink of her voice was enough to get her out of the things she did not fancy following through. But they needed to be finished, so guess who had to pick up her slack?

"It's only a month and then I'll be a major..." I shrugged again to let her know the conversation bored me. I also twisted a knife there, she may have managed to get out of many unpleasant things, but her adulthood only brought her the rank of First Lieutenant. Meaning she didn't even have her own room and had to share with three privates, being the only female with her status.

And I would soon get a cabin.

Whatever this faerie was, I would break the hell out of it.

*Day 0.5*

"Are you really going to check my panties, Michael?" I frowned at the security guard, once a colleague. I have known his family since I was a babe, I had more memories of them than the dreadful place we used to live in before escaping to the Human Realm. Michael was probably three or four when our parents jumped realms, along with a few hundred others, hoping for a better future.

He was given to the army, same as I was, as offering for the shelter provided to the refugees aka our parents, grandparents, brothers and sisters. The Human Realm was no fool. It claimed a young life for the betterment of older ones and kids like Michael and me had to become the tribute.

We were the lucky ones though, able to live long enough to grow and get a job, earn wages good enough to pay for our own maintenance and send the rest back home to the family. Home... it was just a word, trapped under so many piled up dreams it became impossible to recognise anymore.

"You know the deal, Ellyana. I can't let anything suspicious pass through the preparation area," he pressed his lips in apology for a short while and continued to rummage through my thongs, trying his best to hide his surprise.

Yeah...I liked a lacy thong, sue me. They offered enough protection and breathable space, compared to the heavy cotton panties the uniform came provided with. A small splurge I allowed myself every other month. Not for the random guy I found now and then to satisfy my urges, but for myself. Because I loved being comfortable in my uniform without a scratchy ass and because I allowed my body this small mercy. I also slept naked since three years ago, when I got my own room, which turned out to be amazing. Another thing I never knew I could do, but once I did, I found out how much I loved it.

But I did bring a few sets of PJs for the faerie. I wasn't going to let some creepy thing see my vag.

"You know you can ask for leave every other day, right?" Michael looked at me, then pointed at the three boxes of tampons I packed. A trick I had to learn from necessity and not a comfortable one, but effective nonetheless.

No boy would touch you if they saw a string coming out from between your legs. They would just be grossed out and leave. Better to be safe than sorry. Plus, I would get my period in a few days, so a box was truly needed.

"Yeah well, I'd rather not spend my leave hours on grocery runs," I smirked at him, causing the guard to chuckle.

"You truly are one of a kind," Michael shook his head while continuing his search.

I wanted to risk it, I wanted to risk it so badly, desperately needing to know if he had any news. If he knew anything I didn't. But if someone heard two immigrants speaking about the refugee village while on the job, and on location, we could both get in too much trouble.

"I haven't gotten a letter in two years." That was all. All I could say to let him know that I didn't know if my family were okay, if my dad's health had improved and if my sisters had finished high school. All I knew was that they were alive because ninety percent of my monthly wages were sent by the unit to their location to facilitate their life. If there were any changes, the army had an obligation to let me know.

"Eight months for me," he replied, a touch of sadness shadowing his voice.

I nodded, his answer more than enough to know that we were both suffering in the uncertainty.

"So, will you be guarding me, then?" I smiled, averting from the dangerous topic.

His dry chuckle made my skin crawl.

"You know as well as I do it doesn't work like that, Elly."

*Elly.*

My mom used to call me that. My dad and my sisters recognised me by that name.

A name from home.

A name long forgotten.

"Who will it be?" I was afraid to ask, knowing all too well they wouldn't make this appointment trial easy for me. I still felt

Milosh's spit on my neck, even though I hopped in the shower as soon as I got to my room and scrubbed that bastard's DNA from my skin until my fingers went numb on the loofa. He must have assigned someone who despised me as equally as he did. Before Michael even opened his mouth, I knew what his answer would be.

"Your favourite trio." What I'd been through growing up was no news to anyone. The entire unit had participated in some way or another and even though I did not witness it many times, I knew Michael had been through the same. The only difference was that I continued to show up for training every morning, even when the wounds on my back cracked from the effort, even when my clothes were soiled or when my stomach grumbled.

I hadn't stopped. Not when they offered me my first rank, not when they wanted to make me a guard, not when I was appointed captain.

I would go all the way or die trying. I would end up commanding everyone who ever wronged me, and I would look in their eyes as I give them orders they cannot disobey if they value their lives.

"This is going to be fucking fun," I sneered, deciding to open another bag for the guard to check and make my transition quicker.

I had worked intelligence before, I knew how hard it was to crack a case and especially a faerie, who I assumed had been through hell and back before coming to our unit. Surprisingly, we were known to be the soft ones. And if someone decided that non-violence was the best way to proceed with this case, it meant they had already tried everything else. And it did not work.

One hell of a faerie. I almost admired the creature. I knew how it must feel. Plucked away from its home, away from its family, everyone and everything it ever knew and loved. To be dragged from place to place, away from basic necessities and drenched in pain. From every way and every direction.

"Have you heard any rumours? Why they chose me for this?"

Michael was on my last bag, so I had another minute or two to make conversation. Probably the only normal chat I would have in the next month. I did not plan to use my leave, I did not plan to give the faerie any reprieve. I would stay there with it, live and breathe, eat, sleep and shit by its side until it cracked.

"No idea, Elly. All I heard is that orders came from higher up and Milosh was pissed. He didn't want you for this and tried to push one of the captains, but he was overruled."

"And the orders?"

I did not know how many there were or when they would be coming. I hadn't been briefed, hadn't been given any weapons. I was going in completely blind.

"They will come sealed and directly to you."

"To me?" I had to make him repeat, because it didn't make any sense. Generally, depending on the progress of the intervention, a team would stay behind and compare analysis, deciding the best course of action on a daily basis. Not give them directly to the interviewer.

"Who will I be in communication with?"

Michael shook his head. "No idea, Elly. It's freaking weird." Then he handed me the last bag and with a tight smile he wished me luck.

As I placed my bags on the rolling band to be scanned and passed through the metal detectors, I started making mental notes. It was hard to remember everything I had learnt, all the information I found in the books I kept checking out from the library and spent hours examining every chance I got.

The years of self-defence and combat training would kick in when danger was detected, so I did not worry about my own safety as much as I did about this new mission I knew nothing about.

All the notification said was today's date, beginning of assignment and subject. I went ballistic as soon as I read it and marched into Milosh's office, when I clearly should have been worrying about other things.

*Better the devil you know*, an inner voice whispered. The same one that urged me to keep going. To keep fighting. To not surrender and never shed tears in front of them. To live humiliation in my own time and keep my head high every time I stepped in public.

Today was just another one of those days. Where I had to keep my calm and face the situation rationally. If I was to receive direct orders, past Milosh and his band, it meant that they were coming from higher up.

That I had been spotted and observed by someone, somewhere, who decided to give me this, for better or worse. To make me the youngest major in the unit, at only twenty-nine. And a woman, above all that.

Someone, higher up, had answered my prayers.

Day 0.9

"All cleared," one of the security guards who passed my bags through the metal detector announced.

"All cleared," the one who scanned every section of my body with a smaller metal detector replied.

"Ready to go, Harrow?" Milosh's voice echoed through the empty room, the preparation room as we liked to refer to it. I had been there many times in the past three years, during my service for the Intelligence Office, but every time it adapted to the needs of the interrogation. Only the process remained the same, but there was no guarantee as to what I would find on the other side of that door.

Before I even started, I had to pass my final psychological evaluation, which the general in charge had to put his signature on. Hence Milosh looking at me with that disgusted grin I had come to love to hate at 11:55 pm, only five minutes from my start date.

"Move it, Harrow, I don't have all night," he grunted just as his ass fell on a chair.

Without another word, I moved to the table with two chairs, one already occupied by my annoyed superior and pulled it just enough to allow me space to take a seat.

"Sir," I half-nodded, not as much in greeting but to tell him that I was ready to go.

"You already know the drill, so I'm not going to waste my time. Same rules as always, you can do whatever you need to, except kill the investigation. The use of blunt force is allowed in any measure you consider fit, however no objects that would lead to direct damage are to be stored in the room. And you are responsible for its nourishment. I don't care what the fucker will eat, but this time, it's on you."

What in the four gods?

Why the fuck would I be responsible for its food?

It was a well-known fact that the individual's nourishment was included in the mission allowance, and I had to fend for myself. So why did I now have to spend *my* money on the thing? *Fucking hell.*

Having no other choice and with a ticking clock at my back, I confirmed.

"Understood," I spoke as soon as he finished the sentence, fully aware of all the boxes he had to check before letting me in.

"You will have at your disposal a fully equipped bedroom with the utilities you have mentioned in your initial interrogation trial request, which has been passed and approved 38 months ago."

"Understood." Another tick.

"You are granted leave every forty-eight hours for a duration no longer than ten percent of the time spent in the interrogation room. The time can be accrued to reach, but not exceed twenty-four hours of continuous leave."

"Agreed."

"The success of this appointment trial is the full subject cooperation and completion of various elements which will be numbered and announced to you after the start of the process. The orders are to come directly to you."

"Okay…" This tick sounded weird, and I had so many questions about it, but only two and a half minutes to complete this test, so I had no choice but to keep my mouth shut.

"The analytics team will participate in the investigation remotely and inform you of any actions/remarks alongside the elements during their arrival. Web is installed in the bedroom, kitchen and living room area, the bathroom remaining undated for privacy reasons. Should any events happen in the premises not covered by cameras, you are to report them via the audio connection of any of the other surface."

"Wait, they are going to record this? Why not bring a team here, like we always do?"

"Harrow…" the darkness in the general's gaze made me keep my questions to a minimum. He had nothing to do with this and by the looks of it, he was annoyed as hell that his access to me was removed for such a long time. This had to definitely have come from higher up, someone with the power to overrule a general of an entire region.

"Understood."

"Your welcome letter, which is to be destroyed after verbal acknowledgement of receipt and memorization, will contain a secure code to be entered in a secret location that will be detailed in the contents of the same. You are only to use it in case of extreme danger, fire or threat upon your life."

"Yes, sir."

"Are you entering the premises on your own free will?"

"Yes, sir."

"Were you coerced in any manner to enter the premises?"

"No, sir."

"Are you medically fit to satisfy and achieve the tasks of this assignment?"

"Yes, sir."

"State your full name, rank and unit for the record."

"Ellyana Harrow, Captain in the Intelligence Unit of the Human Realm."

The last tick brought a full chorus of cherubs singing in my ears. With a final look to merit his attention, Milosh threw a letter across the table and pointed to the door with his pencil.

"Off you go then, Harrow. Have fun with the faerie."

*Day 1*

The metallic door in front of me slid open to reveal a pitch-black space. My eyes strained to the point of popping out of their sockets, trying to spot something, anything in the heavy darkness but I knew the drill. The location would not be made available to me until I ripped open the envelope.

At the sound of rustling paper, a small light turned on right above me, illuminating over my head, enough to allow me to see the letter, but not anything else around the space. Okay, message received.

Generally, an initial letter told me more about the subject I was supposed to interrogate, the process and their background and any challenges and KPIs I had to follow throughout the month. Truth be told, it never took me a month. Which is why I had drawn positive attention. I hoped.

I understood pain, it had been a constant companion since childhood and I knew, better than anyone, what a person in pain needed to hear. What they needed to be made to feel in order to see me as the friendly face, the only light strong enough to save them from the darkness they had been put through.

Instead, this letter was short, only three paragraphs, telling me what I already knew.

**"Dearest Captain Harrow,**

**We are delighted to learn of your acceptance of this appointment trial, and we take the opportunity to congratulate you in advance for your appointment as Major of the Intelligence Unit of the Human Realm.**

**We also want to pass our congratulations to the youngest female Captain in your region and know that we are delighted to meet you in person and discuss more about your future plans upon completion of this appointment trial.**

**The rules have already been explained to you, so we only take the opportunity to wish you good luck and may you have a fruitful trial. Please wait for more instructions to be delivered directly to yourself. Your secure code is 6803334435/465325 to be inserted on the keypad behind the metal case in the safe.**

**Warm regards,**

**PDD"**

PDD? I did not recognise that unit, as far as I knew there were no PDD units in the Human Realm. Well, whatever it meant and whoever they were, I found myself under their employment for the next month, so I better start working.

6803334435/465325

I repeated the code like coordinate routes, adding meaning to each of the numbers until they remained in my head.

"Memorisation complete," I said to no one in particular, but Milosh had asked for verbal confirmation.

As soon as I spoke the words, another light appeared to display a sink. So, the entrance was through the kitchen. Good to know, because in most cases, this was also the only exit.

The sink was filled with water, a plate resting at the bottom. I knew what needed to be done and stepped towards it to drop the letter inside.

The printed paper started dropping its ink at the contact with water. I inhaled a deep breath to mark my first completed step of this long month ahead. The destruction of the letter.

I watched the ink drip and fade into the water, releasing dark hues against the inox and watched the dirty plate that looked to have been dropped in there recently, by someone who must have been too hungry to wait until all preparations were done. In that very moment, my stomach decided to grumble, reminding me that we haven't eaten in over eighteen hours.

Something to be remedied soon, there was no better bond than sharing food.

"Now where the hell are the lights?"

Instantly, the entire room lit up.

Cool trick. I turned to examine the small kitchen. A table with two stools, a mini fridge and a cupboard with lots of cans. I wasn't sure the food was enough to last for two, but then I also did not hold information about the subject. For all I knew, they could eat trees and I'd have to go out for two hours every other day and forage for their feed.

One step at a time. I walked out of the small room into another wad of darkness, but this time I was prepared. "Can I have some light in here too?"

In the next second, the lights were on. I was starting to like this voice control thing. Uncomfortable that an entire team had to be watching my every move, but it wasn't so different to the screens I had to use before, where the analytics team could hear and see everything I was doing. The only difference was that these PDD people had a bird's eye view. And more funds, clearly.

The living room was massive and filled with...gym equipment? It was not really a sitting area like I thought it would, but rather a fully functioning home gym. Okay, so the subject must really like pain.

"Is there a bedroom?"

New lights turned on in the next room to reveal a small bedroom. I walked to the new area and prepared myself to find my bags thrown around one side of the room, but instead I found a very nice and inviting double room.

With a double bed.

And my bags carefully stored to one side, next to a nightstand.

A double bed sounded amazing.

"Thank you," I heard myself say, the words escaping my mouth on their own accord. I never had a bed this big. Never, ever, in my entire life. I grew up in bunk beds and when I finally got my own room, three years ago, they gave me a single with a worn-out mattress. I could have bought my own, but beds were expensive and delivering one to our unit, in such a remote area would have cost me a fortune. So, I made do with the military supplied one and enjoyed the privacy.

I did experience the joys of double beds on my leave, where I visited the nearby town and got invited to spend the night with some guy or another. But I only used one for sex, never sleep, preferring to leave as soon as the deed was done and my needs sated. For safety reasons.

Unable to resist the temptation, I threw myself on the mattress and splayed my body onto the massive bed, enjoying the feel of soft cotton sheets and the bounciness of a, obviously new, mattress. I could definitely get used to this. I envisioned myself sleeping here comfortably for the next thirty days while the faerie hung onto the ropes of the home gym, exercised its nocturnal energies or whatever it was that said faerie liked to do.

It felt weird not to have the subject with me already, not to know anything about them except their fae origin, but nothing about this appointment trial had been conventional so far.

I decided to make the best out of my spare time and get familiarised with the new location. I checked out the bathroom, the only room with a door which was pretty standard. A toilet, a small cupboard filled with towels and a bathtub with an incorporated shower along with shower gel, shampoo and the necessary elements. Nothing special enough to keep me interested, so I focused back on the bedroom, which I planned to fully occupy.

I unpacked and filled the wardrobe with my clothes and other garments, not leaving much space for the coming faerie. I still couldn't believe they gave me a faerie. My first faerie. The first one in the unit if I remembered correctly. I had been trained on humans only and the faerie folklore lessons kept things to a minimum, so I truly didn't know what to expect.

It would probably be some sort of furry creature or a winged thing that would not need clothing anyway. I placed my uniform on hangers, determined to have it on hand even in this informal setting. It was my mission to befriend and extract information, but one must not forget we were on different sides. First impressions were a priority.

I checked out some of the books in the small cupboard by the wall, all of them novels. I hadn't read a novel since I was a teenager and even then, it was so difficult to sneak them in, that the risk of getting caught did not make it worth it. I read my fair share of romance books, which became useful later on, when I started being alone with men. Had I not learnt about sex from those books, I would have had no idea how to react when seeing a naked man.

And I also learnt that romance books were exactly what they sounded like, an escape from this life, where everything was exaggerated, and nothing was real. Because no man caressed my body like the main heroes of those novels, no man looked at me like his life depended on my smiles and no one took the time to prepare me for the sexual act. They did not even care if I found release.

So yeah...not going to touch those anytime soon.

I focused instead on food. I found the fridge stocked with cheese, meat and vegetables, so I made myself a stir fry and two sandwiches, wanting to make sure I had as much nutrition as I possibly could before starting the mission.

"Is there a clock in here?" I asked out loud, hoping that this supervised home would talk back to me or give me the information I required.

A robotic voice sounded from the ceiling, making me realise that if the speakers were planted everywhere, they must have a double purpose and become mics as well. Which meant that the entire surface of the ceiling was a recording device.

"The time is 4:37 AM."

"Any idea what time the faerie is getting here?" I took my chances and looked up in question.

"Your first instruction will arrive tomorrow afternoon. Please take the time to rest in the meanwhile."

I was on a mission, and I was wasting time. Not much relaxing in that. But I decided to listen to the voice and sat down at the table to enjoy my meal. I normally ate in a hurry and always standing. Sitting at the table felt nicer than I remembered. Once the meal was over, I started exploring my surroundings and once that was finished as well, I decided to catch some sleep.

I had no idea what time it was, but my body felt rested. My bones did not crack when I rose from bed for the first time in forever. I freaking loved this mattress. The sheets were soft and smelled amazing, the pillow was just the right fit to support my neck and keep my spine straight. Basically, I had the best sleep in as long as I could remember.

"Can you tell me the time, please?"

"14:12," the ceiling robot announced.

Shit, I jumped and hurried to the bathroom. Shit, shit, shit, I overslept. To the point of losing an entire morning.

I took exactly three minutes to pee and shower, then jumped in my uniform and grabbed a banana from the kitchen counter to fill my stomach. The over-eating, plus the mattress and having no natural light made my body forget that we had things to do.

"I'm ready," I looked up, circling around the gym to make sure all the cameras spotted me and that whoever was watching gave me a chance to rectify this silly sleep. I looked like an amateur, coming in here, enjoying the good life without giving a damn about the mission. This was not me. Not at all. I had to stay focused and earn whatever PDD planned to entrust me with.

"The first instruction is in the drawer of the right nightstand," my robot friend told me, making me rush to the bedroom. Was someone in here while I slept? Because I had checked every corner last night and found no instruction letters.

The letter was short, containing only two words that did not make too much sense.

**"Welcome Gale."**

Okay...what was I supposed to do with that? I didn't know a Gale. Was Gale supposed to visit? Was it PDD? Hundreds of questions rushed through my mind, but I found my robotic friend silent after I uttered each one. No one was listening. Or if they did, they did not plan on helping me with this issue.

Which again, was odd, because an analytics team was supposed to help with whatever questions and support I needed during the trial. During any trial, for that matter.

By dinner time, my anxiety went through the roof. I baked some potatoes and sausages and opened a fizzy drink, hoping that the sugar rush would keep my heart from pumping to its untimely death and I asked the roof robot what time it was so often, that it decided to give me regular updates.

At ten pm, just as I was prepared to go out of my mind, the ceiling started buzzing slowly.

"New message for Captain Harrow. Please confirm acceptance."

"Yes, yes, I accept," I pointed my full attention upwards, scanning the white ceiling without even breathing from fear of missing a word.

**"Dearest Captain Harrow,**

**Please accept our apologies for the delay in the start of this trial. A complimentary electronic device has been brought to your disposal to keep you entertained while you wait. Please note that some instructions may be delivered to you electronically."**

As soon as the message ended, a metallic creak made its way into the living room. I hurried to check the disturbance and spotted the gym equipment sliding to the side, as if on a conveyor belt to make room for a box to be lifted from underneath the floorboards on some sort of an elevating platform.

I blinked a few times and watched the sliding motion with amazement, wondering, once again, how many funds have gone into these quarters.

"Thank you…" I said to no one in particular but hoped that the ceiling robot heard me and moved to pick up the box to find a tablet inside. One of the new models, which must have cost months of my wages.

To keep me entertained, they said. Fortunately, it came fully charged, so I did not have to waste time with cables and went straight to the bedroom. Very well, if they were going to be late, at least this offered me more preparation time. I went straight to the search tab and typed 'Gale.'

After an hour and a half of reading articles, I still had no clue as to who I was supposed to share these rooms with. There was no type of faerie called a gale, I went through hundreds of pages and even chatted to some online libraries, for them to come up with the same answer. Which meant that it had to be a name.

And if the faerie had a name, it meant that it could openly communicate in our language, which was another bonus for me. Having to use speech detectors only worsened my job. I also searched for PDD but gave up quickly after discovering that it was a lesser faerie kink and many sex pages dedicated thousands of videos to it. Not something I would like to see again. Or try.

My eyes started drooping and I found myself dozing off when another noise came from the living room. This time sounding heavier, as if the load was much more difficult to push through.

"What is this?" I asked again when a massive crate made its way into the room through the hidden system underneath the floorboards.

"Please read the note," the robotic voice I had grown so accustomed with replied.

A small envelope, like one of those delivery cards, was attached to the side of the massive wooden crate, so I picked it up and opened it.

**"Dearest Captain Harrow,**

**Please accept our apologies for the delay. Gale is not best known for his collaboration skills."**

Another delay? Seriously? I hoped they were not planning on taking this time away from my trial, because we had already lost about twenty-four hours.

This was weird as fuck. First, I had no knowledge of the subject, then I had no idea of the premises and no analytics team and now we kept expecting delays as if this was some sort of train station. Unable to contain my rage, I kicked the crate, shoving my boot into the wood and making splinters burst from my anger.

The side popped open, the nails sustaining it too rusty to hold onto the wood. How long had this crate been closed for? I moved to the side, tilting my head to peek through the opening and my heart leaped out of my chest, because inside the wooden box, a bloodied figure trembled at the sight of light.

It was chained.

# Day 2

What in the hell? How was this even...

I shook my head, banning all the questions. They did not matter. Nothing mattered but the shaking figure, covered in blood and wounds, trembling inside the wooden box. By the state of those rotten pieces and the rust around the nails, this figure had stayed inside the box for a long time.

Surrounded by damp and cold.

In the dark.

Of course it shook at the sight of light, forcing its body to retract, surely thinking that whatever happened to it before being put inside those tiny walls, will start again. Poor thing, to think that being buried alive was a reprieve from pain.

My mind registered the instruction only then.

"Welcome Gale," the note had said. They apologised for tardiness. And then this wooden box was somehow delivered to me, with a being inside. I inched a bit closer to gain a better view of the interior, without frightening the faerie. Because it was a faerie, if those chains were what they seemed to be.

Iron.

They had put it away, for gods know how long, without food or water, bound in iron and darkness. I didn't even want to think how their skin must look like, the pain they had to suffer through, possibly for days or even weeks.

Which told me several things:

1. This Gale creature was strong.

2. This Gale creature had been uncooperative to the point of deserving punishment in detriment of collaboration

3. The creature was hurt

4. The creature will most definitely be unable to speak or fend for itself for quite some time

5. This completely messed up at least the first week of the trial

6. I would have to be made responsible to care for it

Fuck me sideways.

I gave myself a minute to force down the frustrations and anger that had no one to be directed at but the one in front of me, and it clearly had more than enough. I was not here to hurt. I was here to befriend.

Putting an imaginary friendship cap on, I tried to think through what it would need. I tried to put myself in its place and think what my first necessities after such dreadful days would be. Weeks? It could not have been months. Definitely not months.

"Hello…" I whispered softly to the box. At the sound of my voice, it started jittering, the wood creaking under brisk movements. I assumed it tried to rip away those chains and escape a new round of torture. A part of me wondered how many times it had to do just that, trapped alone and in the darkness.

"You are safe now, no one is going to come and hurt you…"
*For the next twenty-nine days at least.* I kept that part to myself, no use giving more information that I had to. I did not know what happened to the subjects after their removal from the living quarters, after I extracted the information we needed. In my happy dreams, I liked to think they were set free and could return home to their families, mates and partners. In my nightmares, I knew the cruelty of the realm I had chosen to live in.

I stepped closer to the box, ensuring that my gestures were slow and easy to decipher. The last thing I wanted to do was scare the creature even more. It had the potential to become aggressive and I did not want that. I did not fear for my safety, because after being iron bound for so long, I already knew the faerie had limited to no power. I was mostly concerned by the adrenaline its fear would produce. Which would weaken my new subject even more.

I suddenly become protective of it, for it was mine for the next twenty-nine days and since whomever the people at PDD were, turned out to be merciless bastards, I wanted to offer it a reprieve, even just for four weeks. I knew it did not mean a lot, but it was better than nothing.

Announcing my intention before moving, I took another step closer, my boots touching the rotten wood.

"I am going to open the box a little more, so we can see each other better and to open enough space for you to get out. I promise you are safe, we are in a secure room and there is no one else around."

Grabbing the wood with both hands, I wrapped my fingers around its damp texture and tilted back with a pull, forcing the nails to rip lose and create a wider opening. Almost a full side of the box was now open, but instead of creating a calming environment, the faerie started jittering again, forcing its bloodied body to escape.

"Please, stop, you will hurt yourself." My educated guess turned out to be correct, those were iron chains, pounds of them wrapped around the crouched body. I watched with a grimace how the flesh on the faeries back ripped open from the pull of iron. "I cannot turn off the lights, they're going to be on for as long as we stay here. It's annoying, I know, but you get used to it."

I waited a while, until the faerie calmed down and stopped moving, determined to continue living at the back of that box and avoid the light.

"There is no one else here," I said again, this time adding a softer undertone, trying to make my voice calmer.

"It's only you and me and I promise I won't hurt you. Honestly...I don't even know you, they told me absolutely nothing about you..."

More silence came, crushing my hopes for this evening to go smoothly. The faerie was terrified, traumatised, in pain and unwilling to help itself. I knew that no matter what I did or said, nothing would be incentive enough to make it come out. I didn't even know if it could come out or if its legs were trapped under those chains with the rest of its body.

Some dark part of me understood it, though. It had lived in pain for so long that it became part of it, and once something crawls into your everyday existence, removing it becomes greater than the initial sting of blood.

What I did know, was that any being, no matter how strong, needed water after a long entrapment. Water and food. If I could not make it communicate or come out, I could at least offer some nourishment. To both make sure it did not die and to score some points in the friendship department.

Without another word, I stepped away from the box and went into the kitchen, searching the fridge for items that looked enticing but were also easy to chew or bite into. I did not know anything about the creature, I could not see it from the darkness of the box and the chains that covered its entire body, so I had to make do with whatever my mind sprouted.

What could be an 'impossible to say no to' meal?

Pizza, definitely. Chocolate cake. Ice cream. Pasta. Any form of junk food. Tacos.

I could make tacos, my mom taught me when I was a kid. I loved it when she would let the four of us in the small kitchen we had at home and gave us each a small chore to help her with. Being the oldest, I got to help her with chopping things and my sisters were always jealous of the small chopping board and the knife my mom told me to be careful with.

I remembered the smell of cooking oil, how she would fry a little bit of bread before frying the onions and let us share it between us. Bread was expensive, but she always let us eat as much as we wanted to, many times convincing us, and herself, that she did not like it. Just so we could have more.

I missed my mom. And her tacos.

I hadn't cooked in a long while, but this recipe was pretty simple, and I had all the ingredients. The faerie must have been starving, so I doubted it would make a fuss if my tacos turned out too salty. I did go easy on the spice, assuming my subject had a raw throat after lack of liquids. Everything went smoothly until it came to filling tacos, something I had no clue how to do, so I ended up spilling the filling on the sides.

No matter, they smelled amazing. Not to sing my own praises, but for someone who never had fresh herbs and vegetables at her disposal, I thought I did a pretty good job.

I hoped it liked coriander though, because I added lots of it. Sue me, avocado and coriander with lemon juice and salt and pepper is a match made in heaven.

"Hi, I'm back," I announced.

*Great job, Ellyana, we're now replacing the ceiling robot with a box,* I mentally sighed. "I made dinner," I put on a cheery voice to make the announcement. "We also have sparkling water, a fizzy cherry drink and ginger tea."

Again, nothing.

"It's getting cold..." I announced five minutes later, tired of sitting there with two sets of plates and all those drinks on a tray.

Of course, I got nothing.

Its nourishment was more important than my ego, and deep down I knew my staying there was the reason it wouldn't come out. And it needed to, those chains had probably infected its skin and I

41

did not fancy cleaning putrid flesh. I didn't fancy cleaning flesh at all.

"I'll just leave it here for you for when you are ready. It's late so I'll go to bed, there's a bedroom just here. There's also a bathroom if you want to have a shower and…do other things." Whatever kind of faerie it was, it needed to relieve itself somehow.

After a few seconds of silence, I got tired of waiting and stepped away with my three tacos.

"Okay then, good night. See you tomorrow."

I took a step back and then another, until I got to the bedroom, but my eyes remained on the plate and drinks I had set on the ground in front of the crate.

The alarm I had set on the new tablet did not do a good job at keeping me awake. I heard the countdown buzzing, the volume I had set for the passing seconds having a calming effect rather than keeping me awake and after a while, the sound of time periodically passing, along with the lack of movement from the box sent me into a calming routine of blinking slower and slower.

Until of course, I fell asleep. I must have stayed up till four or five in the morning, but the faerie was either asleep itself or not planning to come out and I surely needed some rest if I was to deal with such a stubborn creature.

"What time is it?" I asked the ceiling robot with a groggy voice, too upset with the tablet that didn't keep me awake to pay it any attention.

"The time is ten forty-eight AM."

Okay, so we both slept for about six hours. Not that bad, I hoped that the faerie at least ate and drank to get some more energy.

I guessed wrong.

The plate of food hadn't been touched, the tea remained a pile of cold mush and the water bottle and can of soda were unopened.

Seriously? I even gave it privacy to come out and freaking eat. I started doubting its intelligence, because who, in their right mind, would refuse nourishment when given the opportunity, and especially, in captivity? Last night was the perfect moment for it to come out, eat and drink, explore, try to escape or even try to murder me in my sleep.

Instead, it chose to just stay there, in the same putrid box that for some reason, had become a shield. Stupid, stupid faerie.

I was especially annoyed because it interfered with my plans. We were already over thirty-six hours in, and I hadn't even met my subject. Hadn't learnt anything about it. And I was wasting valuable time.

Determined to make the first progress of the day, even if I had to force it, I stepped towards the box while slamming my boots on the hardwood floor, just to make sure the faerie was already awake.

"Hey buddy, I'm sorry to steal your thunder, but your box stinks like hell and we can't be living like this. So, brace yourself, because your home is going to disappear soon."

I did not give it time to reply, by this point I was ready to use blunt force and get it out. And what better way than destroying its home?

We did not have any weapons in the kitchen, but a rolling pin would do just fine. I grabbed it and went back to my friend in the box, ready for my morning cardio.

"You might want to mind your head in there. It's going to be noisy."

And with that, I started slamming the box from every side, forcing the wood to crack under the pressure. My every movement threw splinters around like they were fireworks and my eyes got hit a few times, but I tilted my head and continued my work. Two or three minutes later, what used to be a box remained a pile of mess. Still, the faerie did not move, did not even draw breath too loud while I was doing all that destruction.

Not that it had much choice now, it needed to come out one way or another.

"Don't worry, I'll rescue you from the rubble in just a second."

I didn't even know why I bothered at this point because clearly, I would be monologuing for a long time. But I was here for a reason, and I would not let anyone or anything mess up my plans.

Even a stubborn faerie in a mouldy box.

Careful to remove the nails and keep my fingers away from sharp edges, I started rummaging through the pile of broken wood, taking it apart piece by piece until a form started to show underneath. I continued to remove the broken pieces of wood until I reached chains.

Its entire body was encased in iron, even its head and face. No wonder it could not move, or speak, or eat and drink.

I was a fucking idiot. I'd basically tortured the creature, placing warm food next to it, forcing it to smell it for the entire night when its body could not move to reach it. A sharp rock dropped through my throat, down my oesophagus and into my stomach at the realisation. At the stupid, amateur thing I had done.

"I'm so sorry." The words were out before I could stop them, before I could even think them.

A blink, that's all it could do. A blink of acknowledgement, maybe gratitude for someone observing their situation and understanding it. I took a moment to look at its face, or what I could spot from behind those iron chains. PDD had basically mummified the creature in chains, leaving only its eyes, which had been covered in so much blood and grime, it was a wonder it could still see.

Could it?

By the way it blinked at me, I hoped it could. Sight was one of the most precious gifts of this life. I spotted a bit of green in those crimson injected eyes, a shade so deep it almost made me fall to my knees. It reminded me of sprouting leaves, of a lake in a forest, reflecting sunlight and life. It reminded me of home.

"Can you stand?"

Silence and another deep blink, this time heavier, carrying regret. Definitely a no.

"Okay, let's make a system. One blink for yes, two for no, okay?" I stepped closer and placed my face in front of its eyes to make sure it saw me.

One blink. Yes. Okay.

"Can you breathe okay?"

One blink.

"Can you move?"

Two blinks. *No, it could not move you flipping idiot, it was trapped in tons of iron.*

"Can you speak?"

Two blinks.

"You must have enjoyed my monologue a lot last night then, huh?"

One blink. Yes.

"You are a cheeky faerie aren't you?" An involuntary smile cropped on my lips.

It did not gain any blinks. Was that a maybe?

"Right, let's establish priorities. I can move the chains around your mouth and bring you water or I can start unwrapping you, but we both know it will take a while and you'll be in a lot of pain. So, one blink for water, two blinks for removing chains."

This one I already knew and before the one blink even came to an end, I rushed to find a straw and filled a glass with water to bring it back to the subject.

I retook my position and announced my intention to shift the chains across its face to uncover its lips. That got me no blinks, so I jumped into action and shifted a few chains to reveal a mouth. And some very burnt and bleeding lips.

I'd seen faeries in chains before, and I knew how iron burnt their skin. By the deep wounds on this one, it must have not been moved for a while, creating a deep cut into its flesh. Which only confirmed my suspicions, the creature had been locked away for some time.

"Drink slowly, your throat is probably raw, and it will hurt like a bitch," I announced while placing the straw on the side of its lips that was least burnt, doing my best to avoid causing more pain. My advice did not stick though, as soon as the faerie's lips touched water, it inhaled it in a few gulps, desperate to hydrate itself. Its eyes widened, I had to assume because of the pain, but it did not stop until the glass fully emptied.

"Another?"

One blink.

"Coming right up."

My subject did the same with the second glass and a third one. It clearly wanted more, but I stopped offering, I had no idea what to do if it started being sick and choked on those chains.

"We need to start unwrapping you, I'm afraid."

One blink.

Okay, so at least it was being realistic.

"Do you have any advice on where to start?"

Although I knew the technicalities of iron binding and I had to remove chains from time to time from subjects, it had always been around the wrists or ankles, just a small chain or two, enough to keep them grounded. And they had been on regular human skin. This one though...I had absolutely no idea what to do.

And it didn't either because my question did not gain any blinks.

"I would start with your face, so you can start healing your lips and eat something. That's a priority. And then I'd go down and do your torso, so you can breathe better."

One blink.

Alright, food and oxygen it is. I was starting to like this creature, simple and to the point.

Getting it done took us the better part of the afternoon. The chains were so tangled and tightly pressed against its skin that every movement caused a disturbance somewhere else. And we had to take many breaks.

I was glad I didn't eat anything that day because the sight of flesh falling off the chains, and the knowledge that said flesh used to be someone's face turned my stomach. I did my best to keep my disgust at bay and breathe through my nose every time I had to pull away at its muscles, but the sight of it, and the thought of the amount of pain it must be enduring crawled under my bones.

By the time its face was released, only a few pieces of hair were left and its eyes, which seemed to blink a lot better, remained. It missed the better part of its nose and mouth, the lips looking like dangling pieces of meat rather than a proper way to speak or eat.

"Do you want to eat now?"

Two blinks.

"But can you eat, are your teeth okay?" In my defence I'd been invested in this from the start, so I did not think the question odd at all.

Its jaw shifted just enough to open part of its mouth and show me teeth. Human looking teeth.

"Awesome, so we can have meals together from now on."

One blink.

"Do you want me to continue?"

This question merited a small, barely noticeable dip of its chin and I could only wonder how much pain that single action took. Which in turn told me that it wanted nothing else but get rid of these chains.

"Okay, okay," I nodded. "I won't stop until we're done."

"Plee..z..."

*Shit, it talks.* More like it grunts and sounds barely pronounceable, but still.

"Okay," I nodded again, determined, and fully committed to this. "I'll get you out."

I kept my promise, the job taking us both into the late hours of the night.

*Day 3*

The last chain was out. I was so tired my entire body shook, my hands especially, from the weight of the chains I had to constantly pull. A massive pile of bloodied iron remained splayed around me. Around us.

It was finally free, but instead of jolting, trying to run or jumping away, the faerie fell to the ground with a thud.

Nothing much remained of it, only a torso and limbs, all covered in broken flesh. It reminded me of the anatomy lessons I took as a child, where they showed us a picture of the human skeleton and another picture, right next to it, with the categories of muscles and how they curved around the body.

Because that is what it looked like. There was no proper portion of skin that I could spot or analyse, only bones and meat, somehow still put together to reveal a human-like figure. Only those green eyes had remained. Pinned on me since the very moment I started pulling, observing me for hours on end until the last clink of the iron armour they had forced on the subject fell.

"Hey, hey, are you okay?"

I didn't want to touch it, did not want to cause more damage and pain so I followed it to the ground, tilting my head to make eye contact with the faerie. Who exhaled deeply and blinked at me again.

"Sleep..." it spoke before shutting those green eyes that swam in relief.

"Okay, I'll let you sleep," I murmured, lowering my voice.

A few seconds later the faerie was either passed out or deeply asleep. Not that there was a major difference between the two, its body completely shattered from the iron binding.

**"Feed Gale."**

Short and to the point. And very easy to do, were the faerie ever going to wake up. It slept for the entire day and into the late evening without moving once. I mean, who could blame it? Had it even been able to sleep until now, trapped in those burning iron chains?

What in the hell had PDD done to it? And why was it now falling to me to care for it? How could I befriend and extract information from a creature who was skinless, in pain, passed out and half dead? Without even knowing what kind of information I was supposed to get?

This was weird, so damn weird. Someone was either messing with me and pissing themselves while enjoying my struggle on the cameras or this was bigger than all of us and everything was too classified to even be revealed. *Welcome Gale. Feed Gale.*

I fucking would, if Gale could wake up and eat.

# Day 4

Fuck this, I'm going out. "Open the door, I'm taking my accrued leave," I announced to the ceiling robot I hadn't spoken to in two days.

Fortunately, it listened and the kitchen door, which looked like a sealed shut wall, opened some sort of a latch to let me punch in my emergency code. I spotted two guards outside and as soon as they saw me storming out, both of them abandoned their cosy chairs in the hallway to come after me.

"E, what happened?" One of them asked, but I did not reply. I was too pissed off and they could not help.

"I'm going to see Milosh. Where is he?"

"He's out…" I did not have to turn to understand the confusion in his voice. In all my trials, I had never once abandoned my post without prior warning and confirmation of a specific time.

"What do you mean he's out?" Rage boiled in my blood, confirming what I already feared. This was either a prank or I was set up to fail. Because how could the unit's general leave his post during a trial appointment? Such a thing was never meant to happen, not when I could be attacked or killed at any point, not when the subject could escape and wreak havoc around the quarters. And two guards only? This was a joke. Unfortunately for them, the two men found themselves at the receiving end of my fury.

"What the fuck is this?" I did not care if I was shouting, I did not care if my outburst drew attention. Good, I wanted everyone to see this. I wanted them to know how unfair this was. How they thought that I would just take it and not fight back. They should have known better…They should have learnt by now…

"I demand to speak to Milosh right away. I don't care where the fuck he is, bring him back or I go to his house."

"Harrow, aren't you needed elsewhere?" I could recognise that voice in my deepest nightmares, because that was where it belonged. Castro. My partner in training, my enemy in the unit and one of the ugliest men to ever walk this earth. Which is why he felt the need to compensate with pure hatred.

"Oh, you mean that trial that's going to make me your superior?" I snapped, then instantly regretted it. I trained for this, I worked on this for so long. I could not lose my temper every time a bully showed up. In this unit, I would have to live my entire day chasing it back.

"I need Milosh," I added without giving him a chance to respond.

"He's out," Castro confirmed what the guards already told me.

"That's not a helpful answer. Who is in charge in his stead?"

"You're looking at him."

Well, fuck. At least Milosh hated me but did not put his mind into destroying me. Castro and his squad however…

"I need some sort of healing energy," I pressed my tone and forced out the demand.

"Don't tell me you're finally deciding to fix your face? Is pretty boy making you feel ugly?"

*Pretty boy?* If he was referring to the pile of faerie-meat I had left melting on the floor, he would have a big surprise.

"Who do I speak to about trial requirements?"

"Beats me," he shrugged as if he did not give a damn about my worries. I don't even know why I bothered. No one had ever lent me a helpful hand, why did I think this time would be different?

"And what am I supposed to do?" I frowned, thinking out loud rather than expecting an answer.

"Speak to whoever gives you instructions. And try make-up once in a while," he patted my shoulder with a crude smirk.

I turned on my heels and paved an alley of curse words until I got back to the training quarters. Castro's idea wasn't half bad and the only actual chance I had.

"Hello?" As soon as I walked back in the kitchen the door sealed shut behind me, trapping me inside. I stepped close to the home gym to find the faerie still passed out.

"I need some sort of healing energy, something appropriate for this kind of faerie."

Long minutes passed without an answer. Time during which my heart started palpitating with commotion, my gaze scanning the faerie and trying to find at least one improvement from the day before. Nothing. It was not healing. It did not have enough energy left to chew, let alone grow muscle and skin.

"Why are you making this request, Captain Harrow?" the ceiling responded, making me jump. This was not the robotic automated voice I had been talking to, this was an actual person at the other end. A man.

"Milosh, is that you?" It did not sound like him, but I had to try. And hope he was willing to respond.

"This is PDD," the man said after a while.

"Um...nice to meet you. Thank you for the opportunity. I propose a subject inspection sir, its health is deteriorating by the minute." Two birds with one stone. He'll have to come inspect the faerie, which meant he would come in and I would finally get to meet this PDD. "Request denied."

Of course it couldn't be that easy, who was I kidding?

"Sir, this thing is dying, I need something to put it back together or this mission will fail." I looked up, pleading, hoping to spot some sort of camera or monitor that would give me a clue as to what was happening.

"Unless that is the purpose of the trial, to set me to fail? To have this faerie die here?"

Another minute of silence that almost gave me a heart attack. "Cloutie root will be delivered in the next hour along with dosage instructions," the voice, my mysterious superior, announced before shutting the connection.

# Day 7

I groggily gave up my cosy bed to turn off the tablet's alarm and prepare the Cloutie tea, a ritual I had become able to perform in my sleep.

*Cloutie root is going to take effect within twenty-four hours, to be boiled for ten minutes and given to the subject as and when needed.*

That made me excited on the first day and I hurried to make the tea and follow the instructions, eager to get the faerie healed and talking.

I used another straw and placed it gently in the faerie's mouth, urging it to start sucking the healing drink. It took it a while to react and even longer for its lips to start moving, but when it did, I swear I heard angels singing. The mug emptied in a few minutes, and I found myself spending the entire day checking on the subject. On the hour.

To see no improvement.

Of course, I made another tea, and when the second one did not work, I made another. And another. For three days.

With absolutely no effect.

I knew all about the Cloutie trees and how precious they were for the faeries. The purest plants to ever exist, highly protected. Given to them by their Earth goddess, Catalina after her passing as a way to keep them safe and protected. Legend says that the early faeries used to hang their clothes on the Cloutie trees and wait for the connecting energies to discover the injuries in their bodies and regenerate it.

It must have been amazing to have healing trees hanging around and use them whenever you had a scratch, broke a leg or even slept wrong. Not something we could find nowadays. Cloutie trees were protected and kept away, in special and top-secret locations and I wondered how much the bag of roots I had received must have cost.

Which again, raised the question of funding for this operation. Who in the hell had so much money to invest in a full bag of Cloutie and give this faerie as much as it needed to be healed?

I still had no answers about the faerie, but I reached the conclusion that Gale must be its name. The tablet did not help to identify another species and judging by the delayed effect the Cloutie tea had on it, I decided it must have been one of the subspecies of the main faeries. Its muscles started to regenerate, covering the old injuries in some sort of pink jelly, which made me think that it was preparing to grow scales, tree bark or some sort of hard cover.

I had tried to move it a few times, but every time I suggested it and approached the faerie to touch it, it groaned in pain. I also feared infection, dragging it and creating more injury, so I decided to leave it on the floor, just like the first day and offer it a pillow and a blanket. It did not touch them, preferring the hard surface.

The tablet alarm started buzzing again, this time with the notification that announced a new instruction, making me run to check the screen.

**"Meet Gale."**

Only this time, something new appeared: a subtext with grey lettering, barely noticeable on the white background.

*Instruction to be completed in two hours.*

I had already met the faerie and cared for it for four days, so I wasn't sure what this instruction referred to. Nonetheless, I decided to follow my routine and start preparing the morning dose of Cloutie tea, checking the faerie on my way to the kitchen.

Something shifted, the energy in the room buzzed with excitement, even the electricity felt more potent all of a sudden. I instantly hurried to the faerie, expecting to find the pile of growing meat I got used to checking on in the past few days.

Instead, a muscled backside, fully covered with skin appeared from under the blanket, dark hair branching out on the pillow.

A male, I barely breathed. Gale was a fae male.

My fingers tightened, causing the tablet to fall on the wooden floor with an echoing thump. Which in turn caused the faerie to draw a sharp breath. Waking him up.

My legs rooted themselves in that spot, making my muscles unable to move or react. My entire body strained, this new information changing everything, even the way I drew breath or apparently, reacted.

It couldn't be, they could not give me a fae male.

I blinked a few times, eyes straining to spot anything out of place, anything that might make me wrong in my assumption, but every visible part of the new body marked what I already knew. What my eyes refused to acknowledge. Perfection.

"I am not going to fuck him for information," I burst out, not caring who heard me, the message solely directed at PDD. If there was one thing that proved always valid for fae males, sex was like their oxygen. They were made for it, built for it, excellent at it.

And I was the only female captain in my unit, chosen for unknown reasons, not given information about my subject or the purpose of my trial.

"Captain Harrow," the not so robotic voice trembled across the room.

"No! Fuck you! You chipped away years of my life, I endured the unthinkable and did what I never thought I would, but you will not have this. It's the only thing I have left." My heart started pounding, deep palpitations fell across my chest like rocks on the smooth surface of a lake, each one causing more pain.

This could not be happening. They would not squeeze my dignity out of me.

Everything shook. The floor, my legs, the ceiling. My lungs filled with shame, with regret and desperation.

They could not use me like this, they could not command me to do this. I deserved better, my heart deserved better. I would not let them, I would not—

"Breathe…" Fingers locked on my right shoulder, grounding me to reality, the voice dripping smoothly down my body, caressing my inability to draw oxygen.

My chest heaved, claws battling to escape inside of my torso, scratching everything in their path. My lungs, my dreams, my future.

"Breathe," the voice said again, gripping me from the darkness I was sinking into, its strength guiding me towards calm. Towards a new breath.

The shadows from the corners of my eyes started dissipating, giving way to new light. Allowing reality to sink in, transporting me back to the room I found myself locked in. Understanding whose fingers rescued me from the brink of a panic attack.

A new force possessed my ankles, giving them sudden strength.

"Don't touch me," I shifted my shoulder, making the fingers slide away from my t-shirt and down my skin. They touched my arm and part of my elbow on their way to separation.

The brief contact raised goosebumps across my skin, wrapping me in warmth and sweet relaxation. A fire started burning in my chest, sending sweet sensations across my body, to my lips and in between my legs, waves of desire caressing my thighs like velvet kisses. I felt beautiful, sensual and needy. Each pulsation starting in my core demanded release.

Fuck me, he was strong. If one accidental touch sent me into this frenzy, I did not want to imagine what a hug would feel like. What looking into his eyes or seeing him smile would cause me to do.

The part I kept buried all my existence came alive, wanting to be loved, needing to be caressed and cherished, to feel attractive and desired, to relish in this feeling. I had never once been loved, never been made love to properly. Maybe he was the one, the one to take me to places I had never been before. He was a fae after all, designed for love making.

"Fuck it, just stop, okay?" I turned on my heel and shouted, expecting to find him in deep concentration, observing my reactions with a wicked snarl.

Instead, the male blinked at me in surprise, those spring-green eyes taking me in with a dash of care and awareness.

"I'm...terribly sorry," he said, blinking at me as if he had no idea why I was so angry. I had to take a second to do the same because...gods damn me...wow.

What I had in front of me was nothing compared to the plasmatic, recovering pile of meat I had cared for the past seventy-two hours. A tall, dark-haired man stood in front of me, his torso looking like a Greek sculpture, packed and perfectly defined. I definitely understood why the need for a gym now.

His scythe-shaped dark eyebrows arched in wonder, and I only had to look for a second into those emerald eyes of his to know that our viewing experience must be very different. Where I saw a prominent straight nose and angular cheekbones, perfectly seasoned

61

with a mouth adorned by full lips, robust and seductive, ready to drop a smile or to steal a kiss, he saw a skinny face with a sucked in jaw. Nonetheless, I took my time to admire him, suddenly understanding all the mythical allure of fae males.

There were so many legends of women kidnapped by them, taken to faerie territories to be playthings, used for their flesh, and shared amongst the party. Sacrificed as offerings. Seduced and murdered.

They had the appearance of angels, but were cruel, wicked things. The one standing in front of me had to be no exception.

"I demand an operation analysis." My mouth released the words, but my eyes remained pinned on him. I was trapped in those gorgeous features, in that enticingly kissable mouth, in those eyes that had grown to be filled with life.

I never could express the colour of green I liked, never knew how to describe it. It was the first raw leaves of grass under a sunset, that green that defines the birth of nature. The exact shade of his eyes.

Which started to blink at me in confusion.

"I apologise, I don't understand," his dark brows arched, letting me observe how perfectly suited they were to his tall forehead, how they embraced his lines to form delightful features. An excellent complement to his locks, stretching in rivers of obsidian to reach his shoulders.

"Unfortunately, your request is not possible, Captain Harrow," PDD's voice echoed through the ceiling.

"In that case, I will unfortunately have to place my badge on the table and be on my way, sir." I released the words without dropping my gaze from the connection it started forming with the faerie's blinks of surprise. I wanted to see its reaction…his reaction.

By the surprise and wonder in those emerald beauties, he had no idea what was happening to him. Who I was.

A long silence scraped the walls. No one said a word or even breathed too loudly. Not me, not Gale and most certainly not PDD.

"I can accommodate a chat via the tablet you were provided," the ceiling finally responded.

"That would be acceptable."

"The request will be granted upon completion of your first instruction," the electronic buzzing draped the room, forcing Gale's neck to tilt, looking for its emitter.

"There's a speaker in the ceiling. We are being watched. So…it's nice to meet you, Gale," I replied loud enough to hear my own voice buzzing in my ears.

My frown must have demanded a response from the faerie, who dipped his chin once. A short and sharp movement, good enough to be caught on camera.

"First instruction completed; I will direct myself towards the bedroom to continue our conversation."

Without saying another word or even looking at the faerie…fae…Gale, I grabbed the tablet from where I had dropped it on the floor and headed to the bathroom, the only place where they could not record me. Where they could not hear me and waited for some sort of video call.

Exactly two minutes later, a chat bar opened on a white background.

"This is PDD."

"Can this conversation take place via video?" I touched the keyboard to form the words, though I already knew the answer before it came.

"Unfortunately, not."

"This is not okay. I am fairly sure this is illegal. You cannot force me to do this. And watch it? That is some sick shit you are up to, and I don't want to be part of any of it."

"Captain Harrow, I must admit my confusion as to what you are referring to."

The fucker. Seriously? Was he going to make me say it? You know what, fine, I internally sighed and started typing again.

"You put a fae male in a room with a single woman, without instructions or prior knowledge, without giving me information about the asset. What am I supposed to think? As I said initially, I will not be trading sexual favour for information. What you are asking of me is illegal and I am in my right to report it."

A sense of pride blanketed my back, caressing the spine I had just shown. I would not fuck my way through a promotion. I would not fuck my way to a home or better wages.

"Captain Harrow."

A minute of pause made me suffer through a cloud of anxiety until the words started appearing on the screen again.

"Please let me assure you that you have absolutely nothing to worry yourself about. You were chosen for this trial due to your proximity to the fae male rather than what is in between your legs."

"Right, so you expect me to believe that putting a fae male and a woman together was just a coincidence?"

"Captain Harrow, you were chosen for this assignment due to your place of birth, which corresponds to the subject's. We hoped that your proximity in childhood might help force a connection. This is classified information, though I will make an exception this time for your comfort."

Gale came from the Wind Realm. The place where I was born, the place where I grew up. The only one I had happy memories from. They chose me because I was an immigrant, I internally sighed, which I doubted it was better than being chosen due to my sex.

"How can I be protected from him? Be your reasons as they may, I am still left alone with a fae male, expecting to befriend and obtain information from it." I deleted the last word and replaced *it* with *him* before I sent the message.

After all, Gale was a person.

Another minute or two of silence made me think of the next month, of how I would have to live with this freakishly hot guy and how I could become a friend while keeping him away. My hardening nipples moaned at the thought of his skin against mine, of those full lips and all the things they probably knew how to do. Better than anyone I had been with.

"We have a suggestion which we hope will bring you more comfort," PDD finally wrote back.

"Please go ahead," I immediately typed.

"We propose the control of cameras in the bedroom to be connected to the tablet and turned on and off at your will, leaving permanently on the ones in the living room and the kitchen. As well as adding a lockable door to the bedroom. We hope this would offer you more privacy should the need for it arise."

"So Gale only stays in the kitchen and gym?"

"That is correct."

"Can these changes be implemented immediately?"

"Of course."

I took a deep breath, visualising my future. The cameras would be constantly on him, so the fae would be under supervision twenty-four seven, while I could use the bedroom for myself and lock the door so I could rest without him coming in here. I could work on him during the day and come in here and take as many cold showers as I needed to, then lock the door at night and leave him to his own devices.

It did not sound too bad. And it was for only twenty-three nights. Five hundred and fifty-two hours.

I had endured worse. I had endured longer.

"Thank you, I accept," I finally typed.

*Day 8*

The first night of uninterrupted sleep in over a month did wonders for my mood. After my conversation with PDD, if it could even be called that, two sets of workers arrived within the hour.

A pair of them spent the better part of the evening in the bedroom, picking apart the fake ceiling and doing wire work to disconnect the cameras. I lingered around and offered drinks, which they politely refused. I also tried to start a conversation, wanting to discover as much as possible about their jobs and more importantly, their superior, but all four of them were a closed book.

While the works took place, the faerie kept quiet, taking the opportunity to scan its surroundings…his surroundings…rummage the fridge and check everyone and everything. Thanks to our host, and the impromptu visit the workers had to make, Gale ended up with some new clothes as well and finally gave up the blanket he had been nestled in.

When I spotted him next, he wore black jeans and white trainers along with a white shirt that did nothing to cover all his distracting bits. The muscles on his back arched like a feline walking to its trapped prey, making his backside look strong and regal, standing tall and straight, with a perfect and imposing posture. It was a wonder that he could walk at all, let alone stroll around like the entire place belonged to him, after what I'd seen only days before. After what had remained of him after I pulled those chains away from his skin.

He had turned from a subject to an opponent, gaining strength by the minute, which, I had to say, had a terrible effect on his attitude.

He did not speak to the workers, who, compared to me, showed a lot of interest in him, and started asking questions no woman should have to be present to hear. Gale paid them little to no attention, becoming more interested in the gym equipment rather than the people in front of him.

When they finished fitting the door in the late hours of the evening, I took the opportunity to wish everyone a good night, grabbed the key and locked myself in the bedroom.

I was not planning on wasting more of my energy listening to dirty talk or how those stupid men talked about sex and women, all to gain Gale's appreciation and possibly some praise from a well versed sexual being. I had better things to do. Like shower and sleep.

The first thing I did after waking up was check the ceiling.

"What time is it?"

I waited a few seconds but received no answer, so I decided to try again, just to test my theory.

"Can you please tell me the time?"

Again, nothing. Which meant that along with the deactivation of the cameras, they had also taken out the mics, giving me full privacy and my very own bedroom. I could not complain and even felt a smirk curling my lips. Grabbing the tablet, I checked the time there instead, relieved that I would not have to go to the bathroom every single day to change. I had a full bedroom for that from now on.

A quick shower and new underwear, along with a fresh uniform lifted my mood, which remained good as I walked out the door, locking it and placing my key on a chain around my neck for extra safety.

The repetitive clink of metal on metal made me turn around the room and stare at the faerie. Lifting weights. Shirtless. Its muscled back dripping with sweat, summoning instant throbbing in between my legs, my nipples hardening in greeting. And guess who did not think it necessary to wear a bra.

"Morning..." I grunted and headed to the kitchen. I kept listening for the sound, for the repetition of the pull, which hadn't even halted to acknowledge my presence.

*Whatever buddy, I need coffee before dealing with all of that.*

Without throwing him a second glance, I stepped to the cupboard that held the tea, coffee and rest of the drinks, determined to indulge in a sugary treat before starting the day. I would not let some Gale faerie ruin one of the best sleeps I had in a long while.

Only the bastard had already managed to piss me off before I even had a bite of my toast. Because there was no toast, or any bread left for that matter. The same applied to most of the contents of the fridge and the majority of the cans in the cupboard. All empty and drained, their remains thrown around the kitchen floor.

"Excuse me!" I puffed my shoulders in protest, my stance ready for a physical fight should it come to it.

I hurried back to the home gym he had so clearly embraced as his new space, to spot more cans and half-eaten sandwiches laying around the various machines, some weights pressed over empty cans of soda. I stopped three feet away from him, but the faerie was adamant to continue lifting weights. My stomach twisted again at the sight of his arms tensing and the muscles pulling up and down, contracting with every movement.

My eyes spotted the way his wrists held pressure around the handle, his fingers fully wrapped around the metal bar, locked and shooting strength. Of course, my insides jumped to their own conclusion, thinking about what those fingers would be able to do and how expertly they would move in other environments, how the heavy calluses of his fingers would feel against the soft skin of my inner thighs.

Fucking stop! I shook my head to chase away those thoughts.

"Hey, excuse me?" I cleared my throat to draw attention to myself, since he clearly was not planning on stopping.

"You are excused," his voice rumbled, dropping on my skin like a silk blanket, raising gooseflesh in its wake.

"What?" I frowned, throat bobbing, eyes unable to avert from the constant tension of his muscles, the way his back arched with every pull. "What are you talking about?" I had to press my fingers into fists to stop the need to touch his shoulders, to make him turn to me.

Gale dropped the weights, making the room snap with the sounds of his abandonment and making my body twitch before turning abruptly. Those green eyes met mine, long dark lashes fanning at me, looking curious and disturbed by my insolence.

"You asked me to excuse you, twice. I already did. You are free to return to your lodgings," he spoke softly, elongating the words as if I needed further clarification, as though he wanted to make sure I understood.

"I don't want to be excused?" I inched closer, nipping at the shrinking distance in between us.

Annoyed, the faerie abandoned its post on the small bench, twisting its...his...leg to get it free and stood, displaying his statuesque posture and might. Fuck me twisted, he really looked like a statue. Like one of the gods, because who in this damn world could be this absolutely gorgeous? Tall, strong built, freakishly gorgeous and alluring. Even his skin emanated sensuality, his pores dripping sweat in the most delicious of ways, inviting my tongue to want to clean every inch of it and never stop until I licked every part of this man.

No wonder we were always told to stay away from fae males. I came to see now that it was not only their reputation, the fact that they lived for sex and liked to toy around with their food, but because they were simply...irresistible.

"What is it that you want then?" Gale took a step to me, causing my heart to leap out and my pussy to want to take flight and run to him. I needed him inside me, I wanted to know everything he would do, I needed to become his and offer myself to him body and soul. Come what may, a tumble with this man would make anything worth it.

"I am waiting, muffin," he crossed his arms, gazing at me with a half-grin, waking me up from my trance.

"That is exactly what I want," I said angrily, ignoring the silly name he found for me. Ha ha, let's make fun of my dark hair and olive skin. Fuck you Gale, because a chocolate muffin was everyone's choice.

"Muffins, toast, fruit, beans, deli, cheese, tomatoes, peppers. The half cucumber I left after I made a salad at dinner," I bit my lower lip as if I still tasted the dill and sour cream cucumber salad I had thoroughly enjoyed the night before. "Where is all the food?"

By the look of all the cans thrown across the room, the food was already in his belly, unless he made stashes of it somewhere, which made no sense, because all the cans were ripped open.

"I was hungry," his brow arched as if I was asking the silliest question in the world, and he had started to doubt my intelligence.

"You were hungry?" I huffed. "For a week's worth of food?"

He did not reply, his eyes taking advantage to scan me for the first time. I did not want to know what he saw, how I must have looked compared to his god-like appearance, so I did not dwell on it.

"It's impossible for a person to eat this much food in just a few hours. You can't possibly do such a thing, which means that you hid it from me," I furrowed my brows, trying to add an inquisitive harshness.

"As I said, I was hungry," Gale lost his patience and turned to the side, scanning the room for a new machine. He chose the bench press and without another look at me, he started walking in that direction.

Lesson one when it comes to Ellyana Harrow: I don't give up easily, and this faerie was going to learn it the hard way.

"I don't believe you. I think you just messed with it so I couldn't have any," I followed him, determined to get to the bottom of this.

"You have sausages and potatoes left. Milk and two eggs," he replied while positioning weights onto the bar. I watched him add weight after weight, not stopping until the total sum was four times my body weight. He shimmied on the bench, strengthening his back while wrapping his fingers around the metal bar, preparing his muscles for the incoming pressure.

"Anything else, muffin?" he tilted his head to me, indirectly telling me that this conversation would be over as soon as those weights went in the air.

"I don't believe you. I think you are up to something," I confessed, playing all my cards in one hand because he gave me no other choice. "For one to be this hungry and eat that much...you must have not had food in a week!" I exclaimed at the ridiculousness of the thought.

"Three," he replied, eyes focused once again on the bar.

"What?"

"Three weeks," he confirmed.

*They had not fed him for three weeks.*

I remembered the box, the way he had been buried in iron, how his mouth was trapped and burnt, the rust around the nails. "And four days," he added.

Three weeks and four days. Twenty-five days in total. Gale had not had any food in twenty-five days. My anger vanished like a snow angel at the first rays of sunshine, its existence and purpose completely forgotten. This man did not eat in twenty-five days. And still, he thought about leaving some food for me. He left me sausages, milk and eggs.

"Are you still hungry?" my mouth went ahead of me, curiosity overpowering reason.

"I am always hungry," he said as if it was the most obvious answer. I had no idea how much a man of his stature would eat, but I had to assume it was a lot more than I did. And I had to buy it for him.

Add the twenty-five days without nourishment and the energy it must have taken his body to grow back all that gorgeousness. It was a lot. Which meant that my food shopping bill had just massively increased.

"I'll bring some more food," I announced, unable to move as my eyes watched his biceps swell with the weights.

"Great," his voice came out strained, the effect of the heavy lifting stinging his voice out.

I stood there and watched him a full minute, unaware that the conversation had abruptly come to an end and that Gale was a lot more focused on not dropping five hundred pounds on his neck. My brain forced my steps away, already drowning in embarrassment, until Gale's voice stopped me in my tracks.

"Muffin?"

Fuck. I should not have stopped, I should not have responded to the stupid nickname. Part of me wanted to walk away as if nothing happened, the other part knew I had already been ridiculed, so there was no point in hiding it.

"What?" I snapped.

"No matter how much I enjoyed pissing in a bucket, my bowels are going to start working again soon, so a proper toilet would be nice."

I didn't even think of that. I had to share a bathroom with him and there he was, on his first day of gorgeousness, claiming that right.

"There's one in my room, you can use it during the day only." I turned to him, prepared to explain my reasons but his attention returned to his task, ignoring me after granting his request.

It took me three hours to do another week's worth of shopping and I spent half of my month's wages on it. Planning to get nutritious things rather than canned goods, I went all out with my grocery bill. If the way to the faerie's friendship was through his stomach, I would do my damn best to get him lots of the good stuff. Along with some other things I needed for myself, like chocolate, pizza and junk food.

My period was supposed to arrive in a couple of days, so I knew I needed lots of carbs. Especially if my nerves were to be tested on a daily basis.

Twenty-five days without food, the memory came to mind as I was struggling to haul all the grocery bags into the cart. I couldn't even imagine the harm done to his stomach, to his entrails, how much his throat and muscles must have suffered. And he'd been iron bound as well.

What the hell did Gale do? Why were they punishing him so harshly, torturing him in such a rough and merciless manner? In all my years of training and experience, I had never seen anything like it. It looked to be some sort of a personal vendetta, something that PDD's team was willing to put lots of funds into. Just to torture a fae male. Or maybe Gale had something they really wanted. Knowing the interrogation techniques, they must have tried everything in the book to reach the conclusion that Gale needed a reprieve.

"Are you going to help me with this or what?" I struggled to breathe after carrying the bags all the way through the scanning area, through the guards, and pushed them all into the room before the door sealed shut behind me.

Gale hadn't even reacted, didn't even look in my direction to follow the noise, preferring the company of his weights.

I'd been away for hours, and the guy was still at it. I had to admire his determination, but also started fearing that the food I'd brought wouldn't be enough and the gods knew my wages could not sustain us both for a longer period of time.

"You seemed pretty angry when I touched your food before, muffin," Gale remained seated, making no gesture to stand and offer his support.

"Well, that was because I didn't know how hungry you would be. And I bought some more food. Which you would know if you were gentleman enough to come and offer me a hand," I snapped, dropping two bags to the floor, unable to hold them any longer. Luckily, they were corn-starch made, so they did not rip apart at the first sign of pressure.

"Gentle*man*..." Gale's voice trembled, a burst of annoyance flaring through his throat. "Not a concept fae are familiar with..."

"Because there aren't any gentlemen where you come from?" my regard slipped to him, half curious.

A spark of longing painted his features, before he realised and cleared it away. He missed his home. But he would not admit it. Not to me and not to himself.

"Because it is a human concept," he finally allowed his words to drop.

"Well..." I sighed, yanking the remaining bags to drop them on the small counter. "Let me explain it to you, then." I did not care if he looked at me or not, I knew he could hear it and that was the only thing that mattered.

"A gentleman is a man who cares for others and likes to follow the polite rules of society. For example, when he sees a lady in distress, he instantly comes and helps. Or when he sees a lady struggling to carry something heavy, he offers to take the load off her. You know, the way it should be in a civilised society. The way tradition dictates it."

"Is that so, muffin? Gale huffed, the rumble of his echoing snarl raising tingles down my skin. "Is that what you want? For me to follow tradition with you?"

"It would be nice," I snapped again, turning my back to him and directing my attention to the bags filled with food. I started regretting my choice to buy so much for him when the bastard clearly did not want to put an ounce of effort into this.

"Would it now?" The warmth in his voice threaded across the room, filling the distance between us. "Is that what you want, muffin? You want me to be…traditional with you?"

I did not want to turn. I did not want to turn because somehow, I knew. However impossible it might be, I knew Gale crossed the room in a split second to situate his tall and muscly body right behind mine. Inches separated us but I already felt his warmth, the way his skin sizzled with fiery rage, how his muscles twitched from the continuous effort and the scent of his sweat…dripping down his torso. The mere image of those delicious beads pouring down his abs turned me liquid, my panties turning mush with need and instant desire.

"Tell me, muffin…" a finger caressed my arm, the bare skin under my t-shirt, causing a wave of goosebumps to take flight under this touch. "Do you know what fae males used to do when they first met a woman?" Another finger joined into the torturous caress and oh my goodness, my knees buckled, and my stomach clenched, hollowing out so much desire my thighs started shaking on their own accord.

"Do you?" he whispered, his breath so close to my ear, its warmth dropping down my neck.

"No…" I barely replied, my tone coming out in a shuddered breath.

"They would take her away…" his fingers reached my elbow and changed direction, going upwards on my skin to continue the slow torture.

Fuck, fuck, fuck, my mind was wrapped around those fingers. Literally. All I could think about, wanted to know, envisioned, was what those two fingers would do were they let loose on my body. How much torture and pleasure they would bring. How they felt like no one else, like nothing I had ever experienced.

"Far away, to a place where they could not be disturbed…" Gale continued, the pads of his fingers now closer to my shoulder. "And they would have their way with her," his breath expelled, bringing my undoing. "They would fuck her. Senseless. Mercilessly. Until both of them had enough. Until *he* had enough."

Oh my gosh…

As he spoke, Gale plastered his body on mine, letting me feel every hard, sculpted muscle. Letting me feel his growing erection. My heart jolted, my mind becoming strained by the urgent need, the deep desire billowing inside of me.

"Is that what you want, muffin? You want me to fuck you?" His voice pierced through every nerve, caressed every feeling I ever had, all the unsatisfied nights where my mind could not help me reach the pleasure I so desperately needed.

I knew he would do it; I knew he would be so good at it too…

"Yes…" my mouth released a moan, my head tilting to catch more of his arduous breath, offering my neck to him.

I heard a low snarl, a male grumble filled with satisfaction. Gale pressed his erection to my ass, letting me feel all of him and I— what the hell was I doing?

"No!" I finally reacted, stepping away to sew distance in between us. "Get the fuck away from me," I shouted, pressing my hands into fists to force them back to reality, to get blood pumping back to my brain.

"Muffin…" he tilted his head with a smirk, as if to tell me that my reaction had been more than obvious, flagging my betrayal.

"If you ever touch me again, I will kill you," I groaned, stepping even further away from him, and circling the table to escape the closed space.

"There is no need to be like this," he spoke, his voice suddenly even and uncaring.

"Take your fucking food and leave me the fuck alone," I barely uttered. My legs stepped away on their own accord, distancing me from the temptation, from my doom. What in the gods name had I been thinking?

"Muffin…" Gale frowned, suddenly surprised by my reaction.

"I said stay the fuck away," I raised a finger in warning, my other hand touching the wall in search of the door handle. As soon as I found it, I turned it and shoved myself in the bedroom, putting my body back to safety and turning the lock.

I started shaking, wide tears pricking my eyes and finding their way down my face while my hands tried to scratch away the caress of his fingers, shoving my fingernails so deep into my skin that I drew blood.

I did not know how much time had passed, how long I stood there, shaking and hating myself for what I wanted, for the way I lost myself, my goal, my purpose and my mission, when a knock on the door came to stop my breath in my chest.

"I made dinner," the fae announced through the door. No doubt some sort of peace offering or plan to get me out and exercise more of his magic on me.

He knocked again, making the same announcement but I held my breath, terrified that he would find a way inside, that he would come in and make me lose control once more.

Finally, his steps echoed away from the door, which remained shut for the rest of the night.

*Day 9*

Last night claimed my nightmares with a vengeance. Every time I closed my eyes I saw images of Gale, of his muscles, of the way his back tensed while lifting those weights, of his breath across my skin and those fingers that had raised more feeling inside of me than any man lately.

Needless to say, rest did not find me easily. I twisted and turned, my skin too hot to be touched by the soft cotton cover. I felt needy and lit up, new sensations snaking down my belly and in between my thighs. I even considered taking care of that need myself, but I did not want to cause any more trouble for future me. It was public knowledge that fae had incredible senses, so I did not want to put myself in a situation where he would know what I had to do to shake away his effect.

My morning shower took longer than usual, due to a second scraping of my skin demanded by my anxiety to face him again. I needed to feel fresh and brand new, I had to battle away and become immune to the effect he had on me. So extra hot water that turned my skin pink proved to be a great remedy.

By the time I opened the bedroom door to let myself into the home gym, a cloud of steam followed me, along with heart palpitations caused by the prolonged exposure to heat.

Following last night's tradition, I did not say a word or even look in the direction of the gym and headed straight into the kitchen to make myself a cup of coffee. Instinct forced me to look behind my shoulder once or twice to make sure no one suddenly appeared there.

After the first few sips of coffee woke up some more of my senses, I headed to the fridge with the hope to still find something left from the night before. When the fridge door pulled open and the light appeared, I almost dropped my coffee mug.

All the groceries were fitted neatly into the small fridge, sorted into categories and colours, making it look as if it belonged to a fancy restaurant. The meats were piled up together, sorted into cuts and types along with sauces, bread and more bits, all enticing and making my stomach grumble.

"Thanks..." I decided to take the lead and become the friendly face my job demanded me to be. The cameras were on, as well as the microphones, running across the ceiling to reach every one of our conversations and gestures, so I had to keep my wits. I couldn't appear flustered or affected by the night before, especially not when I had another three weeks to spend in the company of this man. Male. Best thing to do was start fresh and set some ground rules.

Keep a foot away must be the first one, because my skin still trembled with unfelt caresses and need.

"Have you had breakfast already?" I asked, taking in a full breath and preparing myself to find those emerald eyes, those adamant locks and that godlike physique of his.

I blinked. Once. twice, my regard slipping across the room, checking the weights, the benches and other gym equipment I had not seen before and wasn't able to name.

Gale was nowhere to be found.

I swung my head across the room and forced my eyes to focus, glowering and dipping to every surface, every corner, every hole. No sign of him.

"Gale?"

Nothing. Radio silence.

"Gale?" I said again, pushing the bedroom door open and running into the bathroom, hoping that the faerie might have gone in there after a full night of being locked away.

"Where are you?"

I ran across the rooms, I even opened my wardrobe should he want to play a prank on me and hide in plain sight. There was no sign of the faerie.

"Oh, my gods..." I started hyperventilating, my legs losing strength, my balance affected and making my body swing to the side. I grabbed the doorframe and leaned against the wooden surface, forcing my body against it and pushing back to hold myself onto something because the world had just escaped from under my legs.

I lost a subject.

I had lost a subject, because I'd been too entitled and unfocused. I put myself first, my needs and terrors had claimed my mind rather than my duty, rather than my mission.

I lost a subject...

The hint of disappointment brushed the air, filled with failure and defeat, all of them wrapped around my name. I had only one mission, one assignment primordial to all. Do my job.

And I had catastrophically failed at it.

Just then the tablet thought to ping for my attention, the sound of a new instruction making me crawl to the nightstand and grip it between shaky fingers. It took me three attempts to slide the screen open and read the new instruction.

**"Keep Gale in good health."**
*Instruction to be completed in twenty-four hours.*

Had they not seen it happen? Were they not present for his escape? What was their plan? Slowly torture me until I drowned in self-defeat?

With a rigid frame, I stepped in the living room to make myself visible to the cameras.

"Can't you see he's gone?"

The words barely escaped me, my throat raw and struggling to keep a wail in.

"The subject will be returned to the living quarters shortly. Please follow the instruction displayed on your tablet," the robotic voice responded, so different from the human tone of PDD. My focus jumped to the information. *"The subject will be returned..."*

On their own accord, my legs led me to the wall where I knew the door would be, sealed shut with no hints of forced exit, no blunt hits or even a drop of paint out of place. As far as I knew, that was the only way out. Not including the moving floor that brought the faerie to me, which I had no idea how to control.

Judging by this, the instruction I had received and the robotic voice that spoke to me as if nothing had happened, I came to one conclusion. Gale had been removed from the room.

And I had nothing to do but wait.

After gulping down some breakfast, which in fact was more lunch due to the time I finally decided to eat because Gale did not seem to be returning soon, I decided to clean the living quarters. I directed my attention to the bathroom first, part of me knowing that it would probably be the place of most interest for the fae, then I cleaned my bedroom and started picking up the cans and remains of food left around the gym machines.

On a tray by the side of the bedroom door, I found a full plate of roast meat, potatoes and steamed vegetables, along with a glass of water and a chocolate muffin.

*"I made dinner..."* he'd announced the night before, his presence scattering my hunger rather than igniting it. No, I was lying to myself. He did make me hungry...hungrier than I'd ever been. Which was why I had to keep my wits about it.

It looked nice though, I would not deny that, and it was a nice gesture to cook for me, after being an absolute dick. Maybe cooking for someone was some sort of faerie apology.

I ended up eating last night's dinner wrapped in a blanket and cosied up in bed with the tablet after deciding that Gale wouldn't return until nightfall or maybe the following day.

The instruction popped into mind a few times, stirring worry in my gut and making me wonder what the new task consisted of. Because I had a full day to keep Gale in good health, but I had no Gale.

Either the tablet was blocked from specific searches or there was nothing on the news or the internet to help me understand my situation better or get more info on PDD. I came to the conclusion that it must have been some sort of shortened identification, but no matter how much I tried to piece it together, sorting puzzles and anagrams had never been my forte. Which was annoying as hell, seeing how I worked in intelligence and all...

I was sound asleep when the entrance door swung open to release a thud, before the sound of compressing into blackness told me they had already shut it. I hurried to the kitchen, blinking my sleep away.

To find a pool of blood and Gale's body twisted on the floor, his limbs shaking with pain. The fae's throat released a dry groan, escaping his bloodied mouth with regularity.

"Oh, my gods," my knees weakened at the sight of the gore, forcing me to fall closer to him. "What...what happened?" I instantly moved towards him, tugging him closer and turning him to the side, afraid that he might choke on the blood seeping through his lips.

Gale tilted his face to me, those wondrous eyes twinkling in agony. Once his hands lifted, his fingers trembled in their struggle to make a fist and display his anger.

Ignoring his possible hatred towards me, towards my race and everything we stood for, I wrapped my hands around his neck, placing him back to the side to let the blood seep out of his mouth and onto the floor while my fingers instinctively moved towards his once adamant locks, now turned crimson and started caressing down his scalp in what I hoped, was a soothing motion.

He jolted a couple of times when the pads of my fingers found something rough and I immediately pulled away, realising I must have touched a head injury and caused more pain rather than calm.

The fae male did not move from my embrace, choosing to lean on the side and continue trembling in pain next to me. I didn't know if what I was doing helped or if he simply didn't have the strength to stand and send me on my merry way. Either way, I had to be there, for both our sakes, the instruction suddenly clear.

"Keep Gale in good health..." Bastards, were they planning to keep me here as a nurse while they tortured and beat the hell out of this man?

Rage boiled in my veins. At the sight of him. Of me.

Of us.

He deserved more than this. *I* deserved more than this.

Another groan from Gale's throat dissipated all my other thoughts. The priority, keep him safe and alive.

"Can you walk?"

His neck barely moved, tilting his face just enough to shake it once in negation.

"Okay..." I nodded, "Okay...hold on."

With the utmost care, I softly released his head, placing it back onto the wooden floor and stepped away. The pool of blood around him turned my stomach, clenching panic into my entrails. He was losing so much blood.

*Okay, okay Ellyana, think logically, you were trained for this*, I tried to settle myself, forcing my analytical brain to take over emotions.

First things first, he had to drink, so I knew his throat worked alright. He'd lost so much blood; he wouldn't be able to heal on his own so one of my priorities was to get him some more Cloutie tea. Fortunately, I still had a couple more roots in the sachet I received after his arrival.

Then, I had to clean his wounds to prevent infection. I needed gauze, clean towels and surgical spirit. I knew there was some in the kitchen cupboard and hurried to my feet to grab all the necessary elements that would help me keep the fae alive.

And in good health, I reminded myself.

Freaking bastards, how could they beat him within an inch of his life and then have the nerve to dump him on me in such a state. For a people that prided themselves for their honourable qualities, us humans truly were savages.

"I need to remove your shirt to clean the wounds. You need to help me here, Gale, you're too heavy for me to lift you by myself,"

I begged the fae after several attempts that made me drop his body to the floor and forced him to groan in agony.

The Cloutie tea started boiling and I had to leave Gale on his own for a few seconds and remove it from the burning surface so I wouldn't overheat it and ruin its regenerative properties. Once I poured it in a mug, ready to be drunk, I turned back to the bleeding fae.

Instead of doing his best to help me, he remained content with bleeding on the floor, his mouth shaping words that seemed more important to him.

"Not...Gale..." he barely mumbled.

"What?" I frowned at the ridiculousness of the situation. Was he more concerned about how I pronounced his name that picking himself off the floor?

"My n...name," he swallowed a gulp of blood, peering at me through crimson blinks. "Not Gale."

"Your name is not Gale?" I repeated, taking a deep breath because I knew he could not, as if I wanted the effect to pass onto him, to help him breathe better.

"Galen...Galenor..."

"Galenor..." I repeated, raising a relieved sigh from his lips.

"Galenor, okay," I nodded again, instantly deciding to never call him Gale again. I knew better than anyone how difficult it was to be an outsider, with an outsider's name. How many documents needed to be redone and repaid for because someone didn't pay enough attention to spell my name correctly. Did not care enough to double check.

Galenor...difficult to pronounce for an untrained tongue, so I assumed the soldiers automatically decided to shorten his name. And he didn't bother to correct them, did not want to give them the power. By the way he exhaled in relief at my pronunciation of his name, he hadn't heard it sound correctly in a long while.

"Galenor, you need to help me," I started again, this time my words meriting his full attention. "You need to pull yourself up so I can remove your shirt. I can't cut it because it's a Human Realm uniform, I am not allowed to destroy the symbol of the realm," I explained, making his chin jut towards me.

"Do you understand?" I asked again, panic thrusting through my sentence at the blood that continued to flow across his torso.

"Okay..." he finally spoke, one of his arms twisting around my neck to help support him while his palm pushed to the ground to force his body to lift.

I made quick work of undressing him and took the opportunity to slip a clean towel underneath his injured torso, which I had already dipped in alcohol.

His deep moan scraped down my skin at the thought of the pain he must be experiencing, his chest, his breath willing out groan after groan as the alcohol invaded his wounds and cuts.

"I'm sorry, but I have to clean them," I spoke the apology while his emerald eyes gawked betrayal at me.

"Here," I hurried to bring him the steaming mug. "It's Cloutie, it will make you better soon."

"Why should I trust you?" he snarled, pressing his lips together in protest.

"Because I'm trying to heal you!" I replied, exasperated. He kept bleeding from a deep cut on the right side of his torso, right below his ribs, which told me his liver must have been affected. And now the fool decided not to trust me and refused healing medicine.

"Why?" He swallowed more blood but kept his lips sealed.

"Because!" I shouted, desperation and annoyance taking control over my voice and impulses. "I'm here to help you," I tried to convince him, and tried to plead with his better judgement.

"No human has ever helped..." Galenor murmured, his gaze blinking away from consciousness.

Determined to pour the Cloutie tea down his throat using force if I had to, I lowered the mug to his eyes, placing it in front of his nose and hoped that the metallic tang of blood did not overpower his other senses and allowed him to examine the contents himself rather than trust my words.

"It's the same one I gave you while you healed from the chains. The exact same batch," I said, dropping the mug a few more inches and tilting it just enough to show him the turquoise root releasing dark waves into the hot water. I always hated Cloutie, it smelled foul, made you sick and came with the cost of lives or lifetime debts.

But when Galenor's lips reached for the mug, I never loved the plant more. Supporting his head with my shoulder and sliding part of myself under his back to gain more support, I slowly poured the contents down his throat, giving him enough pause to swallow and breathe as I did so.

The last drop sent the fae into a deep sleep, giving me the opportunity to examine him and clean the blood and the cuts while struggling to keep my focus and observe his every breath. The way his chest dropped up and down, how his arms relaxed and allowed his body to rest, to find peace.

Involuntarily, I found myself stroking parts of his skin that did not hold injuries, my fingers captivated by the softness and allure of his naked torso.

When I finished cleaning him off, I returned to the bedroom to grab the spare blanket and a pillow to keep him protected from the cold while he healed. I didn't care that I had received clean linen when they came in to install the door. I knew Galenor needed to be comfortable and in that moment, it was all that mattered to me.

The bedroom door remained unlocked that night.

# Day 10

The fae did not have a good night and neither did I, his groans of pain keeping me awake until the late hours, forcing my consciousness to push me from bed with the need to check on him on several occasions.

All my actions were met with more snarls and grunting.

Galenor and I started a tradition that night, where I would express my concern regarding his situation and offer to help, while he grumbled and dropped insults with every word.

"Stop pretending you care, muffin. Go get some sleep…" he'd murmured between heavy breaths, urging me away.

"I just want to know if you're okay…" I had tried to explain, to which he forced a wide smile, obviously fake.

"Splendid."

Another time he called me a cunt, though I was unsure if he wanted to say that directly to my face or if his pain made him talk to himself. *Do they really think I am that gullible? Bringing a pretty little cunt to sweeten the deal…*

That last sentence pissed me off more than anything and I forced myself away after that. Fine, linger there, cold and on the floor, delirious with fever if you don't want any help.

Take that alpha male attitude and see how far it gets you, buddy.

I missed my second pillow and started regretting giving him the blanket, all my compassion and sympathy for his situation suddenly turning into annoyance.

Why did I care what the bastard thought anyway? Clearly, he was one of those entitled brats who thought the world belonged to them and everyone else was put there for their entertainment. Well...if that's what he thought of me, boy, he had a lot to learn.

Commotion made me shake awake, the sounds of footsteps and voices coming from the living room. From the kitchen. Was someone here? Inside the quarters?

"Hello?" I rushed to the door, swinging it open to find four guards in the kitchen, all circling Galenor as if they wanted to grab him while the fae male simply watched them, huddled in his blanket. As if they were of no significance, as if this was his daily routine and four guards waking him from sleep was a matter of no regard.

"What is happening here?" I demanded, instantly gaining myself four sets of eyes, all pinned on my tank top that allowed my nipples to pull the fabric around their shape.

No, scratch that. Galenor seemed to find an interest that morning as well.

"What is happening here?" I asked again, wrapping my hands into fists to hide the need to cover myself. I did not know these men, they were not guards I had grown up with, trained with, shared food with during training. These men proved unknown to me, standing out from any of the units I had worked with.

"Nothing you need to concern yourself with, Captain Harrow," one of them finally replied, though his eyes still lingered on my boobs.

"I will be the judge of that. Identify yourselves," I ordered, fully aware that this was my territory, and I had the upper hand.

"Negative, Captain. Our identities must be preserved in the presence of the subject," another replied.

Fair, we had the right to preserve our identities should we consider ourselves in danger. Which posed the question: was Galenor that strong? Did he really need to be escorted by four guards when his body wasn't properly healed yet?

"Why are you here?" I pointed my gaze to the first one, noticing how he still showed interest in my boobs. On their own accord, my hands slid to my midsection and grabbed the white tank top, yanking it in an abrupt upward motion to pull it over my head. Revealing my breasts.

"Clearly, you boys haven't seen these too often," I jiggled my medium-sized breasts proudly, making them shake in the cold air, my nipples instantly hardening. "They are called tits. All women have two of them. Their purpose is to feed a new-born by producing milk or turn men into retarded beings. Can we now continue our conversation?"

The four of them remained dumbfounded, their blinks filled with boobs but a low inhale pulled my attention towards Galenor. To find him blinking at me, his gaze brushing on my skin to raise goosebumps in its wake. He looked proud. And by that low smirk adorning his lips, he liked what he saw.

"Well?" I drew my attention back to the guards, whose faces had turned crimson, and their dicks had turned hard. Visibly.

I dragged down my tank to cover myself and folded my arms to wait for a reply.

"They... We... Interrogation," the first one said, shaking his head as if he wanted to remove the image of my boobs from his eyes.

"He was interrogated yesterday and was returned to me injured and bloodied. Who ordered this?" I snapped, stepping closer to them and grabbing Galenor's arm to force him to his feet.

"Captain, it is the process. We do not question orders. Gale is to be brought back for interrogation."

"BY WHOSE ORDERS?" I found myself shouting while my fingers wrapped protectively around the fae's arm.

"Captain, we do not question orders. If he does not come willingly, we will have to iron bind him and drag him with us," a third voice appeared into the conversation.

"The hell you will," I threatened, ready to start a war in that small kitchen over this if I had to. I had suddenly become protective of Galenor, hating the atrocities I had cleaned on his skin and terrified of the same happening again. I had to do everything in my power to prevent them.

His fingers wrapped around mine, a soft, understanding voice painting devotion on my skin.

"Muffin...don't waste your energy, we will need it for later," Galenor spoke, his voice pinning waves of hurt into my chest.

He couldn't do this. He couldn't just let them take him...without even fighting back. I turned to find him towering over me, those green eyes that shone filled with life suddenly burning into me. Then, turning to the guards, he dipped his chin.

"I will go."

With no other choice but to watch him leave, I followed Galenor's steps out of the room, terrified of how he'd be returned to me.

A burst of indignation flared through my body as I had no choice but to stand there and watch the door seal back shut. I felt powerless, useless, purposeless. Why in the name of all the gods had I been instructed to care for him, when they were going to do it all over again?

My lips rose in a snarl, powered by my inability to help him.

Not that I cared. I must have repeated that to myself over ten times, each one becoming harder to believe. I had known the guy for three days, without counting the time he spent as a pile of meat freshly out of a wooden box.

He was rude, impertinent and curt, he thought himself more important than those around him and he ate all my food, whilst proceeding to ignore me and work on his weights. Still, panic speared through me at the thought of what they would do to him, what he had to endure throughout the day.

If yesterday was any indication, he was in for the long run, and I'd probably see him back after dinner. Which meant that over ten hours of torture awaited my faerie companion. And there was nothing in my power to change his fate.

PDD, my mind snapped.

"Hello, can I speak to PDD please?" I turned my eyes up to the ceiling, doing everything in my power for my echo to pierce through the morning haze.

"Hello?" I insisted, raising my tone and standing on my toes as if in that position my voice could penetrate deeper into the mics.

"Captain Harrow, how can we be of assistance?" the robotic voice, not belonging to PDD responded.

"I need to speak to PDD. I request a written conversation, same as last time."

A few minutes of silence passed, during which I checked the screen of the device about a hundred times to see if any chat messages appeared.

"He is not available at the moment, if you would like to leave a message..." the voice replied, so distorted, it made it obvious that this was a new person, possibly a woman who tried to alter the voice encryption probably a bit too much.

I sighed, knowing my insistence would be for nothing. "Fine, how can I leave a message?"

"We will add a messaging service to your device shortly."

And that was that. I had to wait.

Wait for them to remotely install whatever the tablet needed.

Wait for time to pass.

Wait for Galenor to return.

Wait and worry.

"For the attention of PDD,

I must express my concern with regards to the development of this trial assignment. Since his arrival, Gale received incident treatment which could be called inhumane. I understand the need to pull information from a subject and the various ways in doing so, however he is now a subject in a trial assignment. We are on day ten and I still haven't received any background on said subject, nor do I have a complete set of instructions that would ease my understanding of this trial.

I must confess my opposition to the way the fae male continues to be treated and I must firmly object to the continuation of this routine, since it leaves the subject injured and unwilling to cooperate. Furthermore, I request information on my role and demand a set of complete instructions to be released at your earliest convenience for the betterment of this assignment.

Should you require more information or wish to have a direct conversation concerning the subject or any other matter, please do not hesitate to contact me directly.

With esteem,

Captain E. Harrow"

"Dearest Captain Harrow,

Firstly, I would like to convey my sincere apologies for the delay in this reply, I must admit the first part of the day was not up to standard and other matters kept me away from the current developments.

I would like to confirm that the temporary release of the subject received prior approval as the fae male in question proved to be a valuable asset in various other projects which are simultaneously running alongside this trial assignment.

Please rest assured that you will be scored on the time the subject spends in the living quarters only, and the completion of this project will not be extended should the subject need to be removed periodically for interrogation purposes.

We take this opportunity to compliment your actions and congratulate you on the brisk completion of the instructions given to you this far.

Captain Harrow, please do not concern yourself with outside matters, your tasks within the living quarters have been stupendous so far, so keep up the good work.

We will see you when you get out, major.

With regards and gratitude,

PDD"

I must have summoned the door to open with so many hours of pacing around. They left me with nothing else to do but wait, so I took the opportunity and polished the floor with my shoes from so much fidgeting around.

"Galenor!" I jumped before the door even opened properly, watching how the guards threw him into the room, and doing my best to reach him and soften the fall, afraid that he couldn't walk again.

"You're okay, you're okay, I got you," I whispered, gripping his back and pressing his chest to mine while my knees struggled under the pressure of his weight.

A heavy groan opened his throat, but I did not know if it tried to express pain or annoyance. Still, his hands wrapped around my shoulders and the fae did his best to grab a hold of his own weight.

"I'm not feeling so good..." he murmured into my ear, his heavy breath draping across my neck to sew concern.

"You're okay, you'll be okay." I tried to encourage him, though his skin looked worse than the day before. His injuries did not have time to heal before the new session of torture, which impregnated into his skin like snow on a dry field.

Pellets of dried blood adorned his shirt and the parts of his skin that I reached, accompanied by deep cuts and heavy injuries. His muscles trembled, his throat bobbed, and his eyes barely kept him awake, probably using the last drops of adrenaline he had left.

"I'm going to be sick..." Galenor announced, his gaze peering out at me while pressing his lips together to hold it in.

"Let's get you to the bathroom," I jumped into action and pressed both our weight into my heels, finding momentum to pull both of us on our feet. Once Galenor regained part of his balance, the trip to the bathroom did not prove as heavy as I expected it, the fae doing his best to strain his muscles into a soft walk.

As soon as we reached the bathroom, he dropped to his knees and buried his head into the toilet bowl to expel the contents of his stomach. Normally, I would have stepped out. Like any sane person, I hated the smell of vomit, but curiosity locked my legs into place, concern forcing me to remain pinned by the door.

I spotted more blood dripping into the toilet, from his throat or from his stomach, I did not know. My nose wrinkled at the thought of his pain, forcing me to suck in oxygen as if the air from my lungs would give him some sort of reprieve. I sat there blinking, watching his back strain with pain, his lungs heaving in between courses of throwing up blood. The process took long minutes, or at least that's what my brain assumed from the amount of blood and the acuteness of the pain Galenor was experiencing.

When he finally stopped, I passed him a clean towel, stepping closer to where he remained seated by the toilet bowl, pressing his lips together and struggling to breathe through his nose.

"Thank you…" he exhaled and moved to wipe away any traces of blood from his lips.

"Can you drink? I'll make you another tea," I offered, causing him to shake his head no.

"Save it for later, there's not much point to it." Galenor straightened his back and moved a little to the side to lean against

103

the bathroom wall, his muscles shaking at the contact with the cold. His head leaned back, splaying his dark locks on the wall to paint tree branches with the crimson remains in his hair.

"It makes you feel better, that is the point," I tried to justify, worried that he might reject my offering. Worried that once more, he saw me as an enemy. *A pretty cunt to sweeten the deal*, his voice rumbled through my memories.

"It won't," he sighed, tired and bothered. "I won't have time to heal before they take me again." His words came out with hatred, with annoyance even, as if what was happening to him was my fault. As if I should use a little more of my brain before bothering him with questions.

"So, what *can* I do for you?" I tried again, unwilling to abandon him. Unprepared to leave him in that state, stuck to a bathroom wall, bleeding and in pain, with no one to care for his wellbeing.

Galenor sighed, annoyance heaving off in waves to cover his entire posture. "Just leave me the fuck alone, muffin."

I wanted to protest, I wanted to refuse and stay there with him, but the fae closed his eyes and leaned against the wall to rest its back straighter. Telling me that he had no use for me or anyone else. That he needed and deserved some peace and quiet.

I stepped away and got out of the bathroom, giving him the space he had required. Shutting the door behind me.

For the next hour, I remained in the bedroom, pacing around and listening by the door, wanting to make sure he was alright, but too afraid to knock and ask him. When I heard the shower running, my heart calmed down a little more.

Reaching the shower meant that his legs worked again, that he could stand long enough to turn the water on, and he was strong enough to clean himself. Or wanted to, at least.

Possessed by instinct and absolutely not thinking my actions through, I returned into the living room to grab his pillow and blanket and bring them back into the bedroom to place them on the floor in front of the bathroom door.

Then I locked my door.

If those guards wanted him for another day, they had to break it down and I was pretty sure it came against my privacy policy recently implemented by PDD. I couldn't do much for Galenor, I didn't even know why I was on his side in the first place, but it was the least I could offer him. A full night of rest.

Before I had a chance to lose my nerve, I knocked on the door and, without giving him a chance to reply, I opened it to shove his belongings inside, while battling a deep wave of steam.

"You're sleeping here tonight," I announced, sealing the door shut behind me.

*Day 11*

I didn't know if he slept well last night, but I surely didn't. Not until the early hours of the morning. I kept my ears peeled to the bathroom door, terrified of what I'd done. Of the decision I had suddenly made, which could not only affect my assignment, but also put me in danger.

What in gods' name had I been thinking, locking myself in with a fae male? Sure enough, the male looked to be more dead than alive last time I saw him, and I didn't even want to think how long it would take me to clean all that blood from the bathroom.

But what if the guards arrived? What if I'd broken rules I did not know about by trying to keep him away from an important interrogation?

*And what if you did, Ellyana? Are you willing to let them kill Galenor?* My empathic self burst the question to life.

No, I wasn't.

I didn't want to think about the effect Galenor had on me. Of how, even last night, even bloodied and miserable, he had raised desire with just a breath, with that damned voice of his that seemed to draw shivers and pebble my skin every time it sounded through the room. It did not seem to matter the situation he was in or whether he was kind or snarky, the mere sound of his voice made me want to abandon everything and fall to his will.

And I had locked myself in a room with him.

At some point, exhaustion must have caught up with me, approximately at the same time Galenor stopped making noises from the bathroom, sleep blanketing the both of us. I did not dream, falling prey to the fatigue and worry I had suffered during the day.

Pressure yanked against my shoulder blade, making me turn in bed and cover my bare skin for involuntary protection. Only to return again, this time with a double press against my shoulder, then once more into my arm.

I groaned, annoyed that something was poking at me when I finally fell asleep.

Another prod, this time accompanied by a fingernail pressing into my skin and a...pinch?

What in the hell?

I snapped awake, turning towards whatever it was that dared bother me.

"I'm hungry," Galenor fanned his lashes at me, eyes twinkling with fresh energy.

My own eyes flew open, realising that the fae sat on the edge of the bed, towering over me. In my room.

"What? What are you doing here?" I protested, pulling the bedsheet over me in a poor attempt to cover my skin, to get away from that closeness and the sensation of him.

"I already told you," he spoke to me, yet again, as if I were an idiot. "I'm hungry." His lashes narrowed in on me, head tilting slightly to the side. "Is your mental capacity affected in some way?" he asked, intrigued.

"Wow, you had to start with that one, huh?" My brows wrinkled in annoyance, my arms instantly folding in anger.

"Forgive me for checking muffin, there seems to be no other explanation. Why else would you keep me away from food then show surprise when I demand it?"

"Galenor, I don't know if you get this a lot or not..." I scanned his face, his interest in what he must have assumed would be a compliment, "but you are a prick."

"I do get that a lot," he nodded, a sly smile curving along his lips, my observation clearly not bothering him. "Now...food?" he repeated, gulping down air for emphasis.

Without another word, I stood from bed and walked to the door to turn the key, wondering why the heck did Galenor feel the need to wake me up rather than letting himself out. When my fingers wrapped around the metal key, I learned the answer.

Of course, the key was made of iron. Thus, making it impossible for Galenor to touch. Well, not impossible, but really, really painful, something I assumed he wouldn't go for again after the days he had. Weeks, rather.

Great, so not only was he thinking I kept food from him, but that I'd also locked him in.

He didn't say any of it though, conforming himself with bursting out the door as soon as I opened it without even a thank you or an acknowledgement. Okay, then...

Terrified of the state of the bathroom, I took a deep breath before turning the handle to push the door open, to find everything sparkling clean. No traces of blood, no clots in the shower, no remains of vomit in the toilet.

Galenor must have spent a long while cleaning last night, or this morning. Had he done all this so I could sleep longer? To give me some time to rest?

It couldn't be, I calmed myself while I started brushing my teeth.

It couldn't be, I had to convince myself again after I jumped in the shower.

It couldn't be, I repeated, forcing the notion in my brain while I dried my hair, slightly aware that I was occupying the bathroom for a long time.

In my defence, Galenor must have emptied half the fridge by then, so a little tit for tat wouldn't hurt anybody.

When I was finally ready to get out and start a new day, after checking the tablet for new messages and making sure no one had come to take the fae away again, I pushed the bedroom door open and let myself into the gym.

The small kitchen table, barely able to fit two people, had been brought into the gym. One of the benches was converted into a tray holder and leaned next to the chairs, filled with trays and drinks.

Galenor already claimed his seat in front of a full plate of food, snacking away with devotion. When he heard the squeak of the door, he stopped and turned, his chin jerking towards the empty chair to form the only invitation I would get.

Wordlessly, I took it and stepped closer to where he'd prepared a makeshift breakfast area for us, doing my best to ignore the taut muscles on his shirtless back.

"Don't you have any clothes?" Of course my mouth had to go ahead and reveal exactly what I was thinking.

"Not really, muffin. The guards keep ripping them off when they poke at me with daggers and such... I only have one good shirt left." His gaze remained pinned to mine, that glower telling me that once more, he questioned my intelligence.

"What are you having?"

"We," he emphasised, pushing a plate in my direction when I took the seat in front of him. "Are having burgers."

"Burgers, huh?" I tried to sound excited, though I worried about the effects the sauces and mayo would have on his stomach after last night's vomiting session.

"I like burgers," he nodded, biting into a new burger with conviction, causing a long line of ketchup to drip down his chin. He didn't bother to clean himself, his only purpose was to discover how many bites it would take to shove as much of the bun into his mouth. Three.

I tilted my head to check the bench of trays he had piled on to spot over a dozen burgers, all filled with cheese, onion, tomatoes, lettuce, jalapenos, and every other kind of filling one could think of.

"How long did it take to prepare all this?" I tried to start a conversation after taking the first bite from my burger. I didn't have to ask to know that I was only getting the one, which already rested on a plate to await my arrival. The rest were all his. Not that I wanted more, I couldn't think about having so much heavy food for breakfast, but I did my best not to upset the fae and start building the friendship we obviously didn't have.

"How long did it take you to shower, muffin? Did you think of me in there?" his throat grumbled, his eyes moving over me, gliding over my fingers as if to show he knew what I had been doing. Who I'd imagine in there with me.

My stomach dropped, breath stopping in my chest. He knew. He knew that just minutes before I had lost control of myself and allowed my fingers to draw pleasure from me. He knew that it was his hands I imagined caressing my naked body, his mouth trailing down my skin, his teeth grazing at my nipples. That my better judgement left my body and the need to be touched and wanted took over my senses.

He watched me for a second, as if daring me to lie to him.

"I miss my boyfriend, so sue me," I snapped, biting a bigger chunk off my burger and doing my best to hide my crimson cheeks behind the bun.

"There's no male scent on you, muffin. You've been cooking alone for a while," he wrinkled his eyebrows and sucked in deeply, wanting to inhale all the oxygen out of the room in a single gulp.

"I don't see how that's any of your business," I snapped.

"Just saying, cupcake. If you need some help in there, let me know," his throat groaned, the invitation provocative and arousing, his voice suddenly turning into invisible limbs that poked and prodded in between my legs.

"Oh, I'm a cupcake now?" I huffed, sick and tired of all these stupid analogies. "How so?"

His eyes flickered across my body, taking me in as a proud smirk grew on his lips. "Because I would really like to see you filled."

"You are a fucking prick!" I voiced out, angrily standing from the seat, making the chair creak with my abrupt movement.

"That, I am," the fae nodded with pride.

"Fuck you, Gale!" I snapped, throwing my half-eaten burger on the table. It was not my intention for the mustard and filling to squirt and splash all across his chest, but I didn't feel bad about it either.

"Anytime, muffin," I heard him chuckle as I hurried back to the bedroom, leaving the subject in the company of his many burgers.

I drowned in my own agony, cursing my life choices, regretting locking Galenor in the bathroom because no one had come to claim him that day, checked my bank account balance about ten times to see if there was any possible way to quit my job, then started cleaning the room and putting all my energy into scrubbing old paint residue I had found in a corner behind the nightstand I wasn't using.

A knock on the door stopped the regular motion I had exerted for about ten minutes on the exact same surface, without caring that the paint marks had vanished a while back.

"Go away!" I shouted through the door, then rose to find the tablet and checked the time, counting the minutes until it would finally be time for bed.

The knock persisted, making it clear it wouldn't go away until I opened. So, with a deep sigh and my nerves stretched beyond their limit, I did.

"What?" I snapped, my regard slipping to those chiselled abs, fully covered in sweat.

"I'm bored," the fae frowned with a reprimand, as if his situation was entirely my fault.

"So?" I tilted my head back, unsure of why exactly he felt the need to give me that information.

"Aren't you supposed to entertain me?" he folded his arms across his chest and leaned on the door frame, expectantly.

"Excuse me?" My eyes bulged out so much it was a wonder they remained in their sockets.

"Aren't you here for my entertainment?" he spoke slowly, pronouncing every syllable as if I was, once again, an idiot.

"What the fuck?" I frowned, amazed by the nerve on this man. Male. Prick.

Clearly my amazement did nothing to dissuade his idea, because Galenor remained there pinned to the door and towering over me as if I'd start dancing ballet or something.

"Listen buddy, just because this mission is weird as fuck, doesn't mean I have to deal with your entitled-ass bullshit, okay?" I found myself raising a finger in the air to tell him off, but it was too late to back down, so I continued. "Go exercise or something, find your own things to do and stop pestering me."

"I already did," Galenor pointed to his abs and sweaty torso as if the subject in question was already obvious. His ability to heal was a marvel my mind had still to understand, his skin looking completely smooth and silky, far off from the fishnet collecting dagger marks from the night before.

"Okay, so...what is it that you want then?"

"Spend some time with me? Talk?" his viridescent irises gazed at me, pleading for attention. How long had he been alone for? How many days or weeks with no one to talk to, apart from the days where he had to be beaten up for information? This time, he was willing to offer a part of himself for free. I would be a fool to reject his offer.

"Okay, I nodded, grateful that he was finally willing to have a chat, that I finally found the moment to progress this assignment. "What would you like to talk about?"

"I would like to tell you," Galenor purred at me, eyes glinting with mischief, "all the positions I would like to fuck you in. I think it would be —"

I shut the door in his face and made sure he heard the lock turning in twice.

"Fuck you, faerie," I shouted through the door.

"Likewise, muffin," he groaned back.

# Day 12

I wondered how my day could possibly get worse and as soon as I opened my eyes and felt the familiar cramps, I knew the answer. My period just decided to drop.

Kill me with a stick, why don't you? I really didn't fancy thirty-six hours of pain, not when I had to deal with the fae next door, improve my mood and not get accidentally fired from the job I'd put my life and soul into.

Hurrying to the bathroom, I placed my behind on the toilet and let the blood drip as I tried to form a mental picture that would settle me enough to get through the day and a half that I had to have my period for every month. For health reasons.

We were injected with various types of hormones since we were kids, to either help us develop muscle, keep us from accidental pregnancies or keep our mood and behaviour in check. I even insisted on getting extra hormones to remove the inconvenience of a period completely, but the medical department were adamant about the health risks.

And anyway, a day and a half was much better than the full week other women had to deal with.

*Let us think logically, Ellyana,* I tried to settle myself and squeeze out as much blood as I could along with my morning pee. I had tampons, I had painkillers, I could get in a hot shower and ease out the pain. One thing I did not have, was patience. Or will to deal with Gale's shit again.

I had decided to go back to calling him Gale, I didn't want the closeness that knowing his full name offered, not when the subject in question tried to compete for the Prick of the Day award. PDD didn't seem to respond to the follow up messages I sent, indirectly telling me that I was here as a nurse. To keep Gale from dying and to bring him food.

Which annoyed the hell out of me. I was a talented captain, I worked intelligence for the majority of my life and had always met my KPIs ahead of term and with the least amount of resources.

I had befriended enemies, I got information about incoming operations and was even interviewed about my skills and technicalities. I was supposed to be the youngest female major of my unit, probably of my region and I was a kick ass woman.

But no, PDD basically hired me to keep his pet company for a whole month. Probably because I was the only female captain in waiting for such a high-end mission and, as the faerie bastard next door had to politely put it, he added a pretty cunt to sweeten the deal.

I had no idea who Gale was, why he was so important and why the rules didn't apply to him. And apparently, I had no right to ask those questions. Even if I did, I got no answers.

So, at least for today, I would give myself time to bleed and take a breath, because clearly, I was no use to anyone around here and, just like the day before, I hadn't heard any guards coming to pick up the fae, which meant that he would spend another day exercising, eating, and pissing me off. Might as well take my time in the shower.

But could I even do that?

Apparently not.

Just as I started relaxing and allowed the hot water to kidnap me into its loving embrace, the bathroom door snapped open, letting the cloud of steam out to reveal a tall dark-haired figure who had no problem entering the space I had obviously claimed.

"What are you doing here? Get out!" I instantly turned towards the bathroom wall, doing my best to cover as much of me as I could and having no other choice but to leave my back and bare ass on display.

"I wanted to check that you were alright..." Galenor's voice pierced through the room before his body fully appeared, his tall frame tightening the small space even further.

"What do you mean? Get the fuck out!" I shouted again, dropping my hair onto my back, desperate to cover as much as me as possible.

"I smelled blood," he blinked. "It can only come from you," he said with a tilt of his head, as though he finally realised that I was naked under the hot stream.

Did he feel a sudden urge to leave? Of course not.

He must have thought I was there for his enjoyment, because the fae leaned against the door frame, leaving the door open to get rid of the hot steam and gain a better view and waited.

A second or two passed, neither of us reacting. Me, too shocked by his impertinence. He, confused as to why I wasn't starting the show. He even felt the need to nudge the air with his chin in invitation and urged me to 'go on."

"Not until you get the fuck out!" I yelled while squeezing my breasts with both hands and doing my best to show him as little as I could.

"As I said, I smelled blood," he did that thing where he started speaking slowly, like one does when addressing a person of foreign heritage and wants to give them enough time to understand the sentence.

"Don't women have periods where you come from?" I snapped, too aware of the bath towel hanging on the door. Behind him.

He looked at me, his focus whispering relief, as if he'd been genuinely concerned that something might happen to me. I must have imagined it, because merely a second later his proud smirk appeared again, peering around my body to uncover every one of my secrets.

"Get away!" I shouted again, swallowing tears that pricked my eyes. I had made a point of keeping my body hidden, preventing anyone from seeing me fully naked.

Even when I had sex, I kept my tank on, unprepared to allow someone to see me like this. To reveal that part of me. Sometimes, I even forgot about it myself.

By the sharp gaze of the fae, he'd spotted my weakness. A deeper tilt of his head as if he wanted to observe me better, told me his focus had shifted from where it was pinned before on my ass.

"What are you hiding, muffin?" his voice rumbled in my stomach, causing my chest to heave under the heavy hot rain of the shower, all of a sudden burning my skin with shame.

"Go away!" I ordered, trying my best to send wet slates of my hair down my shoulders, desperate to cover my back and ribs along with all the memories I did not allow myself to succumb to. The only choice I had was to turn and face him, to turn my back away from his sight. Even though I had shown my tits with so much valour the day before, I couldn't bring myself to uncover all of me. Not to him.

So, I remained huddled against the wall, plastering my fears onto the splashes of water that burned into my skin and let the faerie come closer. He moved to the point of stepping in with me, only the rim of the bathtub separating his feet from mine, bringing me to the same level as he was.

Allowing me to look into his eyes and take them fully in, not just glimpses that my short stature allowed me to steal. They were truly wondrous, the most beautiful shade I had ever seen. I had thought them to be emerald but no, they were pure life, sprouting at me with curiosity and sudden understanding.

"Let me see…" he murmured, his focus still pinned to mine, not dropping to my midsection or in between my legs, even though I had found myself so drawn by him that I fully turned. Displaying myself completely to him, unveiling every part I had kept hidden.

"No.." I dropped the plea, my voice shaking from the instant connection we had forged, too deep to break, too strong to dislocate.

"Please…" he murmured as his fingers reached for my skin, raising more heat than the steaming shower ever could.

I found myself broken by that word, by the sound of his voice echoing it and unlocked my defences, opening myself to him, to the caress that caught alongside my elbow, to the fingers that twisted slowly around my skin, urging me to turn.

To let him see me. The real me.

I allowed myself to uncover, to bloom into his touch like I had never done before, to rip away the chains that had kept me trapped, kept me shamed and small, obedient and hurt. My right hand twisted the shower handle to make the water stop dropping invisible lashes on my skin, allowing only the steam to caress the space between us.

My other hand gripped my hair, forcing the curtain of blackness away from my back as I turned, uncovering my shoulder blades, my ribs and my past to the fae male standing behind me.

I did not need to ask if he spotted them, his sharp inhale letting me know that he had revealed the most hideous part of me. He took a long moment to analyse me, not bothered by the sharp breaths I forced to prevent the sobs that planned to escape without permission.

"How?" One word. It was all I needed to break down, to allow the tears I hadn't shed in years to resurface, to bring me back to those months of pain and punishment. I didn't need him to ask more, to detail the question. I already knew what every person who saw my back must have thought, what they must have questioned. How did I get those scars?

"In the refugee camp, when I was seven," I swallowed a dry lump stuck in my throat like cement, even though the hot steam of the bathroom made vapours of water dance around Galenor and I.

"What did you do?"

Bold of him to assume it was my fault. Though, after spending these few days with me, he must have had a rough idea.

"I snuck food to the faerie children." The confession slammed across my back, bringing the memories of the fifty lashes I had to endure while watching the bodies of my friends burn.

"Tell me," he urged, the fingers that once travelled up my arm starting to slide across my back, covering the scars of the lashes I had yet to heal. The ones I would never forgive myself for getting. Stepping down into the memory, I leaned into Galenor's touch, into calloused fingers that scraped along my back in an attempt to soothe my tears.

"We'd arrived the day before, mom, dad and my sisters. We'd barely escaped the faerie kingdom and received accommodation in a nearby refugee camp. It was the first time I had solid food in weeks."

I pressed my lips together, aware of what I had uttered. That my story from back then resounded so similar to his present situation. But his fingers did not stop tracing my scars, observing and caressing each and every one, so I felt compelled to continue.

"I remember a table, filled with goodies. Bread, fruit, buns and pastries, sandwiches, everything you can think of. And I thought it was plenty. That no one would mind if I took some to share with the kids behind the fence. I knew they were faeries, but I didn't know the situation, the animosity…"

"I took them a platter of sandwiches and when they finished eating, I went in and grabbed some more." My throat coiled on itself, stopping oxygen from flowing freely. I forced myself to continue, leaning more into Galenor's caress.

"I was followed and punished. My family protested, my mother and father both cried and begged for mercy. We were immigrants. Foreigners. We did not know the rules."

"It didn't matter…" Galenor continued in my stead, his voice strained, as if he too was feeling my pain.

"It didn't matter," I confirmed. "They sentenced me to a public lashing. I took about fifty until I lost consciousness. By the time I woke up, arrangements had already been made for me to get a place in the military."

"At least you showed kindness that day, it's not an entirely bad memory," the fae tried to improve the situation without knowing the full version of the events, and part of me wanted to keep quiet, to let him see me as a good person, just for a while longer.

Guilt ravaged my stomach, seeping dread and agony in my chest. Urging me to confess.

"They caught the children that night," I forced my mouth to expel the venom of the memory. To confess my betrayal. "They burnt them at the same time my lashing was scheduled. I had to watch," I exhaled between panting sobs, shame and remorse braiding a bouquet of tears on my face.

I braced myself for the condemning look I would find in his eyes, fully prepared for the blow his hatred would pound on my chest. Instead, Galenor took one step back, distancing himself enough from me to be able to stretch his arms around his hips. And pull his t-shirt up, giving me an eyeful of his sculpted physique.

I wanted to protest, and my arms instantly moved to cover my breasts, my legs shifting to close the gap between my thighs. Only Galenor did not pay attention to me, at least not in the way I thought he would.

As soon as his shirt was up, he turned to give me a view of his muscled back, displaying the deep and taut tissue proudly glistening from the steam.

To allow me to see...

I blinked, my heart suddenly thumping like manic.

The fae must have guessed the question, because he started speaking before I had a chance to react.

"It's an iron lined whip, so the scars never go away, even after rounds of Cloutie. It's how we mark traitors."

His muscles trembled, contracting involuntarily under the weight of those scars. Scars that deepened on his skin, that branded that perfect softness I had admired on many occasions. I had never seen them before, never given myself enough time to observe them.

Unlike mine, his scars were soft, dug into the pores of his skin as if a sharp blade had sown them into his muscles to help them erupt with the passing of time. To help them sprout every time his skin was remade, as if whoever gave these to him knew he would have to regenerate many times throughout his life. I wondered how many times he thought he escaped this curse, how many times he hoped they wouldn't come back to haunt him and had woken up with the heavy memories of whatever those events were.

Copying his gesture, I raised my hand to his back, allowing the pads of my fingers to caress along the many lines, to feel the traces of his regret and the heaviness he had to carry around.

"I'm...sorry," I muttered, the shock preventing me from finding the proper words. I must have said the wrong thing, because the fae's stance hardened, eyes gaping at me with sudden rage.

"You're not special for having those, muffin," he growled, then turned on his heels and headed to the bathroom door. Before making an exit, he turned his focus on me, this time pinning his eyes to my thighs.

"I suggest you give yourself another wash, that blood will stink up the room." Then, he snapped the door shut.

Well, there goes my day...

## Day 13

They caught me, someone grabbed my wrist and started dragging me away from my sisters. I shouted, unwilling to let them go, terrorised by the dread in their eyes.

They couldn't be left alone, they knew no one.

We knew no one.

I couldn't find mom and dad, I shouted for them, screamed their names but I couldn't see them. More people started walking around me, gathering close while the pull on my wrist forced me away. It felt like people were chasing me, following in my steps as if they wanted to see more of me. Somehow, I had become the main attraction.

Maybe the party was for us, maybe they would bring out more cake and sing happy birthday like they did in the old movies. I started smiling, looking at the humans around me with newly found interest, waiting for them to start singing soon.

Only they didn't.

They kept dragging me through an angry crowd, furrowed brows and wrinkled noses checking me as if I was some sort of bug, disgust lining their lips. They acted like I was dirty and left a stench behind me, which was odd because they forced us to shower and bathe when we arrived, they had to cut our hair and lather us in lotions that killed all bacteria.

I cried when they cut my mom's long, beautiful hair, when they threw away our toys and clothing, but soon enough we had new ones.

I received a shirt that was a bit too big for me, but it was pink and fluffy, so different from the grey and brown dirty clothes we wore before.

But now they stripped away the shirt, leaving me naked in front of everyone.

I started crying. I was ashamed. Terrified. Lost.

And everyone started cheering all of a sudden, but I looked around and there was no cake.

Nothing to be happy or excited about.

My eyes blinked quickly to shed the tears and clear my eyes, to allow me to see better and I scrambled my gaze around to find the source of whatever it was that made these people so happy.

My friends! They were here.

Maybe this really was a birthday party because they even invited my friends. My mom and dad and my sisters were probably preparing the presents, just like in the movies!

I was happy, I was excited, I even started jumping up and down, following the cheer of the crowd.

But the words were strange, not like in the movies. No happy birthday wishes echoed through the air, no one sang happy songs or clapped with joy.

Instead, I heard words like 'burn them', 'punish her,' chanting like 'pay, pay, pay' or 'kill, kill, kill." I didn't like it, so I stopped. I didn't want to follow them anymore, I didn't like those songs.

I couldn't go near my friends because someone grabbed them too and pulled them away just like they did with me. I didn't know their names, so I didn't know what to say or what to shout to draw their attention.

But they found me somehow, in the commotion of the crowd. And I waved at them with a little smile, happy to see them. They waved back, only their eyes looked terrified.

They were crying too.

My friends were dragged on a big pile of sticks and wood, which was strange because it didn't look like a table or chairs, it looked uncomfortable to sit in there.

Just then, mom and dad appeared, both of them crying and pleading. Dad was on his knees, his arms lifted in the air to pray.

Someone kicked me, I didn't know who because I couldn't turn, my arms were pulled tight against some straps that kept them wide open, forcing my naked back to expand. It pulled at my muscles. It hurt, and I didn't like it. I must have started crying again because my face was cold and wet.

I couldn't see my parents anymore, my face had been turned towards my friends, they too were strapped to more wood, they too were crying. They had started screaming even, but I didn't know why.

Then I saw the flames. Rising like a hurricane into the night, eating at my friends' legs and making them shout in agony. I started crying even harder, terrified of what was happening, trying to jiggle my arms free to run to them and set them free when the first blow came.

Swishing through skin and muscle, a deep cut made my back arch, my throat instantly howling in pain.

Then another one came, my own screams a new string to the ballad of wails coming from the burning faerie children.

"NO! Please, stop it, it hurts!" I tried to tell them, to shout at anyone who would listen, anyone who gave a damn and had the power to save me. To save us.

"Please, let them go!" I tried again, hoping that, if they couldn't gather enough mercy for all of us, they would at least spare the other children.

The smell of burning meat wrapped around my nose, inundating my chest as more pain came crushing on my back.

"STOOOOOOP!"

"Muffin!"

My shoulders started jolting, forcing my throat to bob.

"Muffin, you're okay!"

I heard a voice calling from a different universe, from a different life, forcing my eyes to open. "You're safe," Galenor's soft voice told me, his emerald eyes shining in the darkness.

"You are safe," he repeated, calloused fingers pressing deep into my shoulders to ground me to reality.

"I'm..." A sharp breath hitched through my chest, forcing me to understand where I was. Who I was with.

It had been a nightmare. One I thought long forgotten, one I had fought to keep from resurfacing for many years, now finally gaining strength and piercing through my brain to wreak havoc. "I'm…sorry," I swallowed hard, my chest still heaving from the image, from the need to take my brain out and wash the memory until it faded into nothing.

My hands shook, my body twitched, muscles trembled with shock and exhaustion, my skin dripping in cold sweat.

"Hey…" Galenor spoke again, his tone of voice the softest I had ever heard it. "You are okay, muffin. It was just a nightmare," he voiced with tenderness, his fingers sliding gently across my shoulders as if to make sure I could support my own weight.

"Ellyana," I murmured.

His gaze lightened. "A faerie name?" He looked both surprised and excited to uncover this new information about me.

"I was born in Wind," I sniffled, trying to pull the dripping snot back into my nose and avoid giving the faerie more opportunities to make fun of me.

"Me too," Galenor grinned, displaying a true smile to me. Probably for the first time.

Instead of bringing me the comfort he might have hoped to spread in me, my body locked, pinning my muscles in place. My bones dissolved into nothing, unable to keep me upright, forcing my back to fall, my head losing balance and following the drop.

"Ellyana!" Galenor's voice followed me, his body tugging me closer, pinning me to his chest. How was he even here? I could have sworn I locked the door. I was grateful for his touch, even if it was the only one I had.

I was not alone, like I'd been hundreds of times when this nightmare returned to rip my sanity away, each time lashing deeper at my consciousness.

Someone was here.

*He* was here, caring for me.

At least for a moment.

Offering me a dash of kindness through the darkness of the night, of our situation, of our souls.

"Breathe..." his voice urged, letting me follow the sensation caressing my body, to follow the waves of calm and protection his closeness offered. Galenor's hands were wrapped tightly around my body, his calloused fingers caressing the lines of my back with patience and dedication, as if he already knew what caused me to end up like this.

Shouting in bed, trembling and sweating from years of guilt.

"Let it go, Ellyana. Come back to me," the fae male urged, his hands lifting to reach my cheek and caress long lines down my skin. His thumb stopped right at the bone of my chin and pressed against it gently, lifting my head to him, forcing my eyes to find his own.

Instead of finding anger or reprimand, I spotted compassion and care.

The heaviness in my chest started to crack, hues of air suddenly bursting into my lungs to allow my raised pulse to settle. My breath to ease. My hands to find Galenor's skin.

I placed my fingers on his shoulder, enjoying the commotion happening under my skin, the deep need and arduous pulsations. I basked in their familiarity, relieved to feel something other than pain.

"How did you get here?"

I did not mean it as a reprimand, rather the need to make sure he was really there, by my side, pulling me from what had been the worst moment of my existence.

"I broke down the door," he responded as if it was no big deal, then shifted his shoulder just enough to let me see behind him. To spot the light from the gym, which did not have an off button. And the door, or what remained of it, in shambles.

Galenor must have pressed his body into the door until he ripped it open, because traces of wood and metal splattered across the bedroom.

How long had I been screaming for to make him do this?

"I'm sorry..." I forced out, my gaze peering around the room. Around his body. Making sure he wasn't injured.

"Don't be, it's my fault."

I had to check my ears because something must have been wrong with my hearing. It couldn't be that the cocky fae male I had shared almost two weeks with had suddenly started to develop good manners. I must still be dreaming.

"Hey..." Galenor's voice raised me from thought, forcing my focus back to him. "It wasn't your fault, muffin, you were just a kid." He exhaled, fingers trailing down my jaw. "You didn't know better."

Unable to avoid the river of tears that threatened to flood my eyes, I started sobbing, allowing myself to set all feelings loose. Unwilling to keep hold of the guilt that lacerated through my system on a daily basis.

Leaning into the fae, I dripped tears down his chest for long minutes, while his hands continued to caress down my back, drawing those scars with a new shade of forgiveness.

I hadn't told anyone this story, only my family and whoever was there that night knew about it. It wasn't in my military reports, and I hadn't confided in anyone, let alone a faerie.

His understanding and caress dragged deeper remorse through my skin, crawling at my veins and scraping at the blood passing through muscle.

He did not hate me. He did not accuse me. All he did was caress my wounds, over and over again, as if his touch was some sort of healing ointment that would take them away.

Little did he know, no one had ever touched my back. No one had ever seen my scars. I had made sure of it. But here I was, letting myself cry in the arms of the enemy, one who had broken through a door to be by my side.

Awareness ripped through me, reason bursting back into my senses. What the hell was I doing?

"It's okay, I'm okay," I said between gritted teeth, not wanting to allow my true feelings to surface.

Because I enjoyed this. I loved being cuddled in big, strong arms, I loved knowing someone was there to care for me, that someone had gone through so much effort to get to me, so I wouldn't be alone.

That female need deeply rooted in my nature liked to be cared for, liked to be caressed and desired. I didn't allow my brain to even consider what I had felt in between Gale's legs when he shifted us into bed. The hardness that hadn't been there when I woke up but greeted me with a massive bulge when its owner grabbed hold of me.

I didn't want to know that I too, had responded to his closeness, that wetness pooled between my thighs and my pussy throbbed, that I had wanted those fingers to go lower than my back, to reach down and grab my need.

I couldn't listen to its calling, I couldn't allow myself to feel what my body begged me to. Instead, I pushed back, trying to separate myself from the fae, doing my best to put as much distance in between us as the tight space allowed me to.

Leaning back and crashing against the bed frame, I did my best to escape Galenor's embrace, my shoulders rolling back to let his hands fall and allow me to escape his grip. Gaining an instant frown.

"What are you doing?" Galenor regained control over my shoulders, his fingers piercing deeper into my skin as if sensing my intention.

"I'm better now, thank you. You can..." I pressed my lips together, unable to say it. Hoping that he understood my meaning.

"Go?" his brows knotted with annoyance. Disappointment? Anger?

I dipped my chin as I swallowed hard, a sudden lump closing my throat. Did I want him to leave? Did I want him to stay? The logical part of me knew the answer. I was a captain, I had a job to do, I had a career to follow.

But the weird thumping in my chest did not care about any of that, reminding me that I'd felt more fulfilled in these few minutes in Galenor's arms than I had been in all my adult life.

"Good night," I barely murmured, the words coming out like spikes from my lips.

Galenor dipped his chin, his dark green eyes gawking at me, as if he expected this to be a joke. He blinked a few times, giving me a chance to reconsider, before he shimmied back from the blanket that remained trapped under his weight.

The fae grabbed it and placed it to the side, moving further away to give me enough space.

Not knowing what to do or how to react, I placed my head on the pillow and closed my eyes, hoping that he would take the hint and leave.

A second later, I felt the cosiness of the blanket pouring along my body while heavy hands fluffed it and arranged it around me, tucking me in. I couldn't help a sob and sealed my eyes shut to avoid more tears from springing.

I heard two steps on the wooden floor before the faerie stopped, the floorboards screeching under his weight and I opened my eyes to find him splayed on the hard floor, by my bed.

"You...you don't have to sleep here," the words rushed from my lips, my heart trembling at the knowledge that he was planning to spend the night a foot away.

"Muffin, you were screaming for minutes, I'm not going to let that happen again." Without another word, he leaned his massive body back on the floor and closed his eyes.

The proximity of him turned my skin aflame, the pounding of my heart unrelenting. My body pulsed, mouth watering at the sight of him, my brain straining with possibilities. I didn't stop until his breath evened out, turning from rigid inhales into soft murmurs. Only then, did my body relax enough to let me drag my mind back into blackness.

When I woke, Gale had prepared breakfast and left it on the small table for me. Then he continued his exercises and ignored me for most of the day.

I remained in the bedroom, supervising the installation of a new door which PDD had ordered without asking for my opinion.

No other instructions came that day.

*Day 14*

"Good morning, muffin," Galenor greeted me when I opened the door to let myself into the living room. He looked sweaty and had probably been working out for a while by the time I woke up and mustered enough courage to get myself into the room.

To find him in the kitchen, preparing breakfast.

This had become some sort of a tradition that neither of us disputed. Furthermore, we both seemed to enjoy it. I had the responsibility to keep the fridge and cupboard fully stocked, and the fae took it upon himself to cook.

For the both of us. True, he was the one consuming ninety percent of the food, but he had a real talent for bringing flavours to life, far better than I ever could.

That morning, he must have gotten tired of a full pound of bacon and eggs and craved something sweet, filling the entire room with the welcoming aromas of cinnamon and chocolate.

"My name is Ellyana," I finally replied with a low grunt, but walked without protest to the small table he'd already cleaned from the night before. It had become some sort of an agreement, Gale claimed ownership of the gym and kitchen while I kept myself mostly to the bedroom and bathroom. He had access to it, twice a day to shower and do his business, which he did so quickly and without trying to make it awkward for me. I appreciated that.

"I know," he turned to take me in and displayed a proud smirk. "But seeing how I am making muffins, it fits better," he chuckled.

"You are making muffins?" My eyes widened in surprise, instantly excited about the prospect of putting something sweet and hot into my mouth, the scent of his baking already enveloping my senses.

"I thought you might crave something sweet these days..." He didn't mention my period again, not after he'd used the excuse to make me feel like crap and saunter out of the bathroom after forcing me to confess the worst night of my life.

"I'm done with that, but thanks anyway," I felt the need to twist the knot, unsure of why it was important for me to tell Galenor that my period was over. I told myself it was because he didn't have another reason to tease me and swallowed the other thought.

"I can make something else if you like, but the food is running low again." His lashes fanned against his cheek with the unspoken request. Basically, he'd made me muffins to bribe me to go shopping again.

"Muffins are fine..." I sighed, my excitement levels dropping at the thought that I had to spend another good part of my wages to buy food for the insatiable faerie. In a way, I did not blame him, he worked out like a maniac, so determined to keep those muscles pumped and he'd been kept away from nourishment for a long while, so it was in part, normal for him to eat a lot. But my budget couldn't take much more of it.

My thoughts started drifting away, thinking about prices and shopping bills, struggling to piece together ways to get cheaper food in bigger quantities. There was another town I could go to where the prices were cheaper, but the drive alone would take hours. And I didn't want to leave Galenor on his own for so long.

Not that I did much when I was here, both of us reserved mostly to keep ourselves to our rooms, but his presence on the other end of the door settled me.

"Muffins for my muffin," the fae male smirked, displaying a proud grin while placing three stunning chocolate muffins in front of me.

"You are something..." I waggled my head, copying his smile, my mouth instantly watering. "They smell amazing, thank you," I nodded, grateful for the treat and took a big bite while watching Galenor bring a full tray for himself.

"How many did you bake?" I looked at him in disbelief, watching how he struggled to carry the massive tray filled with layers of chocolate muffins.

"Thirty-three," a full mouth dropped the reply in between attacks of chewing, the fae too hungry to sit at the table before he started eating.

I snickered, taking a moment to watch how he carefully placed the tray on the nearby bench and started biting from another muffin, while keeping another one at the ready. It was endearing to see him like that. Excited, calm, unburdened by constant worry.

His cheeks looked plumper, a beautiful healthy rosy colour appearing on his skin. His eyes shone brighter, and his mood had massively improved. It was amazing what a few days of recovery could do to the body.

Unfortunately, the joy of our breakfast did not last long. By the time Galenor reached his tenth muffin, the kitchen door unsealed with the familiar noise, forcing both of us to our feet.

My heart jolted as terror crawled down my bones, my feet already locked in place. Unable to move. My gaze jumped to the fae to observe his lips pressed tightly together and the way his throat bobbed with fear, how his back contorted and layered a cape of tension over his body, pushing his muscles from their relaxed stance into a fighting one.

They were coming for him again. They were going to take him away, to hurt him, to damage him, to destroy this new part of him that had just surfaced and that I had grown so fond of in such a short period of time.

I couldn't let that happen.

With sudden strength forcing my legs into action, I moved in front of Galenor, using my body as a shield against the guards that started to enter the room. There were six of them this time, all tall and muscled men in uniforms, armed to the teeth. Their brows were already furrowed as they came in, eyes pointed to their mission, unrelenting and oblivious to anything else.

"No, you can't have him," I sprang into action, extending my arms as if that would miraculously fix the gap between my body and the fae's. But he was at least a head taller than me, his shoulders too broad to hide behind my slim figure, his back too wide to camouflage behind me.

"Stay back," I threatened, forcing my voice into the commanding tone I had to practise in the bathroom so many times since I became captain, to even out my voice and delete all traces of feeling.

"I am ordering you to stay back. This is Captain Harrow that is speaking, you are commanded to step back. These living quarters are under my supervision and the subject is in my care." I took another step, my back scraping Galenor's chest from the abrupt movement. He did not shift, did not change position and remained in the exact same place he had been when the guards first entered.

Amongst the two of us, he was the only one who actually stood his ground. Hell of a captain I was. How could these guards take me seriously when I was the one backing away while giving them more space to inch closer to us? To take the fae away from me.

"Ellyana..." Galenor's voice scraped at my temple, his breath brushing softly against my skin. "I have to go..."

"No," I turned my head for a split second, just enough for my eyes to meet his. To spot the surprise in their glimmer. They lowered to me, as if to show appreciation before his lips uttered a murmured request.

"I need to go..."

"No! I won't let you!" I then turned to the guards, watching how they had already circled us, how I was the only thing standing in their way and preventing them from grabbing Galenor.

"They will hurt you again!" I shouted, unsure of what my best action would be. Unsure of what to say, what my body suddenly dictated me to do. "I cannot let that happen…" I shook my head, fighting back tears.

Tears! For a fae!

"Captain Harrow, please move," one of the men took another step towards me, closing in the distance, his eyes darkening by the second with visible annoyance.

"I will not move!" My voice came out with a threat, the expulsion of the words rising tension in the room.

"Captain Harrow," he insisted, pressing yet another step towards me. Towards us. Raising his hands as if he wanted to move me out of the way and get to Galenor.

Leaving his gun unprotected.

His biggest mistake.

My training kicked in, urging me to take the opportunity. As the man continued to move towards me, I took advantage of his cockiness, the fact that he thought he had the situation handled. After all, he was surrounded by five other men, all of them armed and ready to jump to his defence. Why not let his guard down?

Before he had a chance to realise what was happening, his gun was in my hands, pressed against his forehead, right in between that deep annoying V line he kept displaying so proudly.

My fingers shook slightly against the trigger, ready to release the life from this man while concentration forced a stream of sweat down my temple.

"Tell your men to back down and leave," I threatened, pressing the gun harder against his skin to form a red circle in between his brows.

His eyes remained pinned on me, filled with determination. He wouldn't back down, I could see it from a mile away. He'd been disarmed in a safe environment, by an ununiformed woman. It would be the end of his career.

But both he and I had too much to lose for either of us to back down. "Tell your men to leave!" I asked again, squeezing a finger just a little bit tighter on the trigger. He knew I was milliseconds away from firing. From putting an end to his life.

"Men..." his throat closed, barely allowing the words to come out like blades, each one hurting his future. "Weapons ready!" he ordered, then closed his eyes to wait for the end.

Half a second later, five guns were pointed at me. At us. Giving us no escape, no upper hand.

We were trapped...

"Lower your weapons," I shouted while using the gun to kick the guard in the head. But I already knew I had lost the upper hand.

I hadn't pressed the trigger when I had the chance. Now, even if I did, three lives would be forfeit instead of one.

"Ellyana..." Long, calloused fingers scraped against my shoulder. "Lower the gun." Galenor's voice brushed defeat against my temple, his arms wrapping around me, around my shoulders and torso, covering me in warmth.

"Lower the gun, muffin," he said again, his voice sweet like cotton candy, like a cloud moving away to let the sunshine in.

My hands started shaking harder, only held in place by his arms that were slowly claiming my body, inching closer to my wrists to force them down. To make me lower the weapon.

"Lower the gun, love" he said again, the last word dropping me to reality. Forcing understanding through my neurons. Of what I did. Of what I was about to do.

As soon as Gale's hands moved the gun away, my fingers dropped it to the floor, causing the guards to lower their own and inch closer to us. Five sets of hands caught Galenor, forcing his touch away from me and pinning him in place.

But his eyes never left mine. Darkness and life crashed together, forging a deeper connection that neither of us had ever thought possible.

I'd been ready to die for him. I put my life on the line for his.

Understanding that everything was lost, I launched myself into him, wrapping my arms around his shoulders.

"Galenor," I squeezed him tightly to my chest, not caring about the guards, about the analytics team that would probably demand my resignation as soon as they left, about my future.

"Ellyana..." he whispered my name with conviction, his head moving to lean against my shoulder, his arms already wrapped in iron behind his back. He must have been in so much pain, but he did not show it. Not for a second.

"I don't deserve your tears, muffin." I don't know how he sensed that I was crying, but there was no point in hiding it. I lifted my eyes to his, blinking rapidly to unblur his face from the tears.

"I'm scared they're going to hurt you..." I sighed, my lips trembling at the expulsion of my new reality.

Galenor smiled, his lips curling with a grateful cheer before he pressed his forehead to mine in the only connection we had left. "I'll be okay..."

It had become our motto, the words following us every day. In every situation.

"*You'll be okay*," I had told him when I didn't even know what he was, just a fresh faerie out of a box.

"*You'll be okay*," he'd repeated to me during the night filled with nightmares.

Now, we were adding another moment to the list.

"I'll be okay," he murmured again as the guards forced him away from me and escorted him out of the room.

I remained limp, in shock and alone, watching the door close and the hilt of a gun crashing against Galenor's head.

Time passed and I remained oblivious, watching the door seal and looking into the wall as if my eyes would magically adapt and let me follow Galenor. My heart thumped, chest palpitating with fear, dreading what they were about to do to him.

Hating myself for not being able to stop them.

A rope twisted around my neck as my eyes fluttered upwards, toward the ceiling. Realising all the cameras were watching. That an entire team had witnessed my breakdown, my inability to do my job. The job I was hired for.

The job that was supposed to build my future.

"Hello?" I barely muttered, terrified of what I was supposed to hear from the other end.

"Yes, Captain Harrow?"

I blinked and gave myself a moment. Trying to get a better grasp of my words. Doing my best to find the exact sentence I wanted to utter. Every cell in my body screamed at me to apologise, to ask for forgiveness and a second chance, while my heart ordered me to keep quiet and stand my ground. To stand against the violence Galenor was suffering through.

"What is the process of my release?" I asked instead.

"Captain?" the robotic voice replied, dispersing confusion even through the voice changing software.

"Isn't this assignment terminated?" Of course they wanted me to drown in my agony, to grovel and beg not to be fired. I wouldn't give them the satisfaction.

"The assignment will be terminated in fifteen days and thirteen hours, Captain. There are no plans or requests concerning an earlier termination of your trial assignment."

I frowned, raising my head fully toward the ceiling to let them read the confusion on my face. "What about the last ten minutes?" What about what I had just done? Threatening to kill a guard in defence of a faerie? A human guard? It broke at least ten rules, and should the laws be applied, I had to be flogged and demoted. At the very least.

"As per your last conversation with our sponsor, your assignment is to care for the wellbeing of the subject. We are grateful for your service, Captain Harrow."

My brain stumbled on the new information, which I pretended not to absorb. Indeed, I remembered the last written conversation I had with PDD, where he had basically appointed me as a month-long babysitter. But instead of using his initials, the robot had said 'our sponsor.'

This was new and unheard of. All missions were funded by the military and as far as I knew, some departments had to wait years for approval to hire an intelligence assignment. The sponsorship of this trial, along with all the secrecy and differences from everything I had been trained to do, meant that PDD, whoever they were, had used private funding to keep Galenor here. To put us both together. I did not know why or how, but it was at least a step forward. Something I could start investigating.

Not wanting to use the tablet to make a list, worried that everything I typed in there had a reflection somewhere else and could easily be spied on, I grabbed a pen and one of the romance novels stacked in my room. Galenor started reading one of them the night before and when he got to the intimate parts, which he felt the need to read out loud to me, I snapped at him and shut the door for the night, kicking him out of the bedroom.

I flicked through the book to find an empty page and started making notes before I lost track of my ideas.

1. PDD – abbreviation?
2. G is from Wind Realm. Why me?
3. Sponsor = private funding?
4. Different guards every time

5. One Cloutie root left.

6. No assignments in the past three days

7. PDD not available when G is away

8. Happy with my outburst - why?

9. Why is G important to PDD?

Nine questions I had no answer to. Nine questions I would put my heart and soul into unveiling before the end of this mission.

I didn't have much choice but to pick myself up and start my day. The muffins Galenor had baked remained scattered on the floor after the abrupt entrance of the guards, so I picked them all up and put them in the disposal chute, not having the heart to take one more bite without him to share it with.

He had announced that we were running out of food, so after forcing myself to tidy up the room as much as I could, I decided to go food shopping. This way he would have enough to help him recover, at least.

My movements became robotic, I punched in the code and opened the door but could barely see what was in front of me. For some reason, my trial assignment had caught the attention of the unit, because some colleagues stopped me several times to ask me how it felt to live with a faerie and asked me for information about the subject. They knew I couldn't reveal any important information, but I assumed something was better than nothing and it gave them a chance to go to their bunks and have something to talk about with their roommates.

I walked the hallways like a zombie, too distressed to even care about the questions and conversation around me, about the people who never took an interest in my wellbeing but were suddenly interested in my day-to-day life. My state of mind did not improve in the shop either, where I spent an hour wandering around the aisles and picking up whatever things caught my attention at that moment. I did not have a strategy and must have bought a lot of junk food and ready meals, not wanting to take away from Galenor's free time and force him to spend longer cooking than necessary.

Before I walked to the checkout line, I added a bottle of red wine to my trolley, something to keep me company throughout the day, and blinked away the minutes until I had to scan my card and go back to the car I had borrowed from the unit.

By the time I drove back, sunset pressed a heavy blanket on the town. I watched people drive home to their families, to prepare dinners and enjoy a quiet night in. Whereas I had to return through a corridor filled with curious eyes and hoped that the fae would be brought back soon and in a state that would at least allow him to walk.

My heart thumped when I reached the familiar hallways that would take me back to this month's assigned living quarters. By the way the guards gaped at me, something must have happened, and I had to assume it was regarding Galenor's return. With newly found enthusiasm, I almost frolicked to the door to unseal it, the weight of the carrier bags a light burden compared to the excitement gushing through my body.

My gaze ran across the room, muscles quaking with anxiety, expecting to find Galenor thrown somewhere on the floor, unable to move or even breathe properly. But the living room looked exactly as I'd left it, clean with no signs of blood.

I hurried my steps into the bedroom, scanning my surroundings, taking in the furniture, the bed and the closed door to the bathroom. I opened it in a hurry, not caring what I would find, too desperate to find *something*.

Empty.

Galenor was not here, and it was already dinner time. Which meant they were going to keep him until the late hours of the night or even until morning.

Not really caring about the food but not wanting it to spoil, I filled the fridge with the new purchases, making sure to keep the wine bottle close to me.

Once everything was in its place, I unscrewed the cork and served myself a tall glass. Then I situated my ass on the small chair facing the sealed entrance and started willing it into opening.

The first glass of wine did not have the intended effect, unable to bring Galenor back to me.

So, I served myself another one and when it finished, I poured a third.

Things started to look blurry, and my eyelashes fanned heavier down my cheek with every sip I took. The concern building through my bones started a dance with the alcohol in my system. My feet were heavy, ankles pumping with ineptitude and anguish and my neck struggled to keep my head upright. When the familiar sound of the lock unsealing the door finally tickled my ears, I jumped into action and ran into the kitchen, preparing my spirit for what was to endure. My eyes for what they were about to see.

I bumped against a hard chest, a heavy weight forming a barrier to prevent my advance and I looked up, readying my fighting stance. They would not keep me away from him.

Not this time.

Emerald eyes blinked at me with relief and curiosity, a small smile curling unbloodied lips.

"Galenor," I wrapped my arms around his neck, pressing myself tighter against the hard body. Instantly, heat pooled around me, his returning embrace spreading warmth across my skin. The combination of his closeness and the wine rushing through my blood almost made me pass out from relief.

"You're okay," I exclaimed happily, taking only a step back to scan his body, to check for unseen wounds. Not enough to leave his embrace though.

First things first, he was standing, he wasn't bleeding, and he was smiling. All good news in my book.

"I am okay," he murmured, an octave dropping from his tone with the new meaning those words had for us.

"I'm so happy," I let a deep breath out, joining my chest to his again and closing in the distance between us for another hug. This time, a tighter one. A truer one.

His arms wrapped around my body as his chin dropped to my shoulder to rest. Galenor gave himself a moment to inhale. The air filling his lungs inflated his chest and pressed him tighter onto me, our heartbeats joining in a symphony of caresses. Our hands started wondering on the other's back, taking in this moment and the safety settling around us. We did not know how long it would last, but we were both safe. Together.

We could at least have this night.

"Are you alright?" I unpegged myself from his arms enough to study his body again, as if I couldn't trust my eyes the first time and needed a second inspection.

He nodded, eyes dropping down to his chest.

"It was a talking day today." As he spoke the words, he too realised our unsettling situation, how our first instinct had pushed us into an embrace and took a small step back. Not enough to fully distance himself from me, but further away from my arms.

On their own accord, they released Galenor's shoulders and dropped around my body, forcing my brain to push my legs into a step back of my own. I took another one, separating myself even further from the fae, suddenly realising that this sort of closeness shouldn't be allowed with a subject, no matter the assignment, but the alcohol running through my blood had the mission to wrap me in humiliation.

As I was taking the second step, my ankle turned wrong and my feet stumbled against one another, forcing me to lose balance. As my vision was slightly blurred and my reactions delayed, I did not have time to catch myself on something before I landed on my ass. On the floor. At Galenor's feet.

"Ouch," I frowned, squinting from the pain. Once more, long arms wrapped around my body and hoisted me up, the fae lifting me from the floor with a chuckle as if I was a sack of potatoes.

Mortified, I hid my face in his shoulder, unwilling to look at him and enjoying the soft tickles his hair performed on my skin.

"Are you okay, muffin?" he jiggled my back slightly to force me to look at him and, not having another choice, I did just that.

Wide, curious and glinting eyes blinked at me. A curl of his lips followed my movements as I lifted my gaze to his. And started laughing.

I let out a deep sobbing laughter, my eyes tearing up and my stomach drilling with contorting pain, so much that I had to double down onto Galenor's body again because I couldn't stop myself from letting it all go. All the worry, all the anxiety, the sudden joy his closeness brought on me. The happiness I felt in that moment, all wrapped up in his arms. Even though it must have proved pretty difficult to keep hold of a woman contorting herself with laughter, he did not ease his hold on me for one second, keeping me tightly pressed into his arms. Where I was safe.

He did try to calm me down a few times by saying my nickname, but when I did not respond, his lips murmured my real name, sealing that connection we had both forged, yet neither of us was willing to recognize.

"Ellyana, are you..." his regard slipped from my lips to the room, then returned to me once more. "Drunk?"

I snickered, proud of myself. "Maybe..."

The chuckle rumbling from Galenor's throat did things to my body but echoed deeper in very particular areas. My brain took that exact moment to remind me that his skin was brushing against mine, that his torso was basically shoved into my left boob and that my pussy laid so close to his face.

I turned crimson, the wine in my system sending pulsations all across my body, from my cheeks down to the part of me I really wanted this male to pay attention to.

"Put me down," I swallowed a dry gulp, feeling guilt washing over me. It was weird how the alcohol hit in the most annoying moments. Where was this happiness and relaxation when I needed it? When I spent hours watching the door and hoping for him to get back uninjured?

"Ellyana..." his eyes scanned me knowingly, probably sensing my desperate need for him. No, no, my need to be away from him.

"Put me down," I insisted. "I'm going to be sick." It sounded like a valid excuse, being picked up and held six feet high in the air could turn anyone's stomach.

"I'll carry you to the bathroom," he insisted and started stepping towards the bedroom, but I pushed myself back and shoved my knees into his chest to force him to get away from me.

Galenor quirked an eyebrow, unsure of what would make me lose my temper and jump from the woman experiencing a laughter attack in his arms to the one kicking him, but he did not protest and bent at the waist to allow me to step out of his embrace.

I brushed his touch away and took one step back, forcing my breath to ease. Then I took another and one more, distancing myself from him. From the temptation of his body. Finally, without another word, I turned on my heels and ran into the bathroom.

"Ellyana?" a knock stopped my trance. I'd placed myself in the bathtub and turned the cold water on, then pressed my gaze to the wall, determined not to move until all the warmth torturing my body disappeared into the deepest corner of my mind, to never be allowed again. I blamed the alcohol. Foul, foul creation.

"Ellyana?" I heard the knock again, this time more insistent.

"How come you are not hurt today?" I shouted through the door. I don't know why I needed to have that information, other than to give myself a few more minutes under the cold shower, hoping my body would be numb enough to stop reacting to him the way it did.

He paused, probably surprised by my question, but nevertheless, offered me an answer. "A Wind delegation is in town. They wanted my input on traditions and such. They offered me a day off if I collaborated, so I said yes."

A day off...It meant he'd be here tomorrow. All day. Just him and I.

"Ellyana, open the door." This time, his voice came as a threat and, before I had a chance to react, the handle snapped open and Galenor burst through the bathroom door.

To find me naked, sitting in the bathtub, shaking away the effects of his touch.

Day 15

"I..." he stopped, letting his gaze slide across my body and tickle every one of my senses before he spoke again. "Muffin..." Galenor sighed.

"Not a word," I threatened, but at the sound of my shaky voice, I decided I could do better. "Not a fucking word!" I stood, letting the cold water stream down my body, without caring what parts of me I had unveiled. "Not a word about how you want to fill me or some other shit like that or I'll smack you! If they didn't, I will!"

The fae remained petrified by the door, eyebrows furrowed, and lips pressed together in what I initially assumed was shock, but under longer observation, it looked like he was trying to hold back a smile.

"Fuck you, faerie!" I decided to throw the last resources of my rage, before my feet forced me down again, the cold seeping into my body making my legs shake.

"Come on, let's get you out." He looked unphased by my sudden outburst and was not bothered one bit by the insults he had received in such a short time. It took him two determined steps to

155

reach the bathtub and by the time I had a chance to react, his fingers were already wrapped around my forearm.

Only then his eyes went wide, shock and surprise seeping into his features. "Ellyana, what in fucking Zaleen's name are you doing?!?"

I'd never heard him swear, let alone use his realm's deity to do so. It forced me to draw a sudden breath, which, combined with the accumulation of shivers and alcohol, sounded more like a moan. That single sound unleashed the fae, snapping whatever self-control he'd been exercising until then.

Before I had a chance to move away, or even react, Galenor's arms wrapped around me, forcing me upright. He grabbed my wrists and settled them around his neck before one of his arms pressed against my ribs and the other lowered to behind my knees. Just like that, I was cold, and naked, and shivering in his arms.

The fae did not even look at me or listened to objection and carried me to the bedroom, where he gently placed my body over the duvet cover and wrapped me in it, making sure that every part of my wet body was covered and getting warm. As if that wasn't enough, he grabbed his own blanket, the one I had offered him in those first few nights which had turned into a sort of mattress for him to sleep on, unfolded it and wrapped it around my legs.

Just when I thought I couldn't get more embarrassed, Galenor jumped in bed behind me and spread his legs to cover each side of me, his hips joining mine from behind. His chest slammed into my back, pulling me close to him to offer his own warmth while his palms rubbed against my shoulders and arms to help my blood flow and give me more comfort.

"I can't do this…" I shook my head slowly, too aware that his chin was right next to my shoulder, that his breath tickled my ear, and his closeness made my heart swell.

"I know you can't," he replied as if my words were the most normal thing coming out of my mouth. "You'll catch a cold, and your healing skills are nowhere near as good as mine," he spoke softly, the sound of his voice causing deep ripples inside my heart.

"You don't understand," I shook my head, making my wet hair fly back and forth, the confession eating at my conscience. "This needs to stop." I paused, letting new air flow into my veins. "I can't…" I shook my head again.

"You can't care for a fae," he filled the room with my unspoken words.

My silence must have been confirmation enough, because I felt him nod behind me. Understanding. Still, his hands continued to send warmth through my body, as if the information I had given him was nothing new.

We spent long minutes in silence, me shivering while Galenor did his best to warm me up. Neither of us tried to fill the void the echo of his words had left across the room. It became comfortable, as if both of us already knew this and did not want to speak the truth.

"Is that why you felt the need to bring yourself to the brink of hypothermia?" he finally asked.

Tired of the lies and of hiding, I allowed myself to confess my feelings, enjoying the new freedom my soul had been yearning for.

"You do things to me…when you speak, when you touch me…Add the alcohol into the mix, I was a goner," I chuckled the sadness away.

"I'm tired," Galenor admitted after another minute or two of listening to each other breathe. "To be judged, to be treated like this. Everyone is basing my worth on what I was born as, not who I came to be." He drew in a long, deep breath, as if those words had been hanging down his throat for a decade, then, with a lighter tone, he continued whispering his worries.

"When I was caught, I thought that would be the end. That I would be killed, or burnt… Instead, everyone assumed my worth to be different, simply because I was born in a different place."

His palms stopped caressing down my arms and wrapped around me, squeezing me to his chest in a tight, long hug. An embrace he needed more than I did, one that allowed him to expel the lead settling into his heart. "It's tiring to crave death and to never earn it."

His words completely broke me, shattering every defence, every fear, every barrier I had created to keep me away from him. I wanted to give myself to him completely, to fill up that void in his soul, even if for only a minute. Because he deserved so much better than this life.

"Galen—"

"We should get some sleep," he shut my words down before they even had a chance to spring.

"Okay…" I murmured, left with no other choice but to agree with him.

Wordlessly, Galenor shifted his weight from behind me and shimmied away from my back, making me crave the return of his warmth. I wanted to say something, to apologise but nothing came out. I remained silent, feeling like absolute crap after hearing his confession, after he'd allowed himself to say those words in my presence.

If anyone deserved a day off, it was this guy.

"You should stay here," my mouth went ahead and released the call, one I hoped he would be willing to accept.

"I'll be fine..." he groaned as he lifted his weight from the bed, making the mattress scream for his return. "I got used to sleeping on the floor. It's more comfortable than you think," he turned and added a quick smile, which I already knew was solely for my benefit.

I didn't want to think about his past, how he was kept in chains that burnt his skin, how he then had to sleep on the hard floor without knowing when his next torture session would come. Today, he had gained a break. And he deserved a proper bed.

"There's cameras there, they will keep watching you," I tried, but it raised no reaction in him, probably too used to his every movement being analysed that he stopped caring.

"Good night, muffin," he stepped away from the mattress, away from me, reverting back to that nickname that brought us to our initial roles. That showed our differences.

My heart jolted, pushing me to do something, anything to make him stay.

"Galenor, please!" I heard myself beg. His eyes widened in surprise. Same as my own. Okay, that caught his attention, I might as well carry on. "Please stay with me tonight." I patted the mattress to show him where he would be sleeping if he listened to my plea.

"They only gave you one bed, Ellyana, and you made it perfectly clear you don't want me near you," his head tilted back to rest against the doorframe, like the memory of my words affected him somehow.

"I shared a room with eleven other people. Trust me, I can share a bed with a fae. Plus, it's a double bed." I took the opportunity to shimmy over to one side, showing him how much space was left should he choose to occupy the other side of the mattress. "There's no cameras in here. You can mumble in your sleep, and no one will be the wiser," I pressed a tight smile, which did nothing to comfort him.

"Is this your will?" His lids narrowed on me, trying to spot any lies I ushered through my lips.

"Yes," I said and moved even further to my side of the bed, making more room for him. Then, doing my best to keep my body covered, I removed the blanket he had wrapped my legs with and threw it to his side, suggesting that we would also have separate covers.

One dip of his chin was all it took for my pulse to explode. Without feeling the need to explain his actions, Galenor sauntered back to the mattress and threw his body over it, burying his locks in the pillow. With a single motion from his hand and foot, the blanket stretched over his body. Well, part of it, his shoulders remained uncovered and the better part of his torso as well. Realising that he wouldn't fit in the bed, he bent his legs and made another attempt, this time his body collapsing on itself to make him fit within the edges of the bed frame.

"Good night," his deep voice wobbled through the room with a few deep breaths to follow it.

Taking his example, I leaned over to the nightstand and turned off the bedside lamp, sealing the room in darkness.

One doesn't have to be a scientist to know that I immediately realised the mistake I made by asking him to share my bed. Not that Galenor did not act like a true gentleman. I chuckled internally, he really was one when he wanted to be. But my skin prickled with the awareness of his closeness.

Every dip of the mattress, every time his lungs contorted and exhaled, I felt it deep within my bones. When he moved an arm to tug the blanket tighter around his body, my soul fluttered so desperately I thought I was going to have a heart attack. How would I be able to spend the night with the man I wanted most in my entire life was beyond me.

My throat dried up, closing in on itself from the sheer angst flowing through my body. My nipples pebbled, begging for contact and my thighs throbbed with need. I even considered touching myself underneath my own cover, but I was too scared to move.

Maybe if I got a little closer to him, maybe if I inched into him just a little, just enough to feel his warmth, that would calm me down a bit. Not knowing what time it was or if his even breathing was a sign that he was already asleep, I faked a sudden need to scratch my back and shifted my body closer to his as I performed the motion.

His back against mine set my core on fire. I felt his breath, the way his shoulders relaxed and tensed with the inflation of his ribs, each time leaning into me a little more.

Gods, kill me now...

As if on cue, Galenor shifted from his side onto his back, extending his shoulders below the pillow in a wide stretch. I didn't even breathe from terror, too afraid that I woke him up. That he would find me by his side, wet and craving for his closeness.

I didn't even have a chance to back down because a grimace made him shift again, probably some old injury that hadn't fully recovered. This time, Galenor's chest stood pressed against my back, an arm carelessly leaning on the side of my hip.

I sucked in a breath which remained trapped in my throat, unable to reach my lungs. Galenor was hugging me in his sleep. Albeit not all the way through, it was mostly an arm that wanted to rest on an elevated surface, and I proved to be that, but still. I was wrapped in Galenor's arms.

I felt his chest pressed against me, his arm resting on my hip and his breath tickled the back of my neck. In my book, that was a hug. And I was expected to fall asleep to that, when need urged me to wake him up and offer myself to him, to give up everyone and everything for a few hours with this fae male.

He would definitely know his way around a woman's body. After all, they were renowned for their ability to turn women crazy with their sexual charms. And Galenor was the most beautiful male I had ever seen. Only the presence of his warmth or a breath from him turned me liquid, and he didn't even have to try.

The pads of his fingers arched against my hip, escaping the hold of his blanket and slipping onto my cover, the only thing that separated my naked body from his touch. His palm started moving against me, sliding slowly, motioning me up and down as if we were in a smooth dance.

I bit my lower lip, trying to muffle a moan that threatened to rip his way through the silence of the room.

"Ellyana…" he groaned, his arm wrapping tighter around me, pulling me closer to him, my back against his hard chest, my ass against his pelvis and against his…

"Oh, gods," I moaned at the sudden press of his erection across my ass. It felt so big and hard, it made me lose all self-control. I shoved my ass deeper into him, using my hips to slide up and down, to try to feel more of it.

Galenor released a deep groan, the sound of his pleasure raising so much sensation inside of me. I felt like I was exploding from within. He must have sensed it because his hands jumped in between my thighs to caress the cover that so rudely separated my skin from his touch.

"Muffin, don't you know it's dangerous to tempt the fae?" he groaned into my ear, his tongue tickling my earlobe to raise another moan from my lips. I slid my head to the side to give him better access, all the while grinding against his cock and tilting my pussy into his hands.

"Oh, yeah?" I sighed, my voice guttural. So, so ready for the taking. "And why is that?"

"Because once I am summoned, love, I won't be able to stop."

"Then don't," I pleaded, my throat begging to feel that hardness.

"Mhm…" he paused, abruptly removing his hand from in between my legs and sliding it up to my chin, turning my face to him. I couldn't see much of him, the only light we had was creeping under the door from the living room, which was always lit. I spotted his shape, the curve of his lips and the glint in his eyes. Watching me. Scanning me for the truth.

"Are you sure, muffin?" Just as he spoke the words, his thumb brushed against my lips, opening my mouth to press against my teeth and find my tongue. I started sucking on it, circling my tongue around his finger to show my willingness.

"I need you to say it," he groaned, pushing his pelvis to me while his thumb pressed against my mouth. "What do you want me to do to you muffin?"

One hand remained on my mouth, torturing my lips while the other moved to rip away the cover, to unveil my naked body to him. Through the darkness of the room, I saw a pleased smirk as his eyes dipped down on me, sliding over my legs, taking in my throbbing pussy, lifting to my tits that begged for attention with peaked nipples.

"Do you want me to take you?" He murmured, his figure shifting over mine, the sudden weight of his body over me pushing me further onto the mattress, unable to move from under him. "Do you want me to fill you?" He pressed his groin against me, his hardness almost ripping at his pants. "Do you want me to taste you?" He pressed on me again, this time his mouth opening to allow his tongue to slide down my neck, making me go crazy with need.

"Yes!" I shouted, unable and unwilling to control myself. "Yes!" I said it again as a moan ripped through me at the feel of his erection.

"Yes! To all..."

"Very well, muffin. Let me taste you," Galenor's voice came out rugged, his chest heaving with anticipation. With a single abrupt motion, he ripped the rest of the blanket away from me, unveiling my body to the heat of his own.

My skin instantly turned gooseflesh, a whisper of expectation tickling through my gut. Filling the room with the madness of this moment.

I was about to have sex with a fae male, in a dark room, behind a closed door where an entire unit was spying on our every move. I thanked my lucky stars for asking them to remove the cameras and microphones from the bedroom, because, even with the light off, it was perfectly clear what Galenor and I were about to do.

My eyes had adjusted to the darkness enough to spot his eyes, hazy with desire. He blinked a few times, taking me in, his regard brushing against my shivering naked body while the pads of his fingers started gliding over my skin.

Plastering my body against his, Galenor shifted in between my hips, sliding my legs around his midsection and pressed against me to allow me to feel the pulsations of his desire.

He throbbed in between my legs, allowing me to feel every single thrust of his veins, of his thickness as he ground onto my skin, letting my wetness seep through his pants, telling him how ready I was.

Unable to wait, desperate to have him then and there, I let the last shred of dignity slip away.

"Take me..." I moaned, my fingernails digging into his back, desperate to get him closer, obsessed with the need for him. To have him, to feel him inside of me.

Galenor released a slow breath, as if he too needed the same thing, as if his hips urged him to pin me in place and shove himself deep into my core. Only he stopped, lifting his desire away from my wetness and sustaining his weight on his palms on each side of me, towering over my body.

Then, with heavy sighs, he confessed his fear.

"You may be the last woman I ever fuck Ellyana, let me do this properly..."

My heart sank into my throat, and I remained unable to contain a sob. Without caring that it would completely ruin the moment, I reached up and wrapped my hands around his back, climbing onto him like a spider monkey to give him that hug he denied me, but most definitely needed. He tried to shiver away, to tense his back so that my arms would release him, but I pressed tighter against him, this time using my legs to wrap around him as well.

We remained in this awkward position, with him holding an impromptu plank while I crawled onto him and pegged myself onto his chest while planting small kisses on his shoulder and neck, the only parts of him my mouth reached.

I knew I broke the heaviness haunting him when he started chuckling and relaxing his arms, allowing me to slowly fall back on the mattress and letting his body press over mine, this time with even more intensity than the first time. Neither of us wanted to break this new connection, the bond this confession and the embrace drilled into us, so we remained there, hugging and placing gentle kisses on the other's skin for long minutes.

Galenor's mouth reached my shoulder, his tongue sliding down to taste the saltiness on my skin and started travelling down to my breasts, his palms suddenly interested with the newly discovered territory. My nipples pebbled again, showing how ready I was for him.

I didn't have to wait long for a reaction, because his touch caressed around the line of my nipples and his tongue started curling them with delight, the heat of his breath raising tickling sensations all across my body.

I arched into him, lifting my chest to his mercy to give him better access to me, to show him that I was ready and willing, but before I even had a chance to enjoy the delightful torture his teeth performed on my tits, his attention slid down, tongue drawing a line on my skin towards his new destination.

His tongue marked my navel and lowered onto my pelvis while his elbows settled around my hips, hands gripping me tightly and sliding me open for him, making me ready for the taking. With my legs splayed on either side of his shoulders, I had no other choice but to shiver for his warmth and remained there, open for him to enjoy.

My stomach clenched with expectation, with the urgent need hollowing out any other encounter I ever had from my memories.

None had raised these feelings, none made me feel like he did. And he hadn't even touched me yet.

Gods...

His fingers slipped through my folds to expertly open my core as he descended on me, his tongue immediately swirling around my clit. I moaned, my head tipping back with the sensation. It felt like I was falling off the edge of the world and when his mouth started swirling around me, I needed to cling onto something to keep myself from fainting. Somehow, my fingers reached his locks and wrapped around the loose strands of his ebony hair, holding on for dear life as he started working me, his face buried in between my thighs.

Warmth started spreading through me, my body was coiling around the caresses of that tongue that never seemed to settle on a single place. He circled and sucked at my clit until I was on the brink of pleasure to then move onto my folds and nip at the side, his tongue stroking out pleasure from parts of myself I didn't know could even hold those kinds of sensation. To then unleash himself to the edge of my thighs and bite me to the point of pain and then circle back to sucking my clit while the tip of his tongue performed a crazy dance along my senses.

I was drenched in minutes, I was moaning and panting, barely able to take air into my lungs, but he never once stopped. Never gave me a reprieve. And never let me cum. As soon as he felt I was close, he changed direction and brought me back to the brink of pleasure from another point, only to claim it back again and start from scratch. He played with me like that for a long while, until I had no other choice but to beg for him, to beg for his mercy and for the explosion of pleasure I knew this wicked game would bring me.

"I can't take this anymore," I panted, pleading for him to let the long-awaited wave of pleasure engulf me. To drown me completely. At this point, I didn't care if I died from an orgasm, it was well worth it.

"The more I tease you, the better it will feel, muffin," Galenor removed his mouth from me just for the seconds it took him to pronounce the words. The stubble that started growing on his chin pierced at my skin torturously, covering his entire face in my wetness, something he seemed to not be at all bothered by. He continued to lick me like I was an ice cream cone on the first hot day of summer. Claiming me with savage desperation, like I was only his.

His to have, his to own, his to possess.

And he would not rest until that feeling remained tattooed on every single angle of my soul.

"Please..." I groaned, almost fainting from the accumulating sensation, unable to control the ache in my legs, which started trembling around his shoulders.

His fingers ripped through my core, opening my pussy to a new sensation and a deep rumble of pleasure that pulsated through me from inside and out. I was the offering to his godly talents, and I was glad to burn in the deepest fires of punishment.

For the first time in my life, I had been introduced to true pleasure and my body did not have the capacity to hold onto it, forcing sensation to explode into my core and take me to the deepest realms of madness.

Galenor ripped waves through me for long minutes, slashing orgasm after orgasm until my body remained nothing but a shaking, sweating mess.

With a deeply satisfied smirk, he planted a few farewell kisses on my clit and around my thighs before he wrapped me back into the cover and leaned on the bed behind me. His arms wrapped around my body and dragged me closer to him, one of his legs resting over my thighs while his hand placed soothing caresses on my shoulder.

"Good night, Ellyana," he murmured, his voice gruff, chin still wet with my desire.

I wanted to protest, to take care of that massive erection that still pressed against my back, but the warmth of his body and palpitations in my chest forced my eyes to flutter closed. The last thing I remember were a few kisses on my neck and the warmth of a whisper. He had spent every ounce of my being.

"Thank you," his whisper creeped into my ear.

I mentally chuckled, having no energy to use my throat to do so. I should be the one thanking him.

Soft lips planted a kiss on my cheek, tugging a smile on my lips. I could get used to waking up like this instead of the shouting of the unit on the hallways or the blaring alarm we had each morning. I turned to find Galenor grinning at me, his deep green eyes glimmering with a new feeling. One I hadn't seen in their shade before. It looked like happiness. I let the image guide me to the sweetest rest.

"Good morning, lazy muffin," the fae chuckled and bit playfully at my shoulder, tasting the lingering pleasure on my skin.

"Mhm...morning," I mumbled, my body too shook from last night's events to muster enough strength to properly wake me up. I was left in some sort of hazy state, where I floated through the night veiled in the most pleasant sensation known to man.

Unable to pull myself together and physically move from the bed, I tilted my head to the side to watch Galenor. His transformation had been amazing, he looked like a fully grown Greek god, packed with muscles and filled with energy, revitalised by the rest, food and a good night sleep.

I knew fae were sexual beings so if we took into account what happened last night, it was as if he'd somehow fed from the pleasure rippling through me. His skin glowed, his hair looked shiny, his eyes glimmered, I could only wonder how his appearance would change once he too reached pleasure.

Something that needed to be rectified very soon.

Not that I felt too guilty. Throughout my life there had been lots of times where I left the encounter unsatisfied or had to fake reaching an orgasm to get it over with, so the fact that I came multiple times last night while my partner didn't was not the end of the world. Though my mouth watered at the thought of what his massive erection would cause down my throat.

"There's pancakes and chocolate syrup waiting for you in the other room," he smirked again, proud of his achievement. I took another moment to gaze at his lips and spot traces of chocolate down his chin. His stubble had grown a little from the night before, not enough to need a shave yet, but enough to cover his chin and the sides of his face and hide those melted drips of goodness.

"I..." the thought sprang to mind. "You said they gave you the day off today, right?" I vaguely remembered him shouting across the door about cooperating with some sort of guests.

He nodded, blinking at me with awareness, so I immediately clarified, not wanting to scare him.

"The living room..." I paused, needing to correct myself. "The gym and kitchen are under twenty-four-hour supervision. There are cameras in the ceiling and mics planted all across the walls." I expected him to make some sort of expression, to show anger and shout at me, to curse humankind and storm out. But he remained immobile, as if he already knew or expected all of this, so I continued. "The bedroom and bathroom are off limits, for my privacy."

That raised a proud smirk, no doubt, content with the fact that our activity remained just between the two of us. I also realised just then that I had told him where he could freely do whatever he wanted. To me...

"Seeing how you were promised a day off, it makes sense for them to let you spend the day in the bedroom." I waited for him to confirm, but he did no such thing, only looked at me as if I had the final say in this.

With a burst of energy, I grabbed the long t-shirt I generally used to sleep in, threw it on and stepped out of the room to tilt my head to the ceiling.

"Good morning," I greeted whoever was observing.

"Good morning, Captain Harrow," the voice responded.

"Galen…" I stopped, not wanting to show closeness. Unwilling to reveal his full name to them and give them power over the fae male. "The subject advised contracting a day off from the assignment due to collaboration on facts related to his origin."

"That is correct," they immediately confirmed.

Pressing my lips together to fill my lungs with bravado, I spoke with determination. "Permission to offer the subject a day of reprieve without supervision within the unrecorded rooms."

One second, two, three…

My heart almost stopped beating by the time the buzzing voice started again.

"Permission granted, Captain. See you tomorrow."

I almost skipped with joy at the confirmation of what this meant for Galenor. If they were willing to give him a full day, just for telling them his traditions, what else could he get from the unit? Could he collaborate on something else to ask for more stable living quarters?

For the end of torture?

For freedom?

There was no better moment to obtain information than sitting down with the involved party and sharing food in a friendly situation. Considering what had happened between the two of us only hours before, I would say he already reached that point.

I grabbed the two plates with pancakes and Galenor helped me carry the tray containing drinks, more sauce and two dozen other pancakes, which I assumed would barely be enough for his breakfast. Then, we both sat in bed, on opposing sides of the mattress, watching each other eat.

I realised, just then, that Galenor and I never enjoyed a meal together, even if we sat down to eat several times. Something always happened. He was rude and shoved me away, he made snarky comments that made me swear at him and leave or he was the one dragged away by soldiers.

My stomach twisted at the sight of his passionate chewing, at the way his tongue glazed over his fingers, dirty with chocolate, how the syrup dripped down his chin, but he remained focused on his task, engulfing his food with dedication.

He must have spotted my gaze on him because he lifted his eyes to me and stopped chewing, leaving half a pancake unsatisfied in between his fingers.

"What?" he asked with his mouth full.

"Nothing," I giggled. "You eat like a savage," I laughed.

His brows knotted, suddenly pinned on me. "Is that a compliment or a complaint?"

"Can't it be both?" I grinned and took a small bite from my own plate, using a fork and knife like a sane person and chewed slowly.

"You like it, muffin," he lifted his chin to me, eyes scanning me all over again as if to confirm his assessment. A second later, he nodded. "You like it," he said again, setting the record straight.

"Well yeah...you eat pussy like a champ, congrats," I tried to brave out the words but turned crimson when my own ears heard them. He spared me the humiliation and returned his attention to the abandoned half-pancake.

"So..." I scratched the back of my head, suddenly uncomfortable to start interrogating him, "How old are you?"

Galenor paused, the half-chewed pancake once more forgotten in his mouth. He frowned, gaze slithering to find my meaning.

"Why are you asking?"

"Because..." I folded my arms across my chest, "before that thing of yours reaches anywhere near my mouth, I would like to know you better," I pointed a finger to his midsection.

"You mean my cock?" he chuckled and swallowed the extra syrup and the pancake, his throat making a choking sound, as if announcing my fate should I dare to go anywhere near him.

"Yeah..." I mustered the confirmation. If I got myself into that mess, I might as well get myself out of it. "If that's something you would like..."

*Oh, my gods, Ellyana, did you actually just ask someone if he'd like to slide down your throat? Fuck, fuck, fuck.*

"Planning to show me your skill, muffin?" he smiled, fire lighting his gaze which burnt through the deepest of my defences. Making me confess everything to him.

"Don't get too excited, I'm not expert level as you are...more like...your average encounter. Probably not as good as the many women you've been with..." I grimaced at my own stupidity and decided to shut my mouth for the rest of my life.

I looked down at the two remaining pancakes on my plate, wishing I would take their place. Nothing sounded better right about now than being swallowed alive and forgotten forever. Along with all the stupid shit I ever said.

"Thirty-two," Galenor replied with an overly amused tone.

"What?" I instantly forgot my wish and lifted my eyes to his.

"I am thirty-two...I think," he frowned and blinked a few times as if wanting to make sure. "I was captured right after I turned thirty and it's been about two years."

My eyes bulged out. He'd been a captive for two years? How did this man survive for so long? The longest captivity I ever heard of was seven and a half months, an ogre from the Water Realm. Instead of dwelling on the information, I decided to ask another question and pull at the string he had just offered me.

"Why were you captured?" I dared ask. Then, not wanting to force the answer out of him, I turned back to my plate and took another bite.

"Because humans are idiots..." Galenor sighed. "No offence."

"None taken," I replied and grabbed some more chocolate syrup. If he liked to drown his pancake in that much chocolate, I was clearly missing out. Silence filled the room and both of us continued to eat and watch each other, smiling from time to time when one of our chins or shirts became a battlefield for the chocolate to flow onto.

"I was travelling to Bentlas for a conference my father forced me to attend. I took his vehicle as it was an official visit and I had to represent our side of the realm. It was close to the Human Realm border, but I'd travelled that route so many times I considered it safe. It wasn't..." he replied with a sigh.

My mind swam with all the information that single phrase brought me. Official business, vehicle, conference.

"Are you someone important?" I swallowed and reached out for the glass of juice he poured for me.

"There's no need for flattery, Ellyana, I haven't been treated properly since my capture," he pouted, as if he missed people fussing over him. Which also told me that yes, he must be someone important. I felt stupid and decided to tell him how little information I actually had on my subject.

"They just shoved me in here and told me to wait for a faerie. I didn't even know you were fae or a male until you healed. Hence, the door," I pointed at the closed bedroom door, the only barrier that separated us from the outside world.

"Told you humans were stupid," he chuckled but then continued speaking. "I'm an Earl of the Wind Realm." Then he furrowed his brows, as if the information he'd provided wasn't at all accurate. "Of the Northern Region," he corrected.

"And earl? What exactly is that?" It had been a long time since we studied realm ranks, so my history knowledge needed a little refresher.

Taking no offence in my need to enquire, Galenor explained. "I am the son of someone important, someone who owns the Northern Region, amongst other territories, and when he meets the goddess, I will inherit the lands. If I'm still alive by then…" he corrected, twisting a dagger in my chest.

Trying my best to shift his thoughts, I chuckled, nodding with the realisation. "I knew you must be someone entitled," I grinned. "You are such a smug prick."

Galenor started laughing, his joy filling the room. "I am," he admitted. "Blame it on my upbringing." He turned his attention back to the pancakes to fold two of them, dipped them in the chocolate syrup until they were drenched and shoved them in his mouth.

Why was the unit holding an earl captive? Surely, he must have had enough diplomatic connections to help them in some way, but judging by the way they treated him, something deeper rooted their interest. Something no alliance could offer.

"Galenor…" I pressed my lips together, shoving the words back for a moment. Doubting that I even had the right to ask these questions.

"Say it, muffin. At this point, there should be nothing holding you back," he encouraged.

"What did you do?" My brain swirled with possibilities, making me dizzy and ready to pass out. Was he a murderer? Was he one of those mad fae that sacrificed humans? Did he hold parties at his grand villa where they burnt our kind to the pyre and danced around it? What did he do to deserve this amount of torture and violence on a daily basis? For the soldiers to become so familiar with it and nickname him 'Gale'?

He huffed, dropping the food and pressing his eyes to mine, sudden anger flaring in them. "Fucking nothing, love." he turned on the mattress and shifted to reach the wall the bed leaned against, resting his back against its coldness. "Show kindness, that's what I fucking did."

A long moment drifted between us, resurfacing against the heaviness of the conversation. I didn't even dare breathe too loudly, concerned that it would spike more anger into the fae male, all of a sudden too aware that he could rip my spine in half if he so wanted to.

"My full name is Galenor Dalenth," he finally spoke, his words a whisper brushing away the silence that had caught root inside the room.

I hitched a breath, my heart stopping for a mere second.

"Yes...that's the reaction," he pointed with his chin towards me, not at all surprised. "Imagine when your dear humans learnt that. Do you think I ever stood a chance?"

"The..." I swallowed the knot growing in my throat. "The king's name is Dalenth," I said the obvious, as if he didn't already know that. *The prince's name is Dalenth.*

"Yup," he leaned further against the wall, his hair resting on the cold surface to make his dark hair wave away onto his shoulders. It grew a little bit longer, only an inch or two since his arrival, giving him the regal stance he no doubt had embraced throughout his life.

"You're the prince of the Wind Realm?" My eyes watered with the realisation, shame engulfing my entire body. I deserved to burn for this betrayal. For letting that bastard touch me, for letting him feed from my energy. With trembling hands, I shifted away from the bed, taking a step back. Away from him.

"Thank you, muffin, that's so nice of you," he tilted his head to look at me only long enough to spill his sarcasm.

"The prince wants us all dead. He's responsible for ten thousand human deaths a year. All the terrorism, all the campaigns, the assaults on young people..." I shook my head, tears falling down my cheeks. What had I done?

"Ellyana, calm the fuck down," Galenor sighed. "I am not *him*." He spoke with such a neutral tone, as if he was tired of uttering this exact same phrase.

"Your name is Dalenth..." I barely whispered, my hands scratching at my skin from the need to get his scent away from me, the traces of his caresses and the kisses he had left behind.

"Ellyana!" he shouted, shifting from bed to catch me by the shoulders, shaking me into reality and forcing my eyes to his. "I. Am. Not. Him."

His eyes...

Those beautiful, wondrous, heavenly eyes...looked true.

"What?" I whispered, blinking away tears to let myself fall into that life-giving green.

"I am related to him," he explained, his fingers squeezing hard at my shoulders to keep me in place. "As in, my great-great-great many generations ago great-grandfather and his great-great whatever were brothers. Centuries ago. When the realms reformed, after the return of the goddesses." He took a moment to allow me to breathe, to understand what he was saying.

"Most of the nobles in the Wind Realm have the same name, it's how you know we're nobles," he pointed with a frown as if it were the most obvious thing in the world.

"What are you saying? That you're innocent?" It was my turn to frown at him.

"I'm saying that my father is a Dalenth and his father before him and his father before him and my children, if I ever get to have any, will be Dalenth and their children and so forth. You are only aware of the Dalenth king and prince, the ones coming out in the world, but the name existed for centuries. The rest are protected within the privacy of the realm."

I stretched my back, forcing his fingers away from my shoulders. "What are you saying?" I asked again, wanting to ensure I had the right mindset to listen to what he was about to say.

"I am saying that humans are idiots and that yes, they have the wrong person." He spoke with such conviction that his words must have been true. Or, he had practised this a lot, wanting to make it sound perfect.

Galenor sighed, taking a step back. "When was the last bombing claimed by the prince?" He looked at me as if I was a voice-controlled search engine and he expected an immediate answer. I hadn't even thought about that, hadn't even thought to check this sort of information.

Not saying a word, I circled the bed and pushed him to sit by the leftovers on his plate until I grabbed the tablet and searched for the information. So many attacks were caused annually by the prince's clan that the search proved to be more difficult than just a simple question. Add the fact that the Wind Realm was closed off for visits, exchanges, commerce or even information with the Human Realm and there was very little coming out of there, if at all. When the press caught glimpses of their realm, they tended to print the same information repeatedly. I had to scroll through articles, through news, through geotags, to enter my unit location and personal number which gave me access to privileged information and had to scroll through all the news about my local region before I had access to current affairs.

During this time, Galenor continued eating, as if I wasn't just trying to confirm his innocence. As if he was already sure of what I would find.

"Three days ago," I finally spoke, my eyes darting to him to spot his reaction. His face remained completely neutral, no sign of surprise or any other lingering feeling. "In Vegnoth..." Half a continent away from us.

Galenor pouted. "The most memorable thing I did three days ago was to eat burgers," he shrugged, as if to say I told you so.

I dropped the tablet with the realisation, my hands shaking. "Why didn't you tell them? Why didn't you..." I shook my head again, trying to chase away more tears. "I can help you prove this, we can—"

"Ellyana," he reached to grab me again, this time his arms wrapping around my back. I let him.

"Trust me, I tried everything, but they don't seem to care. Or listen. If I am not the prince, then I share his name and must have some sort of information about him. If it's not one thing it's the other."

"Maybe you can give them something, maybe if you tell them enough, they will let you go," I placed my hands on each side of his cheeks, forcing his face to mine.

"I despise the royal family and did my best to stay away. Trust me, if I could have said something, I would have done it in two years."

"But why don't they believe you?" I sobbed, sharing his pain, the inability to make people listen, to make yourself heard.

"I'm a faerie who begs for death every day, do you honestly think my word matters anymore?" he blinked at me with a sad smile.

## Day 16

I didn't know what time it was, but I had a feeling it was still early. Galenor's even breathing told me that he remained asleep by my side, his hands still wrapped around my waist just like when we'd gone to bed. His closeness enveloped me through the night, but when he suggestively caressed my leg, I bit my tongue to the point of bleeding but faked being asleep.

I knew what he wanted. And I wasn't ready for it.

My body begged for more, urging me to get close to him and let him take me to the highest realms of pleasure, desperate for another world-shattering orgasm. But my mind kept spinning, drunk with the information, with everything he'd confessed.

He sounded so sincere, so careless, that part of me thought his words had been rehearsed. Over and over again until they sounded as harmless as clear water. It was hard to think that the institution I represented and had worked for my entire life would make these kinds of mistakes. And if they did, that they wouldn't rectify them.

Every single subject I had encountered during my assignments had proved guilty, whether their crimes were petty, or the information provided saved an entire region. I had never found someone with a case of mistaken identity.

But everything was so secret about this trial assignment. Private funding, no analytics team, cameras and mics in the living quarters, constant torture of the subject. And they had confirmed yesterday that Galenor spoke the truth regarding his help with a Wind Realm delegation. I had given them those exact details and they even agreed to stop observing him for an entire day.

Never once had a team come to an agreement to give time off to a subject, especially while situated in the living quarters.

I couldn't...my brain felt like it would explode.

Would the unit keep someone locked away and tortured for two years just because they thought he might have information, even if he proved not to be the one they were looking for?

A shiver passed through my guts. I already knew the answer to that.

Yes. Yes, they would.

Everything related to the prince of Wind had become such taboo, some even believed him to be a vampire rather than a fae because of his obsession with claiming human blood. We'd all grown up hearing about his atrocities, ever since he was a child he enjoyed seeing humans suffer. No one knew what he looked like, so he might have been anyone. All the information we had was his name, which was always dropped at the base of every attack, proudly claiming the incident. "Prince Dalenth." The Prince of Death, we called him instead.

It made sense for the unit to distrust Galenor when he had the exact same name, when he spoke with hatred about humans and hated every one of us. What didn't make sense was for these attacks to continue even after his imprisonment. Surely, whomever was keeping him here knew about the incidents, so why hadn't they released Galenor?

So many pieces of the puzzle that my brain was on the brink of a massive explosion.

In the end, I could only go with my gut. Which told me to believe Galenor.

At least for now.

Wanting to let Galenor get some rest, I slowly shimmied out of his arms and leaned against the wall to support my back, grabbed the tablet and slid my fingerprint to unlock it.

I opened the chat box I had saved the last time PDD and I had a conversation and started typing in the hope that someone will be at the other end.

"I would like to confirm information about the subject," I typed quickly and prayed to all the gods for that chat bubble to start moving. I waited long minutes, my chest filled with anxiety and hoping that Galenor wouldn't wake up just yet. Hoping I had enough time to get to the bottom of this.

"Captain Harrow, how can I help?"

Thank you, thank you PDD for getting back to me so early in the morning.

"Good morning, sir. I would like to confirm the subject's name."

"Galenor Dalenth," the next chat line appeared in a few seconds.

"Background?" I typed, not wanting to get ahead of myself.

"Wind Realm, Northern Territory."

So far so good. Everything Galenor told me the day before proved to be correct.

"Capture date and location?"

"40 km from Bentlas, twenty-seventh March, two years prior."

Fuck.

Fuck, fuck, fuck. My heart started pumping with despair. That was exactly what Galenor had told me.

"Reason for captivity?"

"That is above your level of clearance, I'm afraid, Captain Harrow."

Of course it was, I pouted. He wouldn't tell me. He'd confirmed everything else, but not this part. Because if he turned out to be the prince, he knew I would freak out and abandon my post. And if they turned out to make a mistake, they wouldn't admit it. Especially not to a mere captain who was assigned to babysit him.

"Your new instruction, Captain Harrow, is to uncover any particular markings on the subject. Time for completion, five hours."

Before I had a chance to type something else, the chat closed.

What the hell was he talking about? Did he want me to get more information on his scars? They must have had enough time to check those in the two years they held him captive.

With a scrambled mind and lazy feet, I dragged myself to the bathroom and took a quick shower. By the time I got out of the steaming space, Galenor was already awake, stretching lazily in bed like a cat that had enjoyed a full bowl of canaries.

"I'll make breakfast while you shower?" I offered instead of a greeting.

"Sure thing, muffin," he grinned at me, his beautiful green eyes still hazy with sleep.

Before he had a chance to say anything else, I dragged myself out of the room and closed the bedroom door to give him that extra sense of privacy.

His break was officially over, and sheer nervousness spilled through my veins at the thought that they would come and take him again. The silver lining was my new instruction, which had to be completed in five hours. It seemed unlikely for them to remove him from the space during that time, it would come against my own assignment.

The weird part was that I hadn't spotted any markings on Galenor, apart from his scars, and I had seen his back and chest so many times I had already started to learn the curve of his muscles. And why was this important? Didn't they get the chance to discover markings in two whole years?

Something was off about this.

"I'm not sure if it's edible, I got distracted," I warned the fae as I set the plate on the small table. A two-egg omelette for me, with a slice of toast, half a tomato and half an avocado. And a ten-egg omelette for him, with three slices of toast, two tomatoes and two avocados. Looking at his massive plate, I had no idea how someone could eat this much, but the small pout told me he was worried it wouldn't be enough to calm his hunger.

Then, a smirk curled his lips and he gazed at me sheepishly. "I assume you had better things to do than think about cooking. Seeing how I was naked in the shower and all."

True, just a look at the way he had the nerve to come in the room, wet and shirtless, wrapped in only a towel made my knees buckle and I almost fainted on the plates. His dark locks dripped on his shoulders still, forcing my gaze to follow the journey of that lucky drop down his chest and onto those gorgeous abs that made me lose my senses.

I swallowed dry, forcing myself to look back at my food.

"This is becoming a pattern," he noted before shoving half an avocado into his mouth. Curious that he went for the veg first.

"What is?" I barely mumbled, doing my best to bite into my toast like a normal person and not start licking it the way I wanted to do with his body. Because damn…how was I supposed to look at that and retain my sanity?

"This," he pointed at me with his fork. "You. Hiding behind your food." He shoved a massive piece of omelette in his mouth and chewed just enough to be able to speak again. "Struggling to swallow, when we both know what you really want to eat is me."

I choked on my tomato, doing my best to keep the half-chewed piece in my mouth. When I dared look up at him, I watched him continue to enjoy his breakfast as if what he had just splayed on me was as obvious as daylight. Clearly, he was used to the effect he had on women. And did not seem to mind it one bit.

"Speaking of your body…" I grabbed my glass and drank the juice in massive gulps to swallow down the tightness pressing against my throat. If we were going to do this and I had less than five hours, I might just as well dive for it. "Do you have any special marks on your body? I need to see them."

That stopped him from eating, his attention instantly turning on me, fully focused on my features.

"Now?" he frowned, slightly bothered.

"Is that a problem?" I blinked, shaping my features to a neutral portrait.

"I was hoping you would at least give me a chance to eat breakfast before asking to see my dick, but you're the boss."

Before I had a chance to protest or even react, Galenor stood and stepped to the side, his waist only inches from me. Then, with absolutely no warning, he dropped the towel he used to cover his body, displaying himself fully to me.

I gawked, too shocked to even breathe because…by all the gods, he had a tattoo just there and it was massive.

*Everything* was massive.

The black lines slithered from the back of his knee up to his thigh, spiralling onto his hips and circling to the left side of his pelvis and down to his…yup, massive, like I said.

"Wow," I said in amazement, a huge sigh leaving my throat.

"Thank you," he smirked, grinning at me with pride.

He was so close to me, so close to my face that one single push would have us connected. It was so easy to take him into my mouth, to taste him and spread that tattoo, which seemed to go on and on. He must have realised it too because his body started reacting to our closeness, urging me to touch him. To lick up and down all those intricate lines.

"Okay, that's enough," I widened my palm and pressed it in front of my eyes to cover the view. "Thank you, you can return to your breakfast now."

I tilted my head to the side and did not move until I heard the squeak of the chair, telling me that he sat back at a safe distance.

"That was..." I sighed. "Unexpected."

"Why, you've seen bigger?" he raised a brow, suddenly curious.

I shook my head no, not wanting to say it. Trying my best to get that image out of my head and to stop my mouth from producing extra saliva.

He blinked a few times, those emerald eyes pinned on me.

"Did I break you, muffin?" Then, with a smirk, he added. "Don't worry, little one. It's just as afraid of you as you are of it."

"Can we please just eat? In silence?" I snapped, all too aware that I started to compete with the tomato for the best shade of red of the morning.

Before I knew it, I had less than an hour left. I had wasted three ignoring Galenor and gawking at the taut muscles on his back as he did his gym exercises through the open door while I laid in bed. I made up an excuse about needing to do some research and left him on his own as soon as I finished gulping down my food.

If I had any chance to do this, I couldn't waste any more time. Before I called for him, I drew in a few sharp breaths, preparing myself for the incoming closeness of his sweaty torso and all the sensations that would raise in me.

"Galenor?" I threw the calling before becoming paralysed with fear.

"Muffin?" he stopped midway through a pull, his swollen biceps clenching around the weight and turned to face me.

"Can you come chat with me for a moment?" I felt my determination crumble, my voice melting at the sight of him.

With a booming thud, he dropped the weight and rushed to the bedroom door. Then, without an invitation, he threw himself on the mattress by my side, watching me with a curious gaze.

"What is it?"

I sighed, readying myself for all the mockery I was about to receive. Knowing I had no choice but to take it.

Wanting to make it clear, I stated my reasons as if I were back in school.

"Part of my assignment is to receive instructions. I use the living quarters of the subject, in this case you, and I am given specific sets of instructions with a time limit to fulfil them."

The fae remained quiet by my side, dripping sensuality on my mattress.

"Today's instruction is to discover any markings on your body," I decided to spurt out, aware of the little time I had left and wanting to make it clear that my job was the only reason why I was bringing this up again.

Galenor chuckled, his laughter making my cheeks automatically blush.

"You called me to your bedroom to talk about my dick again, muffin?" he grinned at me and turned to the side to better display the ribs and taut muscles he had been working on all morning.

"Galenor, please..." I sighed, both flushed and frustrated. "This is my job."

He tsked, eyes twinkling with delight. "So, your job for the day is to unveil my—"

"Yes! Alright, enough. Please." I said again, pummelling my fists into the pillow right next to me.

He pressed his lips together, observing me for a long moment. "How long you got left?"

"About half an hour..." I confessed, seriously desperate to stop this cat and mouse routine and just get the information I needed.

Just when I thought he would leave me hanging, Galenor stretched his back on the mattress, leaning to the side to find me.

"It's our family history. In the house we grew up in, on this massive wall," he gestured to display the size from his memory, "was a tapestry, dating from five centuries ago. With our family tree."

I barely breathed from fear of missing out, thanking my lucky stars that he was willing to reveal this about himself. "Traditionally, a fae male had a marking ceremony, where he had to choose his mark. It could be anything, a flower, an animal, a cloud even. The only requirement was that the mark had to remain present during their lifetime."

"I remember that," I said without thinking, the image of a history book popping into mind. "They told us that the prince who summoned the gods had a gardenia as a symbol. The flower was celebrated for many centuries after his death."

"It still is. The Earth Realm holds a huge celebration in May when the flower blooms," Galenor confirmed. "So, this tapestry had all the intertwined symbols of our ancestors, up until our father. When we became of age, my brother and I got really drunk and challenged one another to get the symbols on the tapestry tattooed."

"Okay, but why choose that area?" My eyes bulged out at the memory of his fully tattooed member, wondering how the logistics of that even worked.

"Because it hurt like a bitch, and we were stubborn bastards. We even bet on it, that we wouldn't let it reach our cocks. We both lost," he chuckled.

"That must've hurt…" I bit my lower lip.

"Not as much as you might think. We were both drunk to the point of passing out. The most challenging part was keeping the flag high until the tattoo was done," he smiled at the memory.

"What? Did you have to be fully…" I didn't say it, I couldn't say it without ignoring the pooling warmth in between my thighs. My core started throbbing at the thought, at the memory of him naked that very morning, at the image of that tattoo shoving into me.

"Four hours. Try doing that when you're fainting from absinthe," he laughed again, proud of himself.

I had to breathe, I had to breathe, I had to breathe. It was too much. Too much information, too much sensation, too much desire.

Four hours. He did it for four hours while a needle pierced at it. My mouth watered.

"Okay…" I tried my best to look composed, but by his burning gaze, I did the exact opposite.

Feeling his stare on my body, his eyes blinking in my arousal, I launched myself at the tablet, doing my best to input the information before my entire body engulfed in flames of desire.

"I need to do this before anything else," I heard myself say, and wrinkled my nose at the stupidity coming out of my mouth.

"Okay, I'll be here," Galenor groaned from behind me, making it clear that this wouldn't be the end of the conversation.

With shaky fingers, I unlocked the screen and opened the chat box.

"He has a tattoo with family meaning, it represents the marks of his ancestors up to five centuries ago. It was a bet with his brother during their coming of age. It lines the back of his knee, circles his thigh, and expands to incorporate his genitals."

"Excellent, Captain Harrow. New instructions will follow tomorrow."

Blood boiled in my veins, desperate and filled with need. Before I even had a chance to think, I saw the message my fingers typed on their own accord.

"Will the subject be taken to interrogation today?"

I waited, heart throbbing in my chest, desperate for an answer. Desperate for time alone with him.

"I am otherwise engaged today. New instructions will follow tomorrow."

I swallowed hard, locking the tablet and throwing it on the nightstand. I swung my head to Galenor then to watch him sweaty and breathing hard, gaping at me with intent, an erection stretching his pants.

"Did it go alright?" he asked, his desire stifling the room.

I nodded, unable to find my words, both excited and terrified of what would come next.

"We both have free time until tomorrow..."

Galenor bit his lip, the urgency of his need spearing through me. "I'm sure we can fill it somehow, muffin."

My brain stopped functioning; my lungs started heaving at the air around me. Everything was suddenly too hot, burning my skin. I was sweating, my flesh had become goosebumps and the blood in my veins flowed with newly found intent.

I was pure energy, ready to be discovered and unveiled, ready to burst out of my skin. Ready to surrender to his will.

"Galenor...I..." I shook my head, unable to speak. Not knowing what to say.

Every muscle in my body begged for contact, everything I was, all that I believed in, forgotten with one look in those gorgeous eyes. Nothing else mattered but this moment. Not my principles, not everything I had learnt about the fae male, not my pride.

"Ellyana..." he groaned, inching closer to me, the space between us shrinking by the second as he leaned on me, bringing his lips close to mine. "I will kiss you now," he announced, his tone guttural, as if he too had been long awaiting this moment.

I nodded, not willing to say it. Not wanting to hear myself give him permission, but wanting him to take me in every way, shape or form he wanted to.

When his lips touched mine, my heat accelerated, a sudden combustion in my chest forcing me to open to him, to let him in. I spread my lips, giving him free reign to lead the kiss and jolting with sensation when his tongue slipped inside my mouth. He tasted salty and harsh. The way his tongue danced inside my mouth, filling me with sensation and inundating me with the taste of him almost made me pass out. Just then, strong arms wrapped around my body, my waist suddenly supported by new pressure, bringing me closer to him, joining my chest with his sweat.

Galenor continued kissing me, every swing of his tongue becoming harsher and more desperate, claiming more than my mouth. He scraped along my teeth and dripped down my throat, making our mouths clash like two armies on a battlefield, both determined and unrelenting. Once unleashed, impossible to grab hold onto.

I needed to breathe. I needed to breathe but all I could inhale was him. His scent, his taste, his mouth, there was nothing else but him. As if sensing my need for air, his lips shifted to my neck to continue their teasing, licking and biting to trail down to my shoulder while his hands occupied themselves with unbuttoning my pants.

A moan stifled my senses then, the feeling of his calloused fingers in my panties making my bones shatter with desire.

The way his hands grabbed at me, with determination and unease told me that this would be completely different to our first night together. This time Galenor was unleashed, desperate and ready for the taking, his urgency ripping at his pants.

Which flew away as soon as I was out of mine, letting his massive erection spring free and press onto me, my thongs the only thing separating us.

"Mmh..." he groaned at the discovery of wetness pooling between my legs, displaying how ready I was. How desperate to take him in. "I like this, muffin," he smirked, eyes pinned back to me to find me panting, red and completely unravelled.

His lips curled wickedly, proud of his achievement.

"Are you sure you want this, love? Once I'm inside you I won't stop until you see stars." The tip of his cock pressed at my entrance, pushing against the lace that kept him away from fully possessing me.

Without saying a word, my throat closed off with desire, I reached to grab him in my hand and started stroking him with desperate urgency, moaning at the wetness at his tip, which he had scraped from between my thighs.

Thick veins jerked at the touch, his length pushing into my hand, using it to pump himself against the round tightness of my fingers to get him ready. Gods, he was big. Bigger than I ever took, bigger than I ever saw.

Crazed with need, I used my free hand to shove away the patch of lace covering me and led him to my entrance, pressing his tip into me again, ordering it to enter and fill me. Demanding to saturate the ache.

With a voice roughened by desire, Galenor snarled. "So eager, cupcake." Then, without warning, he slid into me.

His sharp movement forced my core to split for him, a burst of pain making my legs clench around his hips. Sharp pain launched at my entrails as he speared through me mercilessly, shoving himself all the way in, touching the deepest sides of me. Then he pulled out as abruptly as he did initially, taking strength in his hips to push into me for a second time, forcing me to split wider for him.

I screamed, unable to contain the pain. It felt like a hot poker kept shoving at me, making my cervix shift into place to make more space for him, my fingernails digging into his back, deep enough to draw blood.

Only then, his hips stopped, green eyes blinking at me in surprise, as if he only then realised I was also there. With a slower motion, he slid back into me, this time taking a moment to let me adjust, his eyes closing with the sensation, as if he could feel me open up for him.

He started pushing again, and again, harder and deeper, rocking his hips against mine and digging into my core with brutality.

He was right, we were a few minutes in, and I already saw stars. Once the pain disappeared and my pussy accepted its new owner, I relaxed enough to allow pleasure to seep through.

It started growing with each movement, piling on and on, crawling into my bones, clenching into my muscles and puckering across my skin.

He took dips into my core, his hips swinging and turning, making his cock caress different parts of me, scraping at my insides until a veil of pleasure ripped from me. I moaned, alert and confused, this new sensation raising an army of shivers all across my body.

The fae's weight covered mine, keeping me prisoner to his mercy, not giving me a moment to adjust to a new position until he switched and turned me, forcing himself in places I didn't know I had, scraping at the walls of my core until I completely combusted.

Like the expert he clearly was, he allowed me to ride my desire and did not shift until I was completely spent, offering me a grin of satisfaction before he hooked my leg around his hips to shift me into a new position.

We performed this dance for a long while, until I didn't know how my body could physically produce any more wetness, Galenor's hips hitting against my thighs like his life depended on it.

After I broke against him several times, climax after climax ripping through me, he removed himself from me enough to spin me and turn my back to him. One arm pressed against my hips to lift them up while the other grabbed at my back for support, his knee pushing against mine to spread my legs and make room for him.

"Any special requests?" he asked, voice gruff and panting, ready to shove himself into me once again.

My brain muted because I had no idea what he wanted from me. I pushed my ass into his wet erection, dripping with my juices, to get him back in. Then it clicked. He was asking permission to fill me up. Like he'd joked about so many times.

"I'm on hormones," I replied, barely able to breathe from the exhaustion, the pleasure, the thought of him cuming inside of me.

As soon as I released the words, his length pressed against my ass, smashing against me like a tall wave onto rock, furious and unrelenting.

He moved so fast, so desperately, that I thought my body would break, were he not gripping my hips to pin me in place. Slam after slam, he thrust into me with brutality and force, making me feel every thick inch of him.

Right when I thought I would pass out, with a final burst, the fae stopped, letting out a violent scream to announce his climax.

Galenor remained inside of me for a minute, his cock slowly pushing into me until his breath evened out. I felt a long line of kisses trail down my back, his lips lowering onto my skin, his body bending to follow his lips, making his still hard member slip out of me.

He allowed himself to fall on the mattress with a thud, his eyes shut, attention fixated on the ceiling. His hands searched for me in his hazy state, finding my body and bringing me to his arms. I rested my head on his chest, listening to the frantic beats of his heart.

*Day 17*

"It's nice to see you smile, muffin," Galenor smirked at me from the side of the bed he had claimed as his own, fully aware that my grin was caused by all the wonderfully wicked things he had done to my body.

After yesterday's hardcore fuck-session, we had dinner and then started all over again, continuing long into the night. My body had been turned and tossed in so many ways and directions, until the fae squeezed every last juice of my desire and took great pleasure in tasting me to the point of making me beg for him to stop. To offer me some time to breathe.

This morning, the quick shower I was meant to take turned into a feral pounding of my insides until all the hot water was gone. And until Galenor was finally satisfied.

"I'd like to see you do the same sometime," I teased. "I only had the pleasure to see grins and smirks, but not a true smile."

"Like this?" He peeled his lips back to show me an extremely forced smile that displayed all his teeth.

I chuckled. "Maybe not that creepy, but it's going in the right direction."

That got me a playful smack on the ass, making me immediately shift away from his reach because I knew what it would bring me, and I was exhausted. Everything in me was still throbbing and my body was on the verge of passing out, so I truly needed a break.

Galenor, instead, looked as fresh as a daisy and as eager as a thirsty gazelle. Part of me envied his genes, that amazing ability to turn women liquid and make them beg for him, but a suddenly jealous other part scolded me for thinking about this.

What the hell was I doing? I couldn't start feeling jealous of other women he had been with, I had already made it clear to him that this was just that, really fantastic, really rough sex. The last thing I needed was to catch feelings for a subject. Be he a stunning, tall, handsome and possibly innocent male.

"What's bothering you, cupcake?" Galenor leaned on the side, displaying his naked torso to me. Ever since he revealed himself fully to me, he hadn't bothered putting clothes on. Which was why I had forced him to stay in the bedroom, behind a closed door, lest there be a team of people watching his sexy ass and massive cock through the ceiling cameras and realise all the nasty and dirty things we were doing in here.

"Just thinking..." I shook my head, willing away dirty images and plans of all the things I still wanted to do to him. Being with Galenor was like eating chocolate for the first time. Delicious, addictive and made things hurt.

"We should get ready for the day," I sighed, every part of me pleading to remain in that bed, next to that man.

He nodded and followed my lead, then grabbed his pants from the floor and put on the only t-shirt he had left. I mentally swore at myself, I hadn't even thought about getting him clothes when I did the food shopping.

"I'll go grab something else for you to wear," I announced as I opened the bedroom door to let both of us out, looking fresh for the day as if we hadn't just completed a sex marathon in there.

"That would be much appreciated, thank you," he sank into his role and stepped away in the opposite direction from me, heading to the gym area while I went into the kitchen.

"Any special requests?" I opened the fridge to check what we had left and almost wanted to cry when I spotted how little food remained. Again.

"No, whatever you have would be great," Galenor started stretching and preparing his body for the lifts. We'd spent the morning in bed and skipped breakfast, so I had the hard mission to try and make brunch. While looking completely innocent and not showing any more familiarity to the subject. I could do that, I was a trained soldier. I settled myself, but my eyes travelled to his back, to the curve of his tight ass, to his hips and the memories of how perfectly they met with mine, making me wet with desire. Yet again.

"Why are you so obsessed with weights?" I asked, feigning curiosity for the cameras I knew would be watching. Better yet, it gave me an excuse to keep my eyes on him and continue salivating at will.

"What else would you have me do, cupcake?" he turned to me with raw desire glinting in those emerald eyes, a wicked smile on his lips. "Read all those dirty little novels you have in your bedroom?"

Gosh, how was this going to work? How would I be able to talk to this man after everything he'd done to me? How could I keep a straight face and be detached when all I wanted to do, when all my body commanded me was to jump his bones?

My eyes widened, silently berating him for the use of that word. Cupcake.

*"Because I want to fill you up,"* he'd once said.

Fortunately, my tablet dinged with the all too familiar noise of a new instruction, picking me up from my thoughts.

"Uncover information about the subject's family."
Completion time: ten hours

My heart leaped from my chest, and I barely contained myself from going over and trapping Galenor in a hug. Fully aware of the supervision we were both under, I turned my attention towards the oven and twenty minutes later, I came out with sausages, eggs and toast.

While he continued to do his lifts, I carried the plates to the small table and filled two glasses with apple juice, cut up some fruit and cordially invited him to brunch.

The fae stepped towards me with a snicker, then he looked at his plate and turned his eyes back to me. "This looks delicious," he licked his lower lip seductively.

"Great," I smiled and took a seat. "Dig in, you'll need your energy," I also grinned at him with an all too obvious innuendo.

"Is that so?" He arched his brows, eyes fixated at me. "And why is that, pray tell?"

"Because you're stuck with me another day," I grinned with pride and excitement.

Keeping our hands away from each other proved to be a more difficult task that I had envisaged, and we ended up finding excuses to go into the bedroom and shield ourselves behind the closed door.

In the late afternoon, I announced very loudly that I had a migraine and needed a nap and then started picking on Galenor about the stench of his sweat, ordering him to have a long bath and scrub himself top to bottom. Something I was more than happy to do once we reached the privacy of the room and I had, once again, reaped the benefits of being alone with a fae male. A very willing fae male.

"Tell me about yourself. What do you do when you don't interrogate people?" Galenor lazily caressed my back while I dried my hair with a towel.

"There's not much to my life, to be honest. I work, sleep, eat, train...don't have sex with the subjects, and then start it all over again."

"Am I special, then?" I didn't have to turn to look at him to know that he had arched a brow to show the inflation of his pride.

"I'm not going to stroke your ego, bad boy," I pressed back at his chest, trying to shove him away but his arms wrapped around my waist, chin resting on my shoulder to plant sensual kisses on my neck.

"Honestly, not much, I don't have days off, unless I need to blow off some steam. Then I drive around to some bar around town and get pissed drunk, maybe find someone, and then come back to base." I had never realised how pathetic my life sounded out loud until this very moment.

"What about family?" he pressed another kiss next to my earlobe.

"I haven't seen my family in a long while. Haven't heard from them either. I work so they can have a better life, most of my income goes to pay for their home." I felt awkward opening myself like that to him, telling him private things about me, about my family and our situation, especially since this was not a subject that I ever stumbled upon. Being the child of immigrants, my life had been hell, but everything I did was for my family, and I never once opened my mouth to tell anyone information about them. Not when I was well aware it could be used against me at some point. Yet, with Galenor, things flowed naturally, and I had no fear of telling him about my life.

I ended up talking about the bullying growing up, about the beatings and the extra work, about how I advanced so quickly and how proud I was to earn my own room. I did not mention about the new home I was supposed to get after this trial, I didn't want him to feel used.

"I grew up on a farm," he confessed, earning a surprised frown from my newly cleansed face. "My father didn't want me around that much, he needed only one son, the second one came as an inconvenience," he shrugged as if the feelings of his father were to be expected.

"Was your childhood nice?" I really hoped he would say yes, because he deserved happiness, especially after the horrible years he'd lost in this realm.

"Part of it. Our mother was not the biggest fan of politics, so she spent a lot of her time with me growing up. She was murdered when I was eleven, so things changed after that," he pressed his lips together and forced a hard swallow, as if the memory was still constricting his throat.

"Galenor, I'm so sorry," I said, a hand travelling to his shoulder in an attempt of a caress, but he waved it away.

"It was a long time ago. But things changed after that, I had to train, I had to take on more responsibility and I had to start living with my father and brother," he sighed, as if none of those years brought nice memories.

"I'm sure your brother misses you very much," I tried to make him feel better, already aware that the 'dad' subject was not a favourable one.

"I doubt it," he chuckled hoarsely. "I believe he's the one who put me in here."

*Day 18*

He is innocent. I know it in my heart, I can feel it in my bones. Galenor has a beating heart and a soul, he is kind and compassionate, he is brave and strong and more loyal than any of the colleagues in my unit.

I couldn't sleep, couldn't stand lying there in bed next to him, feeling him breathe into me when every nerve in my body shouted for justice.

After he fell asleep, I laid there watching him for long minutes, analysing his features, his long lashes, the way he pressed his lips together when he started dreaming. How his arms instinctively searched for me, for the closeness of my warmth and how, once he found me again, he wrapped himself around me and leaned his head on my pillow, breathing into my neck.

I became determined to get to the bottom of this, to find whatever it was that brought him to me, whatever reason they had to keep this innocent male still trapped, beaten and tortured in a confined space. It was as if they wanted to play with him, to punish him in ways I didn't yet understand. Pairing him with a woman born in his homeland, setting a constant reminder of what he had left behind.

And worst of all, he suspected his family did this to him. Set up a trap to get him away, both father and brother settling an alliance to rid themselves of an unwanted son. But why was the Realm playing along? Why the secrecy, the extra funding, why bring him here?

The more I thought about it, the more I understood how little information I had. And the thoughts continued torturing me throughout the night.

I would not be responsible for the suffering of an innocent, not again. I would not put a faerie in pain because of my actions. Because I couldn't stand up for them. Because I was weak.

The sound of the unsealing kitchen door made me jump in bed, causing Galenor to wake up with a fright. We both gazed at one another for a mere moment, our eyes locked, shooting terror through our veins.

They were here again.

They had come to get him.

"The fuck you are," I planted myself in the living room to wait for the incoming guards, keeping the bedroom door shut to protect Galenor. They wouldn't dare step into my private space, it would be a violation of our agreement.

"Good morning, Captain Harrow," the first guard greeted me, adding a slow smile to what looked to be, for him, a cheery morning.

Others appeared through the door behind him, stepping into the room with methodical placement, exuding military training. I took a beat to study their faces, trying to remember if any of them had already been here, but their features told me nothing. They didn't know me, and I didn't know them.

Just like last time Galenor was taken, these men were brought here from the outside. Their uniforms, weapons and stance instantly gave it away. We were a small unit in a remote town, but these six men had the allure of importance surrounding them. They had been in high-risk situations and were not afraid to use violence at the simplest opportunity.

Six of them.

Someone up there learnt their lesson. Unfortunately for them, I wasn't ready to give up without a fight.

"How may I assist..." I tilted my head and raised a brow, indicating that none of them took the decency to introduce themselves after barging in my home.

Fuck, just hearing myself think it caused me nausea. *My home.* What the fuck was I doing? Was I really putting myself in front of six massively muscled, fully armed high-level guards for a fae male? Did I really think I could play house with the guy without any consequences?

*No, don't back down,. not now*, I urged myself, tensing my calves and planting the soles of my feet to get a better, more threatening grip on the floor. He was innocent. And he was mine.

For another twelve days at least...

"Lieutenant-colonel Geoffrey," the first man introduced himself and I almost fell on my ass. Fuck it, he was more senior than me. Which turned everything into high priority, far above my clearance level.

"How can I help, lieutenant-colonel Geoffrey?" I pressed his name with a threatening tone, pronouncing every syllable in his name with a tick, ready to burst out of my skin at the earliest disruption.

"We have orders to escort Gale to the interrogation quarters," he dipped his chin, as if to warn me not to get in their way. "My men and I are ready, please alert him of our arrival," he added.

"What, like I'm a housemaid?" I frowned, shifting my weight from one hip to another. None of the men flinched, their sharp regards pinned on me, ready for whatever was coming their way.

"I am here to fulfil orders and I take time very seriously, Captain. It is not in my job description to care for your womanly feelings," the man pressed, a small step coming towards me. With just a slide of his boots, his men inched closer, forming a semicircle around me and closing in the exit.

"PDD can confirm that I am not in agreement with this," I pressed, fisting my palms, readying myself for an attack. I felt my nerves shaking, adrenaline pumping through me, urging me to jump on him. I could do it. This time, I could do it.

"I will not discuss orders with an inferior officer in rank, please do as you're told." His patience was running thin, and I was stepping on his last nerve by disobeying a direct order in front of his delegation. Little did he know, it was about to get uglier still.

"Like I said, I am disinclined to open that door. I did not receive any orders and I don't —"

A punch swirled across my cheek, shifting my face to the side and my neck tilted with a crack before I had a chance to add another word. My lips immediately started bleeding, filling my mouth with a metallic taste.

I had always hated the taste of blood; I hated its scent and its colour. But none of that would stop me.

Taking propulsion on my heels, which had luckily stayed prompted in the exact same place on the floor, I jumped, using my hips to shift my leg upward and reach Geoffrey's head, pounding straight into his skull. He must not have expected me to fight back, or if he did, he probably prepared for a slap or an attempt of a punch, because he flung back, the loss of his balance pushing him a foot away from me.

Before I had a chance to place both my feet on the ground again, two of his men grabbed me while a third one pushed me back with a firm uppercut straight into the stomach, forcing me on my knees.

More blood spurted out as I received punch after punch, my ribs and stomach forcing the air out of my lungs with every new impulse of pain.

They stopped abruptly, their attention shifting behind me, where I only heard a few grunts and the clang of metal breaking bone. Once, twice, three times.

The two men grabbing my arms released me, hurrying to assist their colleague and I had a chance to turn back and see Galenor fight against three men while using the lift bar of his weights to slam across their bodies and use it as a shield for upcoming kicks.

He was kicking their asses, I smiled to myself, barely able to throw another punch to the man still standing in front of me before a bar of metal snapped against my temple.

Along with Geoffrey's annoyed voice.

I didn't have to look up to know what I would find pinned to my head.

"That's enough," the head guard spoke, putting a halt to the fight behind me. "You come willingly and without any more mess or miss pretty here will have brains for her last supper."

My ears buzzed, adrenaline bursting through my veins. Everything went silent around me, I couldn't hear voices, breaths or movement, only the tension of the gun shoving into my scalp.

Someone moved. A bag appeared out of nowhere, something shiny inside of it.

My eyes seeped darkness along with the tears that started escaping my cheeks as if they didn't want to be present for what I was about to see. For what was about to happen.

"Please, don't do this..." I heard myself plead with soft breaths, my voice too shattered to produce an audible sound.

"Keep your mouth shut, bitch," the threat came along with fingers wrapping through my hair and ripping at my scalp, turning me to face what was happening behind me. To see Galenor full of blood, his skin burning with the iron chains three soldiers wrapped around his wrists, both pressed tightly against his back.

"Galenor..." I cried, desperate to get to him, to stop them from hurting him.

Through all the pain, Galenor looked at me, his depthless eyes sending sparks of hope. "Don't worry, muffin. I'll be alright."

At the words, I started crying harder, letting myself fall with only Geoffrey's hand stuck in my hair to keep me upright. I didn't care about the gun pressed against my temple, not when I saw the burning flesh falling down his neck when they wrapped iron around his throat.

"Please!" I shouted, wanting to run to him, to stop them. To do something, anything to make them go away.

"Fucking idiot," the man spat while removing his gun from my temple. Before I had a chance to move, a burst of pain exploded at the back of my head, turning everything blurry.

I lost control over my body and remained helpless, watching the slow rhythm of their steps while escorting Galenor away before everything around lost its focus.

# Day 19

Everything hurt. My pulse, my stomach, every single time I tried to draw air and I had the headache of the century.

Every part of me felt swollen, like I just woke up after a massive allergic reaction. My throat was dry and itchy and the muscles in my back convulsed uncomfortably.

I opened my eyes to the same bedroom I had started to get accustomed to, in the bed I had spent the last three weeks in. Wrapped in gauze and possessed by pain.

All alone.

"Galenor," I tried to shout for him, but my voice barely came out, dragging out a crude whisper that sounded defeated and dry.

Pressing my body weight into my elbows, I forced myself up. As soon as my spine contracted, sharp pain electrocuted my rib cage, my body begging me to lay back down.

The fuck I will. I pushed myself into the understanding that no matter how horrible and mauled it felt, this was happening. We were getting up. A violent impulse dragged through me as I forced my chest upright, pushing my legs on the floor and pressed my weight slowly onto them, using the nightstand for support. About a minute later, I managed to do it and took my first step in what felt like years.

I had gauze wrapped around my chest and stomach and the back of my head pounded with pressure, another tight wrap pressing against my skull. Instinctively, my hand followed the throbbing pain and touched my nape, feeling something sharp underneath the cotton gauze. Stitches.

Someone had cracked my head open and left me there to rot. I didn't have to think too hard to understand who that might be.

"Hello?" I forced my voice to call out once I opened the door to let myself into the living room and stepped into the light of the hidden cameras.

"Hello?" I called again, this time looking straight at the ceiling, demanding their attention.

"Captain Harrow, we are glad to see you recovered," the robotic voice drilled into my ears.

Recovered my ass. They had stitched me together and dropped me back in bed as if I just needed a good night's sleep. Which immediately begged the question.

"Assignment date and time?" I didn't even think to search for the tablet, my main concern was to find Galenor. Unfortunately, he wasn't back yet. I burst with rage at the thought of what was happening to him right in that moment.

"Day nineteen, time seventeen twenty-two," the voice answered, blowing a hole in my brain.

What the fuck? Had I been passed out for a whole day?

"What time did Gal..." I corrected myself and flattened my tone of voice. "What time did the subject leave for interrogation this morning?"

A very long pause told me something was definitely wrong.

"I asked a question," I blurted out, the anxiety of the weight along with the lack of food mixing with the pain made me feel light-headed. And very, very pissed off.

"The subject has not been returned to the assigned living quarters since his initial departure on day eighteen at ten forty-six."

The air turned into lead.

They kept him overnight. Those high military men kept him overnight and let me rot in my room. No one thought to wake me up, no one cared about my involvement in this assignment, which had obviously surpassed its trial basis. This wasn't about me, about showing my skills or extracting essential information. I had been a distraction. Placed in a perfect setting for Galenor to relax and let his guard down for whatever purpose they needed him to.

He could have fought them off, he could have escaped. He could have definitely hurt me and taken his chances on the other side of that door.

Instead, he showed kindness, he showed compassion and spent the night on the floor to keep my nightmares at bay. How easy it could have been for him to kick the first guards that came to escort him once they were out, if he managed to fight off three highly trained army guards.

He probably waited for me, hoped for someone to get him out of this mess and I had just laid here, unconscious and patched up, until I was ready to play nurse again.

No more.

Anger clenched my bones with a desperate need for vengeance, pushing me into action. I would not let this happen. I would not stand and do nothing, like a scared little girl while humans, the unit I had become part of and grown up into, seeped misery and injustice.

With a new wave of adrenaline rushing through my blood, I changed into the uniform I had left abandoned in the wardrobe as the past days with Galenor did not require much clothing on my part.

I combed my hair and filled it with setting gel to arrange it into the all too familiar bun that had become part of my image since I was ten and arranged my epaulettes to display the awards and titles I had received so far, chiselling myself into my status. That of a *Captain* of the Intelligence Unit, a person whose position demanded a salute.

Unwilling to ask for leave, I entered the code that would open the door in case of emergency and slammed my boot onto the ground, forcing the floor underneath me to shake under my rage. I didn't pay attention to the guards stationed in front of the living quarters and ignored their questions as I headed straight for the general's office.

I passed through a blaze of wandering eyes and whispered questions. Some colleagues even tried to stop me, asking if something had happened to get me out of the living quarters in the evening of a weekend. Apparently, it was Saturday. The day when Milosh hosted a dinner for the other commanders.

Not that I cared.

I climbed the stairs two at a time and stormed through the double doors of his private dining room, making them all turn their heads and glare at me with accusing eyes for daring to ruin their charade of an evening.

Mostly they just sat there drinking until the late hours of the night and talked about how unhappy they were in their marriages and how they would fuck the young women in town. Not that their topic of conversation would have impacted my action in any way, he could have hosted dinner for the royal family for all I cared.

"Milosh!" I demanded his attention as I kicked open the doors, ignoring the other men who looked at me in annoyance, ready to jump and escort me out.

Oh boy, was I ready for that.

"Harrow, out!" the general ordered, looking at me with the disgust one gives a bug that fell into their soup and ruined their appetiser.

"The fuck I am," I reached at my side pockets and exposed the small gun I had kept tucked away in one of the lockers on the third floor, in case of emergencies.

"You and I need to talk." I slid both thumbs over the safety, chambering a round in the gun, ready for the blow.

The small tick sound exiting the weapon made Milosh's features paint a portrait of shock, but I stood my ground.

"Now, general," I snapped, moving the gun into my right hand in a demand that he stood and followed me to the next room, where his office was.

"Please excuse me," he kicked his chair back and stood in annoyance, not wanting to alert a security breach and cause a scene in his own unit. I may be killed for threatening a superior officer, but he would have his ass kicked by his superiors too.

I knew that if I played my cards right, I had this in my pocket. No one wanted to have their careers over with because of an immigrant woman, let alone a misogynistic old man in his late sixties.

"Are you fucking crazy?" he turned to me and kicked my arm, demanding that I stopped threatening him as he slid the doors shut. His voice remained low, probably unwilling for our conversation to be heard from the other room and make him look even worse than he already did.

"Where is Galenor?" I demanded, keeping the weapon locked on him and allowing my dominant hand to reach his desk and desperately slide through papers, hoping to find any kind of information that would help me. He must have knowledge of this. I knew he must.

"Are you drunk, Harrow? What is wrong with you?" He forced his thick brows into a deep frown and threw himself on a sofa filled with old files and ancient maps, losing his patience. He pressed his fingers to his temple as if trying to find it again and sighed deeply, filling the room with the stench of his breath.

"Go back to your post before the team penalises you."

That was it. My breaking point.

I was sick and tired of everyone treating me like a silly young girl, one that could be passed around and told anything, one that would not question orders and do what she was told. I snapped then, slapping both my palms on his desk and using my wrists to push everything on the floor, making his documents and daily work a pile of mess adorning the old mouldy carpet.

"What the fuck is wrong with you, stupid cunt?" he lost his temper and wanted to stand but I immediately directed the gun back at him, forcing him still.

"Tell me where Galenor is." I took the few steps that separated us, stopping inches from his head, the pistol aimed at the perfect distance to blow his brains out.

He swallowed dry, understanding he had no way out of this but to tell me what I needed to know.

"*I don't know who Galenor is*," he spoke slowly, as one does in a hostage negotiation. I attended those lessons; I knew the old man's tricks. "We have no one by that name," he spoke, reassuring me.

"The subject of my trial!" I shouted, forcing his memory back along with a press of the pistol into his forehead. I'd been there. It sucked like a bitch, and I knew the old man wouldn't like it.

"Are you crazy?" Milosh snapped at me, his grey-blue eyes filling with sudden realisation. "That's what this is about?"

"Yes, that's what this is about," I retorted, feeling my face turn crimson from the anger boiling in my capillaries.

"Silly girl," he sighed again, only this time his breath came out different. More calm and regretful. "You are risking everything,

Ellyana…" he spoke softly, making my breath stop with the sound of my name on his lips. He'd never done it, not once. He never recognised my origin, not even when I was a child, abused and beaten every day under his watch. He then started to shake his head. "Don't throw your hard work away for a faerie. It's not worth it."

"How would you know what worth is? All you do is rot in here and complain about how difficult your life is, when you have no idea what real pain feels like," I accused, feeling my eyes sting with tears.

"Harrow," he leaned back into the couch, eyes suddenly sorrowful and pinned on me. "I know what you have been through. I know how hard you worked to get here—"

"But you chose to turn a blind eye!" I shouted, my eyes unable to hold tears back and let them drop on my cheek. I didn't feel their sting, too filled with rage to do anything but shout at the man who saw me grow up. The only one who had had the power to stop all the dreadful things that happened to me. "You chose to leave me all alone. To be robbed from my family, mistreated and abused. Beaten every day. You did nothing, Milosh. Nothing!" I shouted, drying my tears with the back of my hand.

"It helped build your character," he retorted. "It made you stronger, sharper than everyone, always alert."

"Because I had to be!"

We both stopped, long seconds scrubbing away the years of memories. "I wish I would have done something to stop it," he finally spoke, his lips pressed together, features defeated.

His admission did nothing for me, the regret of an old man would not wipe away the years of pain. Still, I decided to give him a chance to rectify his wrongs.

"You still have time, Milosh," I said, making his attention fly to me. "You can do something now, to help erase all those times you did nothing."

The general blinked and dipped his chin, an agreement that my request would be considered.

"Do whatever you must to bring him back to me."

*Day 20*

A waiting game began when I returned to the living quarters. After the conversation with Milosh, I watched him make phone call after phone call while I sat frozen on his sofa, struggling to keep all my emotions together.

He was doing it. He was finally doing something for me and the idea that even this old man who hated me all my life felt the need for redemption told me that he must have known, deep down, that something was very wrong with my assignment trial.

Watching him struggle to bring Galenor back to me confirmed my suspicions. He was innocent. And it was up to me to get him out.

After a while I put my gun back and removed myself from the general's office to drag my steps to the living quarters. The anxieties of the day, along with the punches to my ribs that struggled to heal, prevented me from filling my lungs with the amount of air they needed, making me light-headed. Add the lack of food and the fact that I'd been asleep and dehydrated for a day, I took it as my sign to return and take care of myself, hoping that Galenor would follow shortly after.

The last thing I needed was to pass out somewhere in the corridors and cause a spectacle. I doubted everyone hadn't already heard about my rampage and the gossip about me storming Milosh's dinner party and forcing him out at gunpoint had spread like wildfire.

Back in the living quarters, I decided to halt the anxiety of waiting for a sound and hoping for the guards to return my subject in a fairly safe condition and take care of my own body. I took a long shower and removed the gauze that had been tightly wrapped around my torso and waist, I brushed my hair and added some iodine to the wound still throbbing at the back of my head.

I tried to tidy up the room as much as I could and prepared something to eat. I also made myself some ginger tea and drank two full bottles of water to help with hydration.

Then I lied on the bed with the door open and allowed myself to pass out while waiting for the slide of the kitchen door to announce the arrival of the man I seemed to care for a lot more than I thought.

I must have dozed off for a long while and let myself fall from consciousness and away from the pain.

"Hello, cupcake," soft fingers caressed the side of my cheek, forcing my eyes wide open to spot vivid green blinking back at me.

"Galenor!" I jumped awake and wrapped my arms around his neck, carefully squeezing him to me, too afraid to joggle any wounds. "You're back," I exclaimed the obvious, making him chuckle.

Blood dripped from his dark shoulder-length locks that looked more like a crown around his head rather than damp hair, with big, dried chunks adorning the sides of his head. His shirt had been demolished by small cuts and a few sharper tears, turning it into rags.

But here he was, safe and back, at least for the time being.

"How are you?" I separated myself enough from him to scan him, to drag my eyes over the gore and the injuries and assess his state. I can't say he looked good, though his beauty still managed to shine through all the damage inflicted on him, but he didn't look bad either, as if he had already started to heal.

"I found the last root in the bag on the nightstand and made myself some tea. Thought I'd let you sleep for a while longer," he explained, probably observing my surprise.

"When did you come back? And why didn't you wake me?" I pushed his shoulder back admonishingly, then grabbed his face in my palms to study it up close. His brow had a massive cut, and the entirety of his jaw was bruised; the purple escaped through the dark stubble to make it look like the last shine of the horizon before nightfall.

The way he shifted in my arms told me that, same as in my case, his torso and ribs took the most damage, his muscles slowly shaking with exhaustion.

But he was healing, that's what mattered.

He was back.

And in my arms.

I pressed a soft kiss on his lips, sealing our closeness and settling my heart. I had to feel more of him, I had to tell my eyes that what they were witnessing was true, that Galenor was really here.

He looked at me with surprise, with pride and...something new. Something that had locked between us both without announcing its visit. Something that planned to stay for a long while. Maybe forever. Galenor noticed it too, that new connection between us, like a bond that just snapped into place, making his eyes tremble with realisation. But, instead of celebrating the forge of energy, he leaned back, as if wanting to get away from me, pressing his lips together to avoid uttering something he might come to regret.

"How did you manage to get me released?" he asked instead, a new shade of curiosity lightening his features.

"I..." I shook my head, not at all prepared for the shift in conversation. Had I really done that? Did I really have enough power to make so many higher ranks release him?

"I don't know," I admitted and gave myself a moment to taste the small victory. To appreciate my own power. Then, I had to spill the truth. "I went ballistic after I woke up and threatened my commanding officer, so the general ordered to get you back."

"You threatened a general?" he arched his brows in awe. And pride. Making me smirk a little.

"Yeah...I kinda..." I felt the need to scratch the back of my head in my sudden discomfort but did not realise my fingernails would choose to scratch the exact spot where my head wound laid. Making me shiver with a burst of pain rather than making me look cool in front of the faerie.

"What is happening?" His attention drilled into me at the observation. Before I had a chance to protest, Galenor grabbed the hand that tried to cover my wound and shifted me in place, forcing my neck to bend towards him so he could observe my injury. Judging by the drip of liquid falling down my neck, I had made the wound bleed and probably made it look more horrific than it actually was.

Galenor gasped at the sight of it, awareness waking in his tone. "Why didn't you alert me of this new injury?" he snapped at me, as if I was somehow responsible for not making a list of everything that happened to my body since he was taken.

"New?" I frowned. "This isn't new, it's from yesterday, from those idiot guards."

"Yes, I am aware!" He continued speaking as if he was scolding me like a child. "I know about your right shoulder, the lower ribs on the left side, the bump in the torso and the bruised kidney. But why didn't you tell me about your head?"

"Wow, okay control-freak," I widened my eyes at him. Had he been creeping on my body while I slept? He must have, because that was a very accurate description of what I observed in the shower as well.

"Ellyana, we need to wash your wound," Galenor stood and urged me to follow.

"I already showered," I pouted. I didn't feel like leaving the bed, especially since he was so close to me. All I wanted was to snuggle and maybe ransack the infirmary for some pain relief meds, then snuggle some more. This male had such warm skin and all I felt like doing was to press myself tightly to him.

"Ellyana..." his palms cupped my face with urgency. "We need to clean your wound," he tried again, this time pleading, but I shook my head no.

I was suddenly feeling very tired and sleepy. And even though it was always warm in these rooms, a chill wrapped around my skin, making my muscles clench and shiver.

"Ellyana, please." Galenor's voice was so close yet so far away, hidden in the cloud of blackness that laid heavily on my body. The sudden pressure in my head made me feel nauseated. Things around me started changing their place, moving to get away from my sight and all I wanted was to sleep.

To grab Galenor in my arms and rest.

Heavy clouds appeared and vanished in front of my eyes, drifting away memories and confusing the present. Strong arms wrapped around me, offering the warmth I craved so much while a deep, sorrowful voice filled my ears with sweet phrases, the type one reads about in romance books.

"Let me take care of you, love."

A call dropped from Galenor's lips, after laying a gentle line of kisses on the side of my neck and up my jaw, spreading joy to my lips. "Ellyana..." he said my name like a prayer, like one is supposed to speak when addressing the gods.

"Why are you doing such terrible things to my heart, cupcake?"

I chuckled then, even though I could not control my lids and my eyes remained closed. "Cupcake," I giggled, not knowing if the words came out in my mind only.

"To fill me," I snickered, remaining limp in his arms, and remembering how he had the nerve to tell me such filthy, terrible things the very first day he met me. And how he, later, took it upon himself to show me all the ways his words had been true. And all the ways my life had been changed forever after that encounter.

How, were I in any other situation, I would abandon it all and drift away into the sunset with my faerie lover. "Lover," I snickered again at the word. One I had never used before. One, no one had ever come close to being named so throughout my life.

"Is that what I am?" a deep voice grumbled in my ear, pushing a line of heat down my neck.

"My fae lover," I laughed, shifting to receive more of that warmth, his breath lining hot waterfalls into my skin. "It feels nice," I smiled. Or tried to, at least. "The things you do to me." I tilted my head for emphasis, and he must have realised what I wanted, because he started licking down my throat and sending more of those heavenly shivers.

"That is a fae lover's role," he replied, his tone lower, more honest, somehow.

I forced my eyes open, pushing back the heaviness clinging to my eyelashes to allow me to gaze at him. To find those beautiful emerald eyes pinned on me, absorbing my every breath.

A bitter smile overtook my lips, the realisation heavy. "It sucks to fall in love, doesn't it?" I blinked at him as I shared my darkest secret.

"I wouldn't say so," he chuckled. "I like having an unlimited supply of muffins."

We both laughed then, allowing ourselves to enjoy that moment, to find a beat of peace. I took a full breath and expelled more laughter, but the injury at the back of my head forced me into a sudden jolt and caused Galenor to react.

"Alright, concussed lover, it's bath time for you." Without giving me a chance to protest or even move, he lifted me from bed to take me into the bathroom, where the bathtub was already filled with hot water and bubbles.

"I don't have a concussion," I protested and tried to stand on my own two feet to help him remove my clothes but the fae wouldn't have it. He placed my ass on the toilet seat and peeled my clothes off slowly, taking special care with my head every time he had to slide a garment past my shoulders. Fortunately, I only had a tank and a shirt on, before I found myself naked and shivering slowly, all of a sudden excited to get in the bath.

"I don't have a concussion," I defended myself again, trying to make Galenor stop looking at me like I was a fragile thing. This wasn't my first bump, I practically grew up with a wrecked head. "I know how those feel and this is not it."

Galenor stopped, surprised by my confession, so I felt the need to defend myself even more. "I didn't have the best time growing up, I already told you," I snapped at him, but instantly felt guilty. "I'm just really tired," I said as an apology.

"Then a nice warm bath would do you great," he replied, though his brows had involuntarily furrowed with rage.

"Don't be mad at me," I reached up to caress his cheek, drawing away whatever sorrows ate at him. He leaned in to kiss my palm.

"Never, muffin."

"Join me, your wounds need cleaning too. And I'll enjoy the company," I smiled, shifting into the bathtub to show him how much room was left for him to take me up on the offer.

I said a secret thank you to whomever built these living quarters, who thought about the subject's freakishly tall frame and brought in this massive bathtub, because after taking a few seconds to consider it, Galenor removed his clothes and jumped into the pile of bubbles by my side.

With extreme care, he nestled me to his chest and splayed me on top of him, his arms wrapping around my back and hips to support my weight.

"This feels nice," I wiggled more into his touch, the warmth of his body combined with the warmth of the water wrapping me in a sphere of cosiness. Until I realised, I was placing my entire weight on him, and he was filled with injuries. As if sensing my worries, Galenor pressed me to his chest and whispered a threat. "Don't even dare."

He pulled me so tight that I knew there was no way I could escape without hurting both of us more, so I took his advice and readjusted myself on top of his body, our legs intertwined while his growing erection started pressing on the side of my tummy.

I enjoyed it. I liked knowing that even now, in a terrible state, he wanted me, but if I had to be completely honest, I wouldn't have the strength to do it. Not when my body had been on the verge of passing out.

To my surprise, he didn't hint towards it, completely satisfied to caress my back and the side of my breasts, while sneakily rubbing more soap into my hair to clean my wound. Every touch hurt, the wound throbbing with ache, but I let him and faked not realising what he was doing, while tilting my head from time to time to give him better access.

We stayed like that, nestled into one another until the water started growing cold and Galenor was completely satisfied with the state of my head. Then, he got out of the bath, displaying a perfectly round ass dripping with bubbles and grabbed two towels to help me dry. I also took great care in cleaning his injuries once again.

Then, I kicked the fae out of the bathroom to allow me some space to pee and brush my teeth for bed, which he, reluctantly, accepted.

Not two minutes had passed when a soft, barely noticeable knock on the door announced his return. Before I even opened my mouth to protest, he flicked an envelope to me. Galenor had it grabbed by one of the corners, holding it in between his thumb and pointer finger as if it was something dirty he didn't want to touch.

"It has your name on it, it was in the kitchen," he announced before turning it to me to allow me to spot my name, handwritten with shivering letters.

"That's weird, I never got letters," I remarked while wrapping the towel around my breasts to pin it in place, then grabbed the envelope and ripped it open. I didn't shy away from Galenor, he was well past the point of being just my subject.

**"Harrow,**

**There are issues in command, they won't give you more instructions until they decide on the course of action. Word is you have three days.**

**That's the best I can do for you.**

**F. Milosh"**

*Day 21*

"Fuuuck, muffin," Galenor's desire-roughened voice slid through my bones while his hand landed at the back of my neck to support my head.

I had set myself a challenge that was going to be the death of me, but no matter how hard my lungs screamed for air, I dived deeper, opening my mouth wider to force more of his girth down my throat.

It had all started as a challenge, one of the little mockeries the fae liked to play around me. He enjoyed toying with me, smiling at me with wickedness while doing unspeakable things to my body and challenging me to do the same. I wanted to make him lose his senses, just like he'd done it for me so many times, so I dared myself to discover exactly how long that tattoo truly was while hoping to gain a very pleased smirk at the end of my journey.

Pushing him on the mattress, I slid his pants down with a decisive pull and pinned him with my hips before he tried to escape. I made my intentions overly clear and curled my tongue along his abs, even though they looked stunning as always. Then, I headed straight for the colossal length springing out from his pants, forcing me to use both my hands to keep it upright.

I didn't have to do too much work until his desire pushed up, hardening him into my mouth and making it difficult to slide up and down on his growing cock. I had to use a hand and rub at his base, since there was no way in hell all of that would fit into my mouth, so I focused on the tip and that long line of tattoos, licking and sliding it down my throat with a vengeance.

To my shame, I choked a few times and my eyes watered when he pressed into me, his hips uneasy and filled with need to force more of himself into my mouth, but he seemed to enjoy the effect he had on me and pulled himself out just a few inches to allow me to take a full breath.

Then, as if suddenly possessed, he stood from bed and grabbed my face, shoving himself deeper into my mouth and down my throat, until I could feel him at the back of my head, stretching down to a point no one had ever reached before.

Gods, he was big. Too big. Those throbbing veins down his thickness made it even more difficult to swallow and added to the choking sensation as they caressed the roof of my mouth.

Seeing how I had no option, but unable to give up, I fully surrendered into him, tipping my head back and trying to breathe as and when I could, fully focused on the way his girth made my throat expand with every thrust.

I must have done something right because he started hissing and took control over my neck. I let him, fully surrendering myself to the experience, to how I could breathe only when he allowed me to, how he took full control over his pleasure and used me to claim it, how I had planted myself at his mercy and fully enjoyed his dominance.

My eyes dripped with tears, my pulse pounded into my chest, begging for more air and sometimes I felt I was on the verge of passing out. Instead of pulling back, I clamped my hands on his thighs and pressed more of myself into him, opening my mouth wider to take more of his length in, to force my throat to open wider for him as he mercilessly pumped into my mouth.

"Fuuuck..." he groaned again, while the rhythm of his hips accelerated, the hand at the back of my neck forcing me more into him while he thrusted ferally into my mouth, curling his length down my throat.

I wanted to die. From pleasure, from pain, from the lack of air. I absolutely enjoyed the power I had over him, to see him so devastatingly raw, lost in his own desire, looking into my teary eyes with amazement, those emerald eyes hazed with pleasure.

With a final hiss and a last thrust, one that forced my jaw into a new state of tension, almost to the point of ripping it, Galenor tipped his head back and allowed himself to breathe, to exhale the desire I felt running down my throat, it's warmth the prize I deserved for bringing him to the brink of madness.

He retreated from my mouth shortly after that, pulling away to allow a full storm of air to enter my lungs while my throat swallowed hard, filled with remnants of spit and cum. I gave myself a few seconds to recover, before I pulled my body up from where I had remained on my knees and cleaned my chin with the back of my hand before I turned, wanting to head for the bathroom.

"No, you don't," Galenor grabbed my waist and dragged me back to the bed, by his side. In a single shift, he had me under him, his weight pinning me onto the mattress to prevent me from escaping, while his hardness poked into me once again.

"I like you raw and dirty," he groaned, that wicked charm he displayed at times taking over. My pants were pulled down in the next moment, panties following soon after as Galenor's mouth travelled to invoke sweet torture in between my legs until I forgot everything but his name.

"What troubles you, muffin?" The fae nuzzled my shoulder, drawing my attention back to him. We were both spent, lying in bed to settle the heavy breaths still rocking through our bodies. And instead of enjoying every moment we had together, my mind started thinking about the impending end.

I shook my head and trapped his lips in a long kiss, not wanting to admit something was indeed wrong. Not wanting to say it out loud.

"Ellyana, I've known you for three whole weeks," Galenor pressed his lips together, a deep furrow drawing a V between his brows, making me chuckle.

"I'm worried," I admitted. "I really messed up and I'm afraid they'll take it out on you." At the sound of the words coming out of my mouth, the admission of my terror brought stinging tears to my eyes. I struggled to blink quickly and disguise them, but the fae was faster in noticing them.

Galenor pulled me to him, pressing his forehead to mine and joining our breaths. "We still have two more days," he whispered slowly, a grateful smile lingering on his features.

"I don't know what will happen," I shook my head, unable to contain my emotion. On their own accord, my arms wrapped around his neck to squeeze him tighter onto me, as if my embrace would somehow protect him from whatever would come.

"Whatever happens," his emerald eyes found mine, "you offered me more happiness than I ever hoped, and for that I am grateful."

# Day 22

"What would you do if you were free?"

His question raised me from the hazy state we had both surrendered to, the threat of the following day weighing heavy on our actions. We'd both remained confined to the bedroom and lived behind the closed door, with towels and the blanket he used to sleep in shoved at the bottom of the door to fill the space between the floorboards and cover the sound of our voices and, more specifically, moans.

Galenor and I behaved like a newlywed couple, too obsessed with the other's body to be able to keep our hands away from one another. Our mouths especially liked to initiate the closeness, biting and licking along new discovered territory, each time unveiling specks of desire we both made a point to discover and drill into.

I came out of the room only once to bring food and drinks, enough to last Galenor for a while. I didn't bother looking up at what I knew were cameras watching my every move, I didn't check the tablet for new instructions, and I did not say a word to whoever was watching us. My main concern was to take their subject away. And wait.

"I *am* free," I replied, though the words sounded weird in my mouth, especially when I had explained to him that I could not leave the living quarters and escape, as he'd suggested. First of all, because I would not abandon him. And second, because I would probably be shot at the very first step I took outside of these rooms. I had no idea what had happened after Milosh made the calls, but if something was bad enough for him to write to me and warn me, then I had to listen.

Galenor tipped his chin to me, silently asking me to reconsider. Sighing, I gave his question another thought. "I would go grab my family and get away from this place," I replied earnestly, the weight of this hidden dream bursting open my chest with a newly found freedom. I had never admitted it out loud. Not to myself. Not to anyone.

"Why don't you?" he leaned on his side, occupying more of the mattress and tilting his head closer to see more of my face. I huffed at the sight of him, at the ridicule of our situation.

We were both trapped in that bedroom, doing nothing but fucking and talking, until someone would probably come and kill us both. Still, I enjoyed his company more than anything and even though the dread for our future pulsated deep within my chest, having him by my side, enjoying these moments of nothingness, meant everything to me.

My relationship with Galenor was the realest I had in my entire life.

"Because I belong to the military? Because they would find me, and my family and probably kill us all?" I replied with sarcasm, but he did not seem to mind.

"What would you do if you could do absolutely anything you wanted?" he rephrased his question, giving my mind more space to roam free.

Enjoying this game, I let myself think about the possibilities, but before I let my mind drift, he added a new idea.

"Don't think about what everyone wants from you, don't think about duty or caring for others. What do *you* want to do?" his fingers found my forearm and squeezed gently to accentuate his meaning. I turned to him to find those beautiful green eyes pinned on me, shining with the hope of endless possibilities.

"I would open a shop," I started giggling.

"A shop?" he arched his brows.

"Yes, one of those small corner shops, with retro sweets and scales and those bottles of fizzy drinks our grandparents used to drink," I continued smiling. "And I would wear a bonnet."

Galenor started laughing his heart out. "A bonnet, muffin? Like a cook?"

"No," I elbowed him playfully, "not like a cook, more like a beret, but not a military one. Yuk," I grimaced, sick of the uniform I had to wear all my life. "It will be like hair decor, just on the side, to support a nice, tidy bun. It will tell everyone that I am the shopkeeper," I smiled with excitement.

"A shopkeeper's bonnet," Galenor nodded with a grin.

"Yes," I smirked, pleased that he was following my lead, no matter how ridiculous the dream sounded. "You'll be wearing one too, but mine would be pink. And yours, green."

"Why do I have to wear a bonnet?" he pouted, but continued smiling, pleased that he was also part of this dream.

"So our customers know you are part owner," I replied like it was the most obvious thing. "And you'll help make sales and carry sacks of potatoes to old ladies' cars because you are so kind and generous. And they would blink at you with dreamy eyes and give you an extra coin for your efforts," I smiled wider, the images moving in front of my eyes.

Galenor released a massive chuckle that almost made him fall on his back. "Right, so you're basically renting my muscles to old ladies for extra coin."

I followed in his laughter. "Hey, you are the one who said to dream big," I elbowed him again, this time fully pushing him into the mattress. I leaned on his bare chest and pressed a few kisses, my lips trembling with the echo of his laughter.

"What are your dreams, then? Can you do better?" I motioned with a pout, inviting him to share his vision and hoping that I would find a place in it.

"We're farmers," he relaxed his head and let his hair fall on the pillow while pulling me closer to his chest, an arm wrapping around me to keep me protected and warm. I didn't even breathe properly. He had said *we*. As in he and I, a collective we.

"We have a massive field where you plant crops and take good care of many types of tomatoes. They are your pride and joy."

"Tomatoes?" I widened my eyes in surprise, but he pressed a finger to my lips to shush me. "I like tomatoes," he whispered the explanation before he continued. "We have a decent home by the side of the lake, not too big but decent enough for when our children grow up and the grandkids come to visit."

Now I fully stopped breathing. The idea hadn't even crossed my mind. Children. Not once had I thought about having children of my own. But children with Galenor? It was a new dream I didn't know I needed until this very moment.

"I take care of the animals, so basically I sleep in the sun a lot while they graze," he displayed a cheeky smirk. "And I make cheese," his eyes widened a little with the new idea. "You love my cheese, I am the best cheesemaker in the region," he nodded with pride, pinning his eyesight on me again.

"Are you, now?"

"Yes," he dipped his chin and curled his abs to reach the top of my head and place a kiss there. "Everyone loves my cheese. And we trade with the neighbours and other locals," he smiled. "On Sundays! At the market," he finished with a pleased smile, and turned his attention back to me, checking my reaction.

"It sounds perfect," I leaned in and kissed him deeply, my hands roaming across his chest to find his heart. I placed my palm over it to feel every hopeful beat before I started kissing down his abs and lowered onto his pelvis, my teeth scraping and tongue licking lower and lower, fully intent to show him just how much I had enjoyed his vision of our future.

I watched with amazement how Galenor stepped in and out of the room, each time coming back with more greens. We were lying in bed and enjoying one another when he stopped moving inside of me, his eyes wide and chest heaving. "It's a full moon tonight, I can feel it."

Without any other explanation, he removed himself from inside of me and let me begrudgingly moan for his return, but the fae wanted to hear none of it.

He shifted me from bed and grabbed me in his arms to remove me from the mattress, then moved the bed frame and landed it next to the wall, creating an empty space on the floor. I remained petrified and watched the insanity in full development. Whenever I asked for an explanation, he continued saying how it was a full moon that night.

He even took the trouble to make some sort of nest for me out of the bed cover and blankets, with the pillows situated on each side of me like a fuzzy throne. I had no choice but to grab a long shirt and pull it over my head, while remaining nestled into the corner he had created for me, watching how he prepared some sort of a green circle in the middle of the bedroom.

He'd managed to create a full circle of greens, some of which I hadn't realised existed in the kitchen. He'd brought in broccoli, lettuce, coriander, cucumbers, a cactus he found somewhere, probably forgotten from the last time this area was used, dried rosemary and lavender, and he even used some books that had a green cover.

"What is this?" I dared ask when he finally stopped bringing things in and started arranging them into a perfect circle.

"A pathetic excuse for a forest," he sighed, driving his full attention into creating whatever vision he had in mind. Only when he was satisfied with the outcome, he turned to gaze back at me and carefully left his green circle to grab me from the pile of covers and pillows and place me at the centre of the greenery, by his side.

Then he grabbed my hands and motioned for us to sit, our knees close together while our eyes remained locked on one another. Once we were settled, Galenor finally revealed his plan.

"In my realm, whenever a couple is ready to confirm their relationship, they bind themselves in moonlight," he blinked, those wonderful emeralds shining so bright, it put all the green things around us to shame.

I breathed slowly, dipping my head just once, too scared to say anything. Too scared to let myself dream. Was he saying what I thought he was?

"The couple will travel on a night with a full moon to the nearest forest and swear their love to the night goddess, binding their love. If they do it three months in a row, they are officially allowed to announce their engagement," he explained, but my heart had already stopped beating.

*Their love.* I didn't hear anything after that word, the name of that new feeling that started sprouting in my chest, the one that made me do the unthinkable. Love.

"I would like to bind myself to you tonight," Galenor added, his voice dropping with anticipation, his regard pinned on me, ready to study my every reaction. Even his hands wrapped tighter around mine, as if he expected me to release him or protest. Instead, I felt a smile bloom on my lips.

"What do I need to do?"

With a new portrait of happiness, Galenor pressed his forehead to mine, forcing my back to arch to meet him, our hands wrapped tightly together, joining the very centre of our souls.

"I, Galenor Dalenth, bind myself to you, Ellyana Harrow, on this full moon. Under the eyes of the goddess and the magic of the realm, I confess my love and hope for a future together," he spoke softly, reverently, as if these words were sacred. Each syllable drilled into me, caressing my present and embracing my past, forcing an unbreakable connection within my spirit.

Instinctively, I started repeating. "I, Ellyana Harrow, bind myself to you, Galenor Dalenth, on this full moon. Under the eyes of the goddess and the magic of the realm, I confess my love and hope for a future together." By the time I finished speaking, my voice trembled, and my hands shook, emotion pricking my eyes.

With a sigh of relief and a cheer of celebration, Galenor pressed his lips to mine, the fire in our kiss sealing the union. We allowed our tongues to reach for one another, eager to swim in the familiar taste while our mouths clashed and waltzed eagerly, stealing our promise.

"Ellyana," Galenor unpinned himself from me enough to grab my attention.

"Yes?" I moaned, already needing to reclaim his presence, the warmth of his lips on mine.

"I need you to promise me something." His tone became rugged, demanding my attention.

"Anything," I dipped my chin in agreement, desperate to get back to devouring his lips. His body. His entire spirit.

Galenor swallowed hard, inching himself back to claim my full attention, his eyes burning the demand into me.

"When they come for me tomorrow, don't fight them."

# Day 23

"Don't," Galenor's eyes pleaded while the sound of the sliding door rose us from bed. We'd both been too unsettled to remain under the covers or even try to catch some rest, so after celebrating our promise of love, we got dressed and spent the last few hours in heavy tension, expecting this exact moment.

"Galenor..." I begged, though we both knew there wasn't much either of us could do. They'd probably send an army this time, carrying weapons and suits and, no matter how much we wanted to resist, there was only so much we could do.

"I'll be alright," he said, the corners of his lips sad in their motion. His emerald eyes shone with terror, his breath hitched, and his arms wrapped around me, fingers shaking down my back.

"I love you," I whispered to him, grabbing at him for dear life, in a desperate need to feel more of him, to join our hearts and our spirits. To make us both disappear.

He replied to my confession with a press of his lips to mine, allowing me to feel his taste one more time before he stood and stepped towards the door, opening it in a determined single motion to reveal himself to the guards.

Galenor stepped out with confidence, the slide of his hips making a mockery of the room filled with soldiers. I tilted my head from the bedroom to spot over fifteen men, all carrying patrol weapons, circling the fae as soon as he made his appearance.

"Good morning to you," Galenor said, and I could feel his smirk, the unrelenting disobedience he had always shown, doing his best to piss off these men. Even now.

I didn't come out; I couldn't watch him leave and he didn't turn back either. Keeping his head high and frame tall, Galenor stepped out of the room like a royal, the guards only there to guarantee his safety.

We hadn't talked about it, neither of us wanted to bring up the subject of our separation, especially after confessing our feelings for the first time, but I knew his stance was solely for my benefit. He didn't want to look defeated or scared, that tremble in his eyes before he said his goodbye was the only thing betraying his fear. Even though tears flooded my eyes, burning deep within my heart and everything in me shouted to fight this, I stood my ground as well.

I did not cause a scene, did not put myself or him in danger, did not come out of the room to seek a fight. We were outnumbered, the battle already lost before even starting. All we could gain out of it was more injuries and punishment, and I was determined to make things as easy as possible for Galenor. Not wanting to risk the guards' rage towards me to be inflicted on him.

So I waited, frozen on the side of the mattress, blinking tears away, until everyone stepped out of the room. Until the door slid shut again, sealing me in my abandonment. I wanted to shout, to wail, to punch and kick everything in my way. All my mind focused on was Galenor. All my brain kept repeating was that this might be the last time we see each other.

"It is safe for you to come out, Captain Harrow," a voice pinned my senses in place, stopping my plans and making me jump from the bedroom to discover its source.

A dark shadow flickered in the centre of the living room, part gym, part storage place for everything we didn't want in the bedroom. The place was a mess, I had never left my assigned quarters to reach that state before. But the confinement to the bedroom we had both chosen left everything else in an abandoned state.

Not that I cared anymore...

"Who is this?" I approached the shadow, flicking my hand through it to observe it was entirely made of smoke. Though it had a form of a tall man and a voice that addressed me, I had no other hints on the origin of this person.

"Even though I must keep my distance from you for the foreseeable future, Captain Harrow, I wanted to speak to you as directly as I'm allowed. I believe I owe you an apology," the materialised smoke tilted its head to me, just like a person would.

"What's your name?" I asked, still observing the apparition with awe.

"I am the one who selected you for this assignment. Unfortunately, I am not at liberty to disclose my name, though we have spoken before."

"PDD?" I blinked, looking at the shape in wonder because it had the exact same height as Galenor. Another one of their mind games, I assumed.

It nodded, darkness mixing with shade in its motion. "You do know me by that name, yes."

"Why can't you come speak to me like a normal person?" I frowned, circling around this shape, and trying to make head and tails out of this strange moment.

"I do not have long, Captain, so you will have to content yourself with following the conversation rather than imposing questions. First of all, I must apologise to you. I am aware the instructions you received were not delivered in a clear manner, but we had our reasons."

"Your reasons," I huffed. "Like putting an innocent male in confinement and torturing him on a daily basis?"

"Galenor is everything but, Captain. Though that is not the reason why I owe you an apology."

"Oh, really?" I folded my arms and shifted my weight on one hip. I didn't know if the shadow could see me or not, but the motion came instinctively. "And what do you need to apologise for, pray tell?"

"We lied to you," it replied. I wanted to ask more questions, but the explanation arrived on its own. "Your bedroom was never cleared of recording devices, nor was your bathroom. We felt you would be more comfortable if said information was relied to you."

I wanted to faint. Fuck. Fuck, fuck, fuck fuck fuck. They saw everything. They saw all our conversations, all our plans, every time we fucked.

"You bastard!" I shouted, instinct urging me to punch the shadow but once I did, it flickered and recomposed in front of me. "You are an absolute creep. A miserable, lying piece of trash!" I released a few more curses and the shadow took them all in without protest.

I didn't know what I was thinking...of course they would know something was up. Galenor and I had been locked in that room for the past three days. But it was one thing to cause rumours and another to watch our every move. To study us.

"Captain Harrow, you have a choice to make," it finally spoke after I took a break from swearing. "We realise part of the failure of this assignment lies on our shoulders for placing a single woman in a confined space with a fae male. We were advised your personality and work ethic would strive over any sexual allures that would be put on you and we trusted the information we received. However, judging by your reaction in the first week, we understood the way this trial would go, and we offered you the freedom to make your own choices."

"Yeah? Was watching us fuck entertaining for you? Did you jerk off at the sight of us? Did my moans make you horny, you sick bastard?" I spurted my rage at the human shape.

"Captain, I am here to offer you a way out of this, so I suggest you listen." He started to sound annoyed and part of me took great pleasure in that. At least I was getting on his nerves.

"I'm listening," I snapped, widening my eyes in anger.

"Galenor has reached a point of no return in our meetings. The information he has offered proved inaccurate and we have reached the end of his use." With a deep breath, I allowed myself to finally relax. They were going to release him. Finally.

"I agree," I instantly replied. "Galenor is ready to be released."

"You, however, have broken various codes. In behaviour, civility, rank…"

"So I am to be demoted?" Three weeks ago, the possibility of demotion would have ended my world, but now, it sounded exciting. I could be free of this place. Galenor and I could make our dreams a reality. I saw myself living on a farm growing tomatoes, I saw my family finally having a home. I saw us happy.

"We reached the conclusion that it would be a shame to lose a member of your quality, so we decided to offer you another chance."

"And what do I need to do?" I asked with awareness.

"We are willing to offer you a final instruction, which, upon completion, will set a positive mark on your record and would allow the career progression you are seeking."

"And what is the instruction?" I snapped at the figure, the distrust for this male growing by the second.

"You must terminate the subject."

# Day 24

If I don't do it, they will.

I kept repeating this exact phrase, over and over, for hours on end as I prepared myself for Galenor's return.

If I don't do it, they will.

After listening to the tempest of rage and insults coming out of my mouth at the news, PDD had offered me the choice. Galenor's life could be ended in peace, by someone who loves and cares for him until the very end, or he could be sentenced to a public execution.

It was all I needed to hear before accepting. I would not let him suffer alone, caged like a beast and trialled in public, I would not let him be stoned or injured by the passing crowd and especially, I would not let his beautiful frame be destroyed by fire.

A public execution had shaped my fate and brought me to where I was today. And I would not, for the life of me, do that to the man I loved.

After the disappearance of the shadow figure, I cried, trashed the place and when there was no energy left in me, I was left with nothing other than to accept my new instruction and make the necessary arrangements.

Only a few minutes till midnight. Until Galenor would be returned to me. Until I had to pierce a knife through his heart.

PDD did not make any requests, leaving me to my own devices as long as the instruction was completed within thirty minutes from the subject's arrival. They didn't trust me to spend more time with him, probably fearing that I would be too weak to fulfil my duties.

But they thought wrong. I was exactly what they raised me to be. A soldier through and through. And I would fight till the very end.

I settled my nerves as the sliding of the door rushed my senses into action, hurrying my step towards the kitchen at the exact moment a pair of hands pushed Galenor into the room, forcing him inside and making him fall on the ground, his body unable to hold its own weight.

He was wrapped in iron chains. Delivered to me like a present. One that I was supposed to slice through.

"Galenor," I rushed to him, my arms instinctively wrapping around his body to bring him closer to me.

"Ellyana," he murmured, his voice strained with pain and exhaustion. I did not want to know how his day had been, I did not have the strength. I could only focus on one thing and one thing only.

I summoned all the training that had been drilled into me since I was seven years old, the control of my emotion, the pain and suffering I had to conceal every single day and the strength to start it all over again. Nothing could get past these few minutes, no emotion I ever felt, not the sound of my pleading heart and my crashing soul, not the heat in between my legs that even now, reacted to Galenor's presence.

I had to stay focused, count my steps and calculate the exact movement that would take him away without adding more pain. The knife concealed at my back, buried into the waist of my pants, burned my skin, making me aware of every heavy second that passed.

"Come, let's get you settled," I helped him stand while doing my best to keep my tone even and my eyes pinned anywhere else but him. I could not look into those beautiful emerald eyes while knowing what I was about to do.

Without protest and fully trusting me, Galenor limped slowly from the living room and into the bedroom, placing himself on the side of the mattress, careful to make enough room for me.

His eyes remained on me, covering me with endearment and hope. Like he was preparing to breathe easy, knowing that he'd reached safety.

Me.

*Ellyana, don't fucking give up now!* It took every shred of strength remaining in my body not to drown in sorrow right then and there, to beg him for forgiveness and to take that knife and punish my own heart for what I was about to do.

"Muffin," he sighed, his arms still wrapped in iron, preventing him from moving comfortably and keeping his chest perfectly stretched for me to insert the blade.

I had to do it, I had to do it now, while he was still hazy from his return, while he still didn't understand what my new instruction was. I had to do it.

"Galenor," I raised my eyes to his, feeling the sting of new tears. No matter how much I'd tried, I could not contain them.

"You can start working on the chains when you are ready, muffin," he said, his voice a half sigh, the pain he was in due to the chains audible in his tone.

On their own accord, my hands lifted to his jaw, cupping his face and caressing his skin while my fingers shook from urgency and despair.

Wordlessly, he leaned into my touch, his head tilting to the side to allow his lips to shift and place a gentle kiss on my palm.

Gods, make this end now, I howled on the inside, my bones shredding into pieces under the weight of guilt dripping through my veins.

Forcing myself to act, I pushed Galenor back, making him fall onto the mattress, his arms still wrapped in iron, bound together.

What a bunch of cowards this entire unit was. They didn't even allow the man a chance to defend himself.

Cutting the agony short, I launched myself at him, straddling him while my hips pinned him in place, preventing his pelvis to jolt.

A grin appeared on his lips, the smirk of a lover who knew how much he'd been missed.

Yet, he had to abruptly awake from that dream.

His eyes widened at the sight of the knife, jiggling in my shaking hand.

"What are you doing?" the fae cried out, smile frozen, a new line of betrayal appearing on his features. His emerald eyes burnt into me, consuming me with a sudden slash of mistrust, the realisation on his features painted like a scar. Understanding dawned on him. I was not his safety. I was his pain.

"It has to be me who does this…" I felt my voice break, words barely coming out in between sobs. The air remained petrified in my lungs, too afraid to escape.

A straight palm from the collarbone. We'd been told many times where to find the heart, how to slice through bone and enter it at an angle to cause irreparable damage.

My arm slid with the force of lightning, slicing through both my heart and him. Without explanation.

At the perfectly rehearsed angle.

It took a beat for blood to start gushing out of his chest, for Galenor's eyes to fly open, flickering with betrayal. For his throat to escape a wail of pain.

I leaned to his chest, ripping the knife away to make way for more blood to abandon his body. His heart pounded with desperation, howling from the impact, from pain and betrayal while his eyes remained pinned on me. Filled with dread. Blinking with pain.

My cries stamped out through the room, scratching at the corners with the talons of my pain while I remained pinned to his chest, the side of my face drowned in crimson as I listened to the sounds of his flickering heart. Each time beating slower.

"I love you..." I cried out, my voice inaudible, crawling with agony. Before his chest stopped beating, I risked a final glance into those once emerald eyes, now pale and slipping from life. "I will see you soon."

Galenor's pupils shut his gaze away before I finished the sentence.

The sound of my heart breaking was overshadowed by a storm of applause coming from the ceiling, the entire team of observers clapping and cheering the death of an innocent man. It made me sick to my stomach and all I wanted to do was explode and take them all with me.

# Day 23.5

The males acted too relaxed to be in this room. In this unit. And in this realm. Which meant that they were clearly faking it. Which also meant that they were smart enough to keep their senses sharp and hopefully, help me with my plan.

I scoured the unit for information about the Wind delegation, I went to Veronica, who, as always, had no interest to discuss something that would benefit me and started asking questions about the fae male locked in my room and how tempting it would be to jump on that dick.

*Yeah, girl...already done that. And look where it got me.*

I went back to Michael, my friend, who for once was off duty and I had to walk all the way to the Eastern side dormitories to find him, running through whistles and all sorts of name-calling and promises of what they would do to me were we alone. In another situation, I might have been terrified to walk through there on my own, to open every dorm room and potentially find naked and horny men who didn't care one bit about my safety or pleasure, but not anymore. Determination urged me to kick open door after door, until I reached my friend.

He laid in his bed, covered in an old grey duvet, with an open book and had started dozing off on his pillow, a large lump of spit dripping from the side of his mouth.

"Is that how you spend your days off, Michael? I expected more." The sound of my voice made him jump. He scanned the room for a second, probably not understanding how a woman's voice got in his head, but as soon as he saw me, his gaze settled, the back of his hand wiping away the drool while his cheeks blushed a warm shade of crimson.

"Ellyana," he murmured my name, surprised to see me there. I took it as an invitation and planted my behind on his mattress, leaning forward as I sat so my head wouldn't bump against the bed above him.

I pitied him, getting the lower bunk sucked.

"What do you know about the Wind delegation?" I didn't have time to dwell, so I went straight to the point. Plus, the man was on his day off and if he wanted to spend it drooling on his pillow, who was I to stop it?

"What do you mean?" he frowned. Then it clicked. "Wait, how do you know about them? You're supposed to be locked away with a faerie."

"Michael, believe me when I say I don't have time to explain and that if you help me with this, I will owe you big." I tilted my head slowly and arched my brows to suggest how big the favour would be.

"I don't know much," he shook his head, fingers scratching at his forehead as if it would stimulate more memories. "They are guests, invited by the territorial commanders and hosted here for some reason. They spent a morning with Milosh and received the tour, but they mostly come and go as they please. Always with an escort, one of the high-ranking guys."

High ranking guys. Alarm blipped through my brain. The same ones that took pleasure in kicking in my ribs. The ones who came for Galenor that very morning.

"They take their lunch here, though. Every day," Michael added, and a choir of angels sounded in my ears.

"Where?" I placed my hands on his shoulders and shook him a little, as if the information would drop out of him.

"The canteen by the garden."

"My friend, I owe you big time," I grabbed the side of his head and leaned in to stamp a massive kiss on his forehead before I hurried to the gardens. Lunch was reserved for two hours, from one till three, which gave exactly forty-three minutes to get to them and ask for help.

And there they were, eating, drinking and chatting away, acting like they had the most wonderful time of their lives. Clearly a facade to anyone who knew better.

Several males huddled together around the only round table in the cafeteria, not wanting to display rank or disloyalty towards their comrades. They all stood tall and even though I could only see the faces of three of them, they all looked extremely handsome. With human features and their elegant stances, it wasn't hard to understand why all the women coddled them with attention and kept bringing plate after plate in a desperate attempt to please them. I couldn't even understand how the unit had allowed fae males to be left on their own in the company of women, especially judging what had happened with Galenor and I.

My best bet was to engage in conversation with the fae males. Judging by their flowing sexual energy, they were guaranteed to give me more attention than their group. Thanking my lucky stars that the waiters were all dressed in our daily uniform, which I was wearing as well, I skittered through the tables and grabbed a canister of wine and a few glasses, placed them on a tray and made my way to the round table.

"Two more dinner parties and we're out of here," a blonde male with tanned skin cheered to his comrades as I approached, downing his glass of wine. And giving me the perfect opportunity.

"Let me refill your glass, my lord," I slowly bowed my head in reverence and motioned to my tray to the full carafe I had grabbed.

He didn't even acknowledge me, acting like I hadn't even uttered a word and continued talking to his colleagues.

"If we manage to leave in one piece and Fratnuk doesn't piss off the lieutenant-general again," a gorgeous chestnut haired, blue eyed male chuckled.

"Fuck off, Valeyan, you know how I can't stand these bastards," the man defended himself while he continued to cut into his steak as if he didn't have a care in the world.

"What matters is that we leave here alive and well. All of us," the third fae male spoke. Impulse pushed through my mouth before I had a chance to think. As I heard the words coming out, I realised that it was too late, that I had laid myself completely at their mercy without having a plan B. I was gambling both our lives on their whim.

"How would you like to get one more out of here?"

They turned to me in unison, seven sets of eyes drilling into me. Filled with observation and curiosity. It took them a few beats to react, time during which I remained frozen. It was the man who enjoyed his steak, Fratnuk, that addressed me first.

"How dare you speak to us, human? Did you not receive the orders?"

Fuck, fuck, fuck. These men…males…could kill me in the blink of an eye. My knees buckled and I had to lean against the table, pinning one hip against the round surface for extra support. What the heck was I getting myself into? My first instinct was to vanish, to run away as far as I could and put myself back to safety. After all, they couldn't get to me. Not yet at least. They didn't know my name or what I wanted. Worst case, they could report a waiter blabbing around their table.

But it wasn't just my life that was at stake here.

"Galenor Dalenth," I pushed his name out of my mouth while my heart squeezed with urgency. "I can help get him out."

It was as if I uttered a magic enchantment. The men instantly settled, frozen in place, as if their brains were trying to understand the name I had just released. They all stood silent, watching me with sudden interest and awe.

"He is alive?" the second male, the prettiest one, Valeyan, finally asked.

I nodded, not prepared to offer more information until I was sure I could trust them.

"Where is he?" The male spoke again, displaying his position within the group. He must have been their leader.

"Can you help get him out of here?" I pressed my lips together and locked eyes with him, letting him know that it was not a request. It was a life-or-death situation.

"Galenor has been my friend for many years," the male uttered, his regard swimming with memories. His blue eyes shone brighter, with newly found hope. Revealing the truth in his words. "I would do anything for him."

The others breathed in unison, keeping their movements natural while their full attention remained pinned on me. To an outsider, it looked like we were having a conversation about food or whatever insignificant thing, the males continuing to drink, eat and act like nothing had changed. But none of them spoke, none of them made a noise. Expecting more information, begging for it.

"Not here," I took the carafe and moved towards the male, filling it very slowly as I leaned more into him. "Go to the toilet at the end of the hall. I'll meet you there."

He grabbed the wine and drank eagerly, making a show of finishing the glass in a few gulps. "Let us praise the humans for their wine!" he lifted his empty glass and started cheering, gaining the same gesture from his comrades as they started talking loudly once more.

The distraction allowed me to slide out of the room while the eyes of the rest of the servers remained pinned on the Wind delegation, all of them asking for more wine.

Once I reached the bathroom at the end of the hall, I locked the door from within and waited, praying to all the gods that I had made the right decision. That the male coming to meet me would not just slice my throat as an act of defiance for keeping his friend a prisoner.

Not a minute later, a knock on the bathroom door announced the male's arrival and before I moved to open, his threatening whisper followed.

"Open the fucking door before I'm hung for treason." He sounded rasp and annoyed, tension lining his vocal cords. Mechanically, I twisted the lock, allowing the door to open with a click. As soon as the male stepped inside, he pushed the door closed and performed the same motion, sealing us in the dirty bathroom.

"My name is Ellyana Harrow," I heard myself speak. Once again, before my brain had a chance to press its seal of approval.

"Valeyan Brebod," the male replied with a curt dip of his chin. "Where is Galenor?"

I understood his urgency. Michael had said they were always under escort, so he didn't have much time. If I wanted his help, this was my only chance.

I kept the information brief, not feeling the need to give him more explanation about his earl. Gods willing, my future mate, if we were somehow getting out of this together. I fully planned on renewing my bond to him for the following two months.

But those dreams were for the living, something I had to ensure continued happening to both of us.

"At the moment, he's in an interrogation room, but he'll be back with me at midnight. And I have to kill him."

Valeyan's eyes bulged out and his fists clamped together, while a vein started pumping angrily from his temple all the way down to the side of his neck.

With a hiss, he replied. "Then why call me here at all?" I recognised that look, filled with hatred and need for revenge. He really cared about Galenor's fate.

"Because I'm assigned to do it. If I don't, they will arrange a public execution. I expect you know what that entails."

Valeyan ground his teeth in anger, his lips pressed together so tightly they almost vanished from his face.

"Again, why call me here?" he pressed.

"Because you are my only hope to save him." The male's eyes sparkled with newly found hope and I heard his chest heave with relief.

"What do you need?"

"I need to make it look like he's really dead, we'll be locked in a room filled with cameras. Whatever solution you have, I will take."

"Are you his lover?" the male asked.

I frowned, not understanding what this information had to do with anything. Nevertheless, I nodded and he followed my gesture, remaining quiet for a few beats.

"Stabbing to the heart would be most believable, make sure you puncture between his heart and lung. You can nick the lung a little but stay clear from the heart. What healing solutions do you have?"

"I have a Cloutie root," I immediately answered, thanking all the gods that I hid the last one in my wardrobe to keep it away from PDD.

"It won't be enough; he needs to appear dead." Another long pause where Valeyan's brows furrowed so deeply, I could almost touch his worry. "I can get river berries potion. The weapon needs to be boiled in it. It will regenerate the tissue from within and place the body in a stillness while it does so, but it cannot heal fatal wounds."

I shook my head, confused. River berries potion? What the hell was that? Sensing my confusion, Valeyan explained.

"We use it to transport hostages, if shot through the bloodstream, it makes the bearer remain in a catatonic state."

"For how long?" I enquired, filled with hope.

"Ten to fifteen hours. Sometimes a little more."

"Then I also need your help to get his body out of here, while he's still passed out," I urged, plans already developing in my mind.

"I will do whatever you ask to bring Galenor home," the man replied, his words braiding a cape of hope around my heart.

Day 25

Disgust swam through my body. My stomach clenched, barely keeping its contents together as I walked out of the living quarters with a full round of applause, bowing my head to several officers and guards who formed a passageway through the corridor and cheered for my success.

They cheered for murder.

I was once one more of them. I stood idly, sometimes felt happy, for colleagues who'd successfully completed assignments, without having actual details of their mission. This may not even be the first time a subject loses their life in those damned rooms, it may be a common occurrence which we were all, in one way or another, privy to.

As I forced my steps to plant themselves one in front of the other, I received handshakes, congratulations, pats on the back and appraisals, some going even as far as already calling me Major. Through it all, I forced a polite smile and kept it plastered for the next hour, until everyone who had participated in this assignment in one way or another disappeared and allowed me to take a full breath for what seemed like forever.

Not that my lungs enjoyed the oxygen when I knew Galenor's body was barely getting any, if at all. The air around me felt dirty, putrid, unable to sustain the beating of my heart. With heaviness and despair caving on my shoulders, I walked to Milosh's office, where I was told he would be expecting me to declare the trial assignment officially complete.

Night lurked on the hallways, whispers and traces of steps sounding from the lower floors while I trotted my way up to Milosh's office. I was so tired, my eyelids were heavy, and I struggled to keep opening with every blink while my feet turned into lead, the weight was heavy on both my body and conscience.

I didn't know if my plan worked, I had no idea if I hit the correct area with the knife I had received merely minutes before midnight from the Wind delegation and especially, I had no idea how and if Galenor would wake up. The potion might last a few hours only, making him wake up right under the cameras or it might take forever. I had no way to know. Only the last thread of hope that struggled to keep hanging onto my chest.

"I must insist, general. Given the situation and our recent findings, this visit has reached an abrupt end."

I heard a voice creeping from Milosh's office as I knocked on the door and, without waiting for an invitation, I let myself in. After all, I was the person keeping him awake at three in the morning, so the sooner we got this done, the better for the both of us.

I painted the perfect picture of surprise as my eyes laid on Valeyan, sitting on the chair in front of Milosh's desk, the general leaning on his wide leather office seat, looking tired and very pissed off.

"Is this…a bad time?" I pressed my lips together in apology and took a theatrical step back to show my intention of leaving and allowing the conversation between these two to continue, but Milosh flicked his fingers to stop my movement.

"Not at all, I was expecting you," the old man replied with a curl of his lips. The bastard was smiling, just like everyone else. The number of times I would have given anything to see even a dash of pride, of acknowledgement from this man was uncountable. But here I was, killing an innocent and everyone was ready to throw a parade in my honour.

This was not the best moment to lash out at him, however. After all, I owed him for using his connections to bring Galenor back and for that warning that offered us three days of supervised bedroom porn.

"If you would excuse us," Milosh turned to Valeyan with dismissal in his tone, but the fae stood his ground, leaning back on the chair to make himself comfortable and folding his arms across his chest, a sign that he had absolutely no intention of leaving.

"The conversation can be continued after I speak with Major Harrow, it will only take a few minutes."

*Major.*

Major Harrow.

This was it. The confirmation I needed, the seal of approval that came with my position. The mark that would improve my future tenfold, the rank that would help me get my own cabin, a better life and enable me to be of better support for my family.

I should have rejoiced this, it was a moment I had worked my ass off for the past twenty-two years, ever since I was first recruited. Yet, none of it mattered. Not when my soul was cracked in two, the other half lying dead three floors down.

Instead of gratitude, I felt hatred for these people. Disgust. Shame for being a part of this unit and despair to get myself free from them.

To take Galenor and leave this life far, far behind.

"What is happening?" I innocently asked, shifting my attention from one side of the desk to the other to observe the two men.

"Nothing of importance," Milosh replied with a harsh tone while Valeyan turned to me and started ordering his offences.

"What is happening is that even though we are working towards a peaceful future, we travel to find out that one of our nobles was held captive under this very roof and, even after he was executed, we are not allowed to see his body and perform the rites," he snapped his hand on the desk for emphasis, redirecting his attention back to Milosh.

"As I already advised," the general's voice turned thick, fully aware of the uncomfortable situation he was trapping me in, "an escort is not available at this moment to accompany you to the border. We expect a convoy to return in three days, after which you are free to perform the appropriate rites."

Valeyan's face turned grave, and he risked a shift of his head to gaze at me, his eyes widening for a second as if to announce we were screwed. The potion he gave Galenor wouldn't last that long, which meant that the fae would wake up still under the supervision of the cameras or in a dark room somewhere, where we had absolutely no control over his escape.

"Is it just the body that needs to be transported to the border?" I kept my face blank, allowing a part of my regret to seep through so the guilt became recognisable on my face.

Valeyan nodded, and by Milosh's furrowed brows, he must have already known what I was about to offer.

"No," he replied before my mouth opened. "I will not allow a newly appointed senior member of my unit to travel unaccompanied with unknown fae officers," the general snorted.

"Very well," Valeyan replied and made a show of standing and towering over the desk, his movement regal and his stance imposing. "My name is Valeyan Brebod, I am the commander of the Northern Legion of the Wind Kingdom, and I am the head of the Annual Convoy of Peace. I am pleased to make your acquaintance, Major Harrow." he bent at the waist in my direction. Then, as if his words would sort out the situation, he turned back to Milosh. "How about now?"

"As I said, commander," Milosh pressed his words, becoming tired and pissed off. "An escort is not available."

"General," I stopped him. "I believe my new rank comes with a duty towards the Wind Realm. And to the male I...cared about," I bit my tongue to stop the word 'love' coming out in front of an insensitive old man. "If you would allow me this, I would take it as payment for my ascent in rank."

I knew I had captured his attention. "You would ask for this instead of the cabin you've been rambling about for years?" His eyes turned into slits, surprised and offended by my words. Seeing how I cared more about a faerie I knew for three weeks than a dream that spent almost two decades in the making.

I dipped my chin and gained myself a heavy sigh from my superior officer.

"You have forty-eight hours to report back, major."

Taking the win, both Valeyan and I headed towards the door but before I opened it, I turned to the decrepit old man in the chair.

"General Milosh," I captured back his attention. He looked so tired and sickly, I doubted he would last more than a few years, but he seemed to be determined to become one of those officers who occupied their rank until the very end. Unable to let go of the ghosts of their dreams. "Thank you, sir," I dipped my chin, the only goodbye I could say to the only authority figure I had in the past twenty-years.

At five thirty, with a new official rank and a tonne of guilt hanging around my shoulders, I met the Wind delegation in the unit parking lot. They had to pass various security measures which lasted over an hour, so I took the opportunity to take one last trip around the unit, sensing that, one way or another, this would be the last time I would walk the hallways.

I strolled through memories and realised that even though I had called this place my home for the past two decades, it was nothing of the sort. I did not have friends that I could say my goodbyes to, apart from Michael, the only other outsider in this part of the unit. I walked around the training rings, the stables, the menagerie, remembering days and nights throughout my life, where these walls seemed the only refuge I had. But they were just that, walls. Layered bricks covered in tainted yellow that never could become a home.

I felt more at home these three weeks with Galenor in a small bedroom and a tiny kitchen than I had since my arrival in the military and none of the dreams I had forced myself to draw managed to push back my determination. My desire to escape and start a new life.

With him.

"Are we ready?" I asked in the form of a greeting while I made my way down the stairs and into the parking lot, where four guards scanned a silver crew van with tinted windows. The back doors were opened, and one guard was inside, pushing in a white body bag.

I bit my tongue and tensed my shoulders at the sight of it, forcing my body to remain still and planting my legs firmly on the soil beneath my boots, struggling to keep myself from passing out.

Valeyan's eyes darted to me for a mere moment before returning to the array of documents he had to present to the chief guard, showing various signatures and stamps, which I assumed, allowed us to leave the unit.

"Are we ready?" I asked again, forcing my voice even, uncaring. As if the man I loved wasn't shoved in a plastic bag. As if my hands weren't the ones who drove the decisive blow. As if the new epaulettes that got delivered to my room that night, carrying my new rank, had been worth the slaughter of an innocent.

The guard lifted his attention to me and for the first time, dipped his chin in greeting. "Almost ready, Major Harrow."

That was it, that's all it took. An extra star on my shoulder to merit the respect of men who kicked me, mocked me and made me cry myself to sleep night after night. I didn't know the name of this particular guard, but he had been in one of the upper classes, one of the group of boys who had always taken pleasure in kicking our lunch trays or spitting in our food. Now he found himself bowing to me and listening to the orders of the very girl he spat on.

"How long?" I pressed, my features annoyed that I was made to wait.

"Two minutes at the most, major," the man dipped his chin again and I nodded, leaving him to complete the checks on Valeyan's documents while I headed towards the van.

My heart jolted, palpitations increased severely, making me feel like blood was about to gush down my face instead of tears. Galenor was in that bag, and I needed to get him out.

It was all I could think about, all I could care about.

Without acknowledging the other fae males in the delegation, I slid into the back of the van and took a seat on one of the side benches, right next to the body bag that laid in the centre.

My eyes remained pinned on the zipper, hands shoved into fists during the time the males settled themselves and the engine started. I continued to lock my full attention on Galenor's body as the car started moving, the motion of the wheels jutting us along with the bag.

"Be fucking careful!" I shouted at the driver and his co-pilot while Valeyan pressed his foot against the side of the bag to keep it from getting injured.

"How long?" the commander looked at me with eagerness, probably as desperate to release his friend as I was.

"Ten minutes till we exit the village and twenty-two until the unit's fence clears," I replied instinctively while tapping my fingers against the bench and watching the body bag intently, sharing the same desperation as Valeyan.

All of us kept quiet, too focused on the road ahead, on leaving this place. Some of the males were restless, tapping their feet on the floor or sighing heavily, all of us counting the minutes that would take us to freedom. That would allow me to open that fucking bag and get Galenor out.

I kept quiet and waited.

Did I ever think I would willingly lock myself in a small space with fae males? Not in a fucking million years. But here I was, watching them with determination and distrust, hoping that we all had the same goal.

I waited until the first set of gates opened for us after a brief document check and head count and I waited again until the second gate, the surveillance one, closed behind us, letting us share the journey with the meadow resting on both sides of the road.

The way to the Wind Realm was a long one, at least ten hours' drive but the final control would be at the realm border, giving Galenor plenty of time to wake up by then.

I didn't wait for the go ahead from the driver and as soon as I heard the gates close behind us, I launched myself at the bag, ripping the zipper to reveal Galenor's body.

The air around froze at the sight of his beautiful face and my heart started pulsating at the sight of him. The engine of the van rattled away while the males in the back exclaimed various sighs and curses, but all I could do was smile.

When I pulled the zipper of the body bag down, I expected to see whitened, colourless flesh, I expected him to look like a body, all traces of blood washed away from his skin. Instead, Galenor was his beautiful self, fanning those long dark lashes with his mouth slightly parted, something I had always observed about him when he spoke, and small bubbles of air danced around his mouth while his chest flowed up and down in a barely noticeable motion. His cheeks became rosy once again, colour returning to form the portrait of beauty on his face.

I risked a glance at Valeyan to see him gazing at his friend with longing and pride. "It worked," he confirmed my hopes with a gentle nod, as if to reassure both me and my heart that he would soon wake up.

"Don't just stand there, help me," I heard myself ordering the males while I did my best to lift Galenor's head out of the body bag and held him in my arms to protect him from any bumps and curves on the road.

Instantly, the males moved and as one, lifted him and placed him on one of the side benches, allowing his body to lay flat while his head remained supported on my thighs. They were kind enough to give up the comfort of their seat, two of them moving on the other bench while the other two crouched on the floor, their backs resting against the wall separating us from the driver's seat.

We must have travelled like that, in silence, all eyes pinned on Galenor, for hours, none of us daring to say a word, too focused on monitoring the state of the fae. I ripped part of his shirt to observe the wound my dagger had caused and cleaned the dried blood with my sleeve, while watching in fascination how the injury was slowly closing.

How, with every invisible breath, his chest became stronger, his muscles more tense and his sleeping movements sharper. After a while, he started looking like he was taking a long nap, so I remained content to observe him and pray to all the gods that he woke up soon.

Given any other situation, I would have ran for my life. Who in their right mind would travel with eight faerie men, in a car with no security, with no plan and no weapons? But, during the long hours of silence, a sort of camaraderie bonded between us. We spoke with our eyes, first observing curiously, then analysing and finally, sustaining gazes and questioning looks, nodding at one another in warning at sharp bends on the road or even sharing a smile or two when Galenor shifted in my lap.

Sleep started taking over me, the fatigue and accumulated stress making my eyes droopy. With the addition of the lack of conversation and constant rumbling of the engine, I found myself dozing off for a few seconds or minutes, all the while my hand continuing to caress Galenor's hair or forehead. I found myself unable to stop, desperately needing the contact of his skin, hoping that I would transmit some sort of peace to his induced sleep.

Until his eyes flew open, large emerald shards stabbing into me.

"Galenor," I exclaimed, my hands paralysing on his skin.

With an abrupt shift, he lifted his upper body, his gaze scanning around, trying to grasp the details of his new reality.

I spotted the exact moment he recognised his friends, because his lips curved, a wide smile blooming.

"You bastards!" he laughed harshly, in a combination of joy and admonishment.

"Took you long enough, brother," Valeyan jumped from the other bench and placed strong arms on Galenor's shoulders, shaking him in an embrace, both of them brimming with joy at the reunion.

Next came the other fae males, Fratnuk and Orynth, both of them following the same structure, patting Galenor's back and exclaiming either insults or brotherly greetings. Galenor took the time to greet and thank everyone by name, including the driver, who had kept silent for the entire journey. I even thought he wasn't able to speak, until he turned to us, looking Galenor dead in the eye and dipped his chin reverently in greeting.

"My prince."

The smile that had been plastered on my face while observing the exchange vanished. Why was this man greeting Galenor like he was his superior? As if he was meant to be treated like royalty.

"What is he talking about?" I stopped being just a spectator to their reunion and pushed myself to the centre of attention, demanding an explanation. "Why did he just call you prince?"

The blood in my veins grew thick when Galenor finally turned his attention to me. I expected to find the same love he had gazed at me with for the past week. I expected him to smile, to reach out to hug me or give all pride away and kiss me in front of these males. After all, I was his and he was mine and we were finally free.

Icy cold rage blew through his eyesight, daggers of disgust directed at me.

With a sigh, he closed his eyes for a second, as if the sight of me hurt his eyelids.

"Someone make her shut up," he waved in annoyance. "Her voice is starting to give me a migraine."

"Yes, my prince," I heard Fratnuk's voice. From the corner of my eye, I spotted a shadow coming towards me, just as pressure collided against the back of my head.

I started losing balance, the daylight around me darkened and my eyes closed on their own accord, forcing my body to fall to the side as my world fell apart.

"Galenor..." I wanted to shout his name, but my mouth would not open.

*Day 26*

My back was killing me. There was a sharp stabbing pain digging under my right shoulder blade that made the tendons pulsate with ache and spread it towards my neck and my lower back.

My head pounded, making my vision blurry. With prickled skin, I tried to feel around me through the darkness, the cold seeping through bone and tissue. It was freezing.

Everything around me felt cold, the ground, my skin, the air that entered my lungs like mud water. I started to blink with desperation, trying to remove the cobwebs over my eyes and sharpen my gaze, but no matter how much I tried, things remained draped in darkness.

I searched around, trying to feel my environment and discover more of my surroundings. The ground was wet, with some sharp edges and piles of smooth surface mixed with mud and water. Some sort of cobblestone. My hands instinctively reached around, trying to grasp something to help me stand. Some sort of wall touched my left hand, made from the same smoothness with forgotten edges, frozen at my touch.

I followed it and felt my way around the cold stone, hoping to find some sort of exit. After four steps, the wall curved, leading me to the right side where I continued to follow it blindly, until I reached another bend. Another four steps led me to an opening.

My body eagerly tried to step into the darkness but halted against heavy lines. I felt my way around again to discover tall bars, arched upwards to make some sort of enclosure.

A cell.

I was stuck in a cell.

Why in all the gods would I be stuck in a cell?

The pounding pain at the back of my head forced me into a sitting position, so I clawed against the cobblestone and rested my back against the bars, doing my best to keep my body away from the water on the floor. By the smell of it, nothing around me was clean.

What was happening to me? Who would put me in a cell and why? The last thing I remembered was being in a car and Galenor's eyes opening to me.

*Prince.*

*Someone make her shut up. Her voice is starting to give me a migraine.*

Galenor's voice dropped the weight of truth over me.

They called him prince.

The male I had fallen in love with, the one I thought was innocent. The one I betrayed my realm for...

Was a liar.

Tears dripped down my cheek, caked in the darkness I found myself wrapped in. My muscles started trembling all over again, but this time, not with the cold. Betrayal weighed heavy on me, chipping away at the pieces of my heart that hadn't been utterly shattered by the realisation. He'd tricked me. He made me fall in love with him to get free.

*Prince*, the sound haunted my memories, drilling remorse through my brain.

*Prince. Prince. Prince.*

"Of course, Your Highness," a distant voice trembled through the darkness, the sound of opening locks and sliding metal doors shattering the silence of my broken dreams.

A line of torches illuminated the area, allowing my eyes to catch a glimpse of my surroundings. I was indeed locked in a cell. No wider than seven feet, barely allowing me space to stretch my body on the floor, with chipped iron bars and a heavy ceiling, filled with mould, blood and some sort of fungus that had started growing in the corners.

Their idea of a toilet was a small metallic container in the corner of the room, right next to the fungus decoration and I also spotted a tattered blanket, so old that generations of moths had inhabited it for what looked like many years.

I forced myself into a stand and stepped to the cell wall, pressing my back against it. The pulsations in my chest threatened to rip through my ribs and my knees were on the point of buckling, but I did not want to show weakness. Not when he was coming to claim his victory.

To reveal his master plan and enjoy my tears, which were continuously dripping, the ultimate sign of defeat.

I listened to his steps as they advanced towards the battlefield he had already claimed, clad in victory and elegance. Various sets of boots stomped through what seemed to be a long corridor. Uniformed soldiers appeared from everywhere, each carrying a torch to illuminate the way for their prince, turning the defeat of darkness into unnatural daylight.

I settled my pulse and waited, all the while scanning every single detail I could about the soldiers. They were all tall, fae males. All carried the same dark crimson uniform, their shoulder length hair tied at the back with the same colour string as their uniform.

The same hair length Galenor had proudly exhibited throughout his stay. Somehow a prisoner of two years managed to keep the fashion of his realm. Fucking idiot, I swore at my own stupidity. He lied to you from the moment he arrived.

"Good morning," his voice pierced through the darkness before his body reached my cell, not wanting to give me a full view.

"Fuck you!" I shouted through the bars and the line of soldiers that huddled with their torches. I did not have time to practise my reaction, to force myself to remain guarded, to even think about what I was going to say to him. One thing was clear, I was not going to let him enjoy this. I would not look defeated and broken, I would not cry for mercy, and I *would not* let him take that sweet victory sip. Not as long as I had breath in my lungs.

"Feisty," I heard a chuckle and more steps echoing on the wet stone. Even his voice sounded different, sharper, merciless. Nothing like the sweet, gentle male he had pretended to be with me.

"Say what you came here to say and let's get this over with," I spat. Rage boiled through me, the adrenaline giving my body more support, urging me to move forward. To step right to those bars and look him in the eyes.

"I simply wanted to meet you," he finally appeared, a sharp smirk planted on his beautiful features.

He even looked different, his hair loose, two strands braided on the sides to keep it away from his face, allowing the rest of his dark locks to flow down his shoulders. There was something odd about his cheeks, they weren't as sharp, and the curve of his upper lip looked harsher, slightly different from the lips I had tasted so many times.

And his eyes...were black. Onyx black, night sky black, perfectly combined with the darkness of his hair.

"What is happening?" I questioned in a hushed tone, the sound of my voice barely escaping.

"Curiosity," he shrugged, making the simple gesture look royal, his shoulders giving an unbecoming elegance.

I kept my mouth shut and forced my gaze to take all the details of him, to see everything that was different from the male I had spent so much time with. I had learnt his body inside and out. I knew every scar, I knew his every gesture. I was trained to observe small details, and the change in his appearance hit me like a storm on a small, deserted island.

"Of course you realised, how foolish of me to think otherwise," he chuckled, displaying a proud smile. "You are indeed magnificent." The way he dipped his chin, the way his lips curved. This was a completely different person.

"Who are you?" I mustered the courage to ask, gaining myself another proud grin.

"I thought you would recognise my voice," he pouted theatrically. "After all, we have spoken many times..." he let the words flow, as if he wanted me to piece it together.

Spoken many times, what was he talking about? The only person I spoke to was Galenor. Well, him and...

"PDD?" I released a trembled realisation.

'*I'm sure my brother put me here...*' Galenor's voice struck through my memories. "Twins?" I finally breathed out.

With a reverent dip of his chin, PDD smiled again. "Beautiful and bright, no wonder my brother brought you home."

"Where is he? Where is Galenor?" I demanded, hope blooming once again inside my heart. Maybe he hadn't been a part of this, maybe he too was a prisoner of his brother. Maybe...

"Galenor is busy enjoying his harem at the moment. Those fine ladies waited a long time for my brother, so they were a bit anxious to get their hands on him. You know how he can be..." he tilted his head as if the explanation were enough. As if he hadn't just shoved another dagger into my heart.

Galenor had a harem. Of course he did, I huffed at my own stupidity. He was a prince of the Wind Realm. One of two, apparently.

My face dropped with understanding.

"PDD. Prince Dalenth of Death," I said the words out loud while tears spurted from my eyes. "Both of you were PDD."

I couldn't contain my voice from shaking, heartbreak pulsating through every beat. Through every muscle.

"Friends call me Dorian," he bowed low, his forehead almost touching the iron bars.

Thousands of questions inundated my mind, making my nervous system implode. How did they manage to get into the realm? Why choose the unit? Why request me for the assignment? Was any of it real? And most importantly, what had I unknowingly helped them do?

"I presume you are going to dispose of me?" I pressed my lips together and forced the ripping pain in my throat down with a swallow.

"So soon?" he furrowed his brows as if he'd freed his morning for this and I was a rude host, shutting the door on our conversation. "Don't you want to ask for a plea? To be returned to your realm? Propose a hostage exchange?"

"I would rather die than help you murder my people!" I shouted, bubbles of saliva exploding from my mouth and onto his precious uniform, but he did not seem to care.

"Yes...I expected you would say that..."

"Kill me then." I kept my head high. I would not give them the satisfaction to see me beg for my life. Not when I had nothing else to live for.

Dorian lined his fingers and stretched his hand through the bars, careful to keep them away from the iron and touched my skin, caressing down my cheek.

"I would," he tilted his head with the admission. "But my brother bound himself to you, so I am forced to keep you alive until the next full moon."

His fingers lowered and gripped my chin hard, pressing my jaw. "After that," he sighed, "it's his decision."

My bones screeched under his touch, pain making its way under his fingers as if summoned by a master. When he released me, I fell back, my feet unable to support my body any longer. Dorian freed his hand from between the bars and rubbed his fingers in disgust, as if he'd touched a slimy frog.

"Meanwhile," he turned, the guards already stepping away to lead him out of this miserable place, "enjoy the windling hospitality. After all, we are renowned for it."

**Follow Ellyana's journey in *Locked, The Realm of Wind Book 2***

For an indie author, reviews are everything, so if you enjoyed this book, please give it some stars!

You can find Xandra on:

Amazon

Goodreads

TikTok

Instagram

YouTube

Facebook

Printed in Great Britain
by Amazon